Gorbals Tale

Gorbals Tale

Ron Deen

The Pentland Press Limited
Edinburgh • Cambridge • Durham • USA

© Ron Deen 2000

First published in 2000 by
The Pentland Press Ltd.
1 Hutton Close
South Church
Bishop Auckland
Durham

British Library Cataloguing in Publication Data.
A Catalogue record for this book is available
from the British Library.

ISBN 1 85821 787 3

Typeset by CBS, Martlesham Heath, Ipswich, Suffolk
Printed and bound by Antony Rowe Ltd., Chippenham

To the Good People of the Gorbals,
Past and Present

I dwelt within a gloomy court,
Wherein did never sunbeam sport;
Yet there my heart was stirr'd –
My very blood did dance and thrill,
When on my narrow window-sill,
Spring lighted like a bird.

'Glasgow' by Alexander Smith (1857)

ACKNOWLEDGMENTS

My thanks to Chief Constable John Orr of Strathclyde Police and his Personnel for their help in my researches, including Superintendent Iain Gordon and Valery Chism-White of Media Services; Kate and David of the Oxford Street Training School Library and Superintendent Alastair Dinsmore for guiding me round the Black Museum.

Special thanks and appreciation to those retired stalwarts of the old Glasgow Police Force, former Chief Inspector Eddie Hardie, Inspector Jim Sinton and Sergeant Gerry MacAllister, not forgetting the late Sergeant Jimmy Clark – a true gentleman and lover of Burns's poetry, all of whom kept me enthralled and amused with reminscences of pounding the beat as young cops in the era described.

Thanks and appreciation to the Staff of the Glasgow Mitchell Library, and Staff of the Pollokshaws and Barrhead Libraries for their help in seeking out relevant information.

To Campbeltown (The Wee Toon) my appreciation for the contributions of Mr and Mrs Ken Holland of Fort Argyll, Mrs Efric Wotherspoon of Martin's Bookshop and Sharon Harvey of the *Campbeltown Courier*, not forgetting Sue Fortune of the Campbeltown Library.

Thanks to Mrs Ada Harrison of the Gorbals History Research Group for introducing me to their informative pamphlets; also to John Clancy of the Laurieston Bar and old-time characters like the late Chick Flettin for recounting their hilarious experiences and to Lydia and John Fleming, not forgetting Mrs May Baker, widow of my old Gorbals pal the late Arthur Baker, for their constant support.

To Mrs Ida Berkeley, my gratitude for her help and encouragement. Ida, well known as actress Ida Schuster, is the widow of the late Dr Allan Berkeley who was my family doctor over forty years and widely loved throughout the Gorbals.

To the many others who have supported my efforts in writing this book, my regrets that limitations of space do not allow for individual mention. To those, and the genuine and helpful people of the Gorbals, I extend my heartfelt thanks and appreciation.

CHAPTER 1

One Friday morning, a thin distraught man with mousey hair could be observed standing at Gorbals Cross peering up at the clock. The person in question, Sandy McKillop, commonly known as Sanny, was distraught. He had run round a half dozen pubs looking for Tim Riley, otherwise known as Twinkletoes. These were quick 'in-and-oot' visits, not the unhurried sessions of a normal 'bevvy night'. Sanny's questions were always the same.

'Hae any o' yees seen Twinkletoes? Ye ken, wee Tim Riley?'

The answer was always the same: no hide nor hair of the wee devil.

Sanny had searched all Riley's favourite pubs. The Hole in the Wall in Abbotsford Place, the Clock Bar in Bedford Street, the Seaforth and Hugh Boyle's Bar in Gorbals Street, and finally the Mally Arms in Eglinton Street. No luck there either, not a sausage!

As Sanny approached the corner of Norfolk Street and South Portland Street, he met Runner Flett, the bookie's man, who told him that Tim Riley was in a hell of a state, and needing him badly.

Seemingly Twinkletoes, so named for his fleet-footedness at the dancing, was in the gents' toilet in Nelson Street under the railway bridge, as drunk as a sailor and screaming for Sanny McKillop!

Hurrying to the scene of distress in the gents' toilets, a bizarre drama unfolded as Sanny communicated with his befuddled crony, Tim Riley, in the toilet cubicle there. Unbelievable as it seems, Twinkletoes was due to be married that very afternoon and was just recovering his *compos mentis* after a night on the binge with the boys, celebrating the very occasion he had now forgotten.

At two thirty that afternoon Sandra McCaw, with family and friends, would be waiting before the Registrar at Eglington Toll and it was now

1

approaching noon.

'Tim, do ye no' ken to-day's yer weddin',' shouted Sanny over the closed cubicle door.

'Cheeses Christ,' came the wail from the toilet cubicle, followed by, 'God, noo ah remember. Ma weddin' day tae Sandra!'

'Ye bluddy stumer, Riley, come oota there noo. Let's get crackin',' roared an irate Sanny.

Several patrons, fumbling with their flies at the porcelain urinals, tried to swivel their attention towards the bizarre wee man talking to the cubicle door, thus causing their streams to spray each other's trousers.

'Sanny, son,' wailed Twinkletoes, " Ah need ma best suit. It's in the pawn roon in Oxford Street. Here, ah've got the stub in ma troosers, take it.'

The sound of rustling ended as the door flew open revealing a bedraggled Tim Riley, in simmit and drawers, holding a tatty pair of trousers and jacket folded over one arm. He thrust a hand forward at Sanny saying:

'Here, Sanny, take these claes and ma da's old gilt watch. Here's the ticket tae fer the pawn. Ye can redeem ma guid suit, and get a coupla quid tae.'

'Ah'll run an' be back in ten minutes,' Sanny quipped, 'an' chuck that bluddy VP bottle away.'

'Aye, hurry, China. Ah need tae chin big Shuggie for a bung as weel!' croaked Riley.

Meanwhile, in a ground floor room and kitchen in nearby Coburg Street, Riley's long suffering mother Theresa waited, puzzling over her son's absence from home the previous night. Theresa Riley was a formidable woman, with a top bun hairstyle and a face like a bull terrier when in a rage, but a teddy-bear in normal repose.

At two o'clock, the wedding party arrived at the Registrar's Office at Eglinton Toll. First there was the peroxide blonde bride, Sandra McCaw, dressed all in pink. The eighteen year old bride was accompanied by her twenty-five year old bridegroom, Tim Riley, clad in a crumpled serge suit, blue shirt and red tie. He wore a pair of unpolished black shoes. Also in attendance were Sandra's mother, aunt, and her three hefty brothers dressed in smart dark suits, white shirts and dark ties, all wearing black patent shoes. The party wore tulip buttonholes of various colours – it was all Sanny could obtain in the limited time available. Missing only was Sandra's best maid. She just hadn't turned up.

'Sanny, nip oot an' see if ye can see the best maid. Maybe the lassie's got lost?' said Tim Riley tersely.

As Sanny observed the clock, it showed five minutes to go for the ceremony to start. Out of the corner of his eye, he noticed an approaching young woman, wearing a head scarf and trailing a crying toddler as she laboured with two heavy string bags. Sanny had his mind made up as he approached the woman.

'Missus, would ye help me oot. We need a young best maid. The real wan hasnae turned up,' exclaimed a breathless Sanny McKillop to a totally bemused woman.

She paused in thought. She liked that he had said 'young woman' – that was flattering.

'Aye okay,' the woman said simply, to Sanny's great relief.

Looks of sheer disbelief and gasps greeted the sight of the newly found best maid, who entered wearing a headscarf and old raincoat, trailing a girnin' wean and heaving two string bags. Agnes, as she was called, had now warmed to her task. She really liked weddings. Besides, Sanny had promised her a ten bob bung.

As the Registrar intoned the familiar, 'Will you, Sandra McCaw, take this man, Timothy Riley, to be your lawful wedded . . .' and so on, Sanny the best man fumbled for the ring which Tim had hurriedly slipped him earlier. Soon a gleaming ring was being placed on the bride's finger, to the admiring glances of the assembled party. Sanny smiled when he recalled how Tim had come by the ring.

'It was a tanner ring ah bought frae Woolies in Argyle Street, for the weddin',' had been Tim's hilarious comment.

At the conclusion of the wedding ceremony, the wedding party adjourned to a local pub lounge at Eglinton Toll before making their way by taxi to the reception. The taxis would be courtesy of Sandra's brothers, whilst the reception was to be held courtesy of Mrs Theresa

Riley at her residence in Coburg Street. So Tim had informed his bride a week earlier.

When Theresa opened the door of her ground floor room and kitchen that unforgettable day in Coburg Street, Gorbals, she was not only surprised, she was totally 'dumfooneered'!

'Mrs Riley,' announced a tipsy Tim, kissing his mother on the cheek and pointing to a red-faced Sandra, 'meet Mrs Riley!'

'Whit, in the name o' God!' shrieked Theresa Riley, 'Whit, ye're merrit!'

'Ay, that's right, Ma. Me and Sandra finally tied the knot, ye might say,' smiled Tim, hugging his mother tightly.

'Fer pity's sake, son. Ye might hav' tolt me, yer ma,' sighed Theresa. 'Ah hivna onything set for a' these folks, whitever their names are. An' the hoose is in a mess. Whit aboot the weddin' meal and drinks?'

'Dinna worry, Mrs Riley,' interjected Sandra, taking Theresa by the arm, 'we'll all muck in an' get things organised.'

'Seems helluva funny, two Missus Rileys, an' I've never been introduced afore to my ain daughter-in-law!' laughed Theresa, slowly recovering her composure, whilst the totally bemused guests looked on in amazement, trying to make head-or-tail of Tim's strange arrangements.

'That's oor nutty Twinkletoes for ye,' was Theresa's only comment.

Tim finally said to his mother, 'Look ma, me an' the boys here, Sandra's brithers, will nick oot for fish suppers frae Grace's Fishey – a dozen should be enough. We'll go doon tae the Mally Arms for a crate o' screwtaps, a coupla' bottles o' whisky, and sherry fur the ladies.'

'We'll fix the table for yees coming back, son,' smiled Theresa, adding, 'ah'll put on ma purple dress tae,' as Sandra, her mother and her aunt prepared to help.

A friendly neighbour from above soon appeared with a wind-up gramophone and a stack of popular dance band records of the day. The Rileys intended to hold a real 'hooley' that night! After demolishing the tasty fish suppers and swallowing the first lot of drinks, the McCaw boys went out for another of 'the same again, all round!' Soon the loud, brassy sounds of Glenn Miller's 'Moonlight Serenade' and Joe Loss with his 'In the Mood' and 'Woodchopper's Ball' blasted through the open windows and front door, out of the close, into the street. There was no doubt that the Rileys were holding a real hooley that night!

It was not long before the goings-on at the ground floor flat in Coburg Street attracted the unwelcome attention of the dreaded Clatty Mob. Like rodents whose sensory perceptions are honed to incredible limits, the Clattys were soon on the scene, attracted by sounds of music and promise of food and drink. The Clatty Mob, led by Ben Clatty and supported by his five 'mingin' brothers were party gatecrashers *par excellence*, and well known locally. The sound of music and raucous laughter emanating from open windows was like cheese to rats.

It was not long before a full-blooded Donnybrook erupted – a stramash of monstrous proportions as the clatty Clattys entered through open door and windows. Immediately the place resounded to the smashing of furniture, the crashing of dishes and the smashing of window panes; the screaming of women and the cursing of oaths rent the air. Even the neighbours, accustomed to the usual weekend 'stooshie', knew this was first division stuff.

'Take that ye Bastart!' followed by 'Yer cruisin for a bruisin, pal!' and 'Goodbye Vienna!' were quickly followed by several Clatty bodies being propelled horizontally through the air, like yon new fankled jet-engines, courtesy of the three battling McCaw brothers – stalwarts of the local LMS Boxing Club. Although lighter than the battling McCaws, Tim and Sanny gave a good account of themselves, swinging their empty MacEwan's beer bottles as clubs. Even hefty Theresa had laid out the big Clatty with a couple of massive bangs of her cast-iron soup pan, leaving the victim covered in green pease-brose.

In the interim, Sandra, her mother and her aunt had fled the close to summon the Police.

With the place like a bomb-site, wreckage and empty bottles, smashed glass and furniture everywhere, Tim sat on the floor with two black eyes. Sanny, minus two front teeth with a bloody nose, sat beside him. They still held empty screwtop bottles and looked in a trance. The McCaw brothers stood regarding the three recumbent Clattys who lay on the kitchen floor, the other three having flown out of the window. All three looked totally immaculate, with not a scratch on them!

'Poor silly bastarts,' was all they murmured as they drank their screwtops.

It was not long before the running steps of the police resounded along the hard pavements, through the close and into the house, as Sergeant Ratley, Constable Auchterlony, and another two cops rushed in, amazed at the scene before them. Finally, looking out of the open windows at the three Clattys lying on the pavement, and at the utter chaos inside, Sergeant Ratley simply remarked, as he took out his black notebook, 'Aye lads, looks like a clear case of forced entry and assault.'

A tall figure moved slowly, like a schooner in a night fog, the cold, dank mist swirling in from the nearby River Clyde, chilling him to the bone as he patrolled his night beat. Missing only to Angus Auchterlony's senses was the foghorn's mournful wail, but this was not the lighthouse at the Mull of Kintyre, where warnings of hidden dangers were announced in advance. This was the South Side, or the Sou'Side as the locals called it, the infamous Gorbals district from whose sprawling and teeming slums dangers came suddenly, without warning.

To the new constable from Campbeltown, the experience was like a scene from Dante's 'Inferno' which he had studied as a pupil at the High School, before the War. The Gorbals, with its endless canyons of black, grimy tenements, with its pubs, drunks, street bookies, tallymen, shebeens and brothels, was akin to Hell mused Angus, when compared to the wide, inspiring sea-scapes of Kintyre and home. He wasn't aware that the Gorbals vied with Naples as the worst slums in Europe. They didn't teach him that in the Police Training School where he learned the rudiments of policing and where he boarded in communal barracks. There was no need to, since after two year's probationary service on the beat, Angus and his colleagues would find out for themselves – there among the unsanitary overcrowding, stinking tenements and culture of violence. It was no stroke of chance that the Glasgow Police Training School found itself right in the middle of the Gorbals, for what better place to learn one's trade as a Police Officer?

Angus Auchterlony had joined the Glasgow Police in mid 1946, aged twenty-four years, after his service in the recent War where he had served with the Argyll and Sutherland Highlanders (The Thin Red Line) in North Africa, Italy and Europe. Through it all he had been very fortunate, the only damage he sustained being a badly sprained ankle as he jumped into a foxhole during one of Rommel's deadly 88-millimetre artillery attacks, and later from a bad case of dehydration in the desert. Many of Angus's comrades had failed to return home, so he always considered himself blessed.

As Angus proceeded down Bridge Street rattling locks and checking shop doors, an unexpected voice behind him spoke.

'Auchterlony, let's be having you.'

Turning round quickly, the young probationer was confronted by his Senior Cop, Horace Sharkey, known as the Fox in the Southern Division.

'What's the trouble?' queried Angus as they hurried down towards the River Clyde.

'At Carlton Place, a tip off about an assault,' was all Sharkey would say.

As the two constables turned into Carlton Place they heard a raucous female voice rendering the strains of 'Nellie Dean', broken every so often by loud sobs. Constable Sharkey knew right away. 'Saints Alive,' he cried as he spied the dejected figure nearby, 'it's Laughing Mary – one of the local *girls*!'

Seated on the top step leading to a rear court where she habitually serviced her clients was Laughing Mary, her skirts above her knees, and legs wide apart revealing her bloomers. She looked up with tearful eyes, sobbing into an old rag.

'Ah've been punched by yon bastart ower yonder, look at ma bleedin' mouth. He tried tae rob me,' cried the poor soul, 'but ah wouldna gie him ma red purse. The swine knew ah had a few bob in it.'

The Policemen looked across at the suspension bridge, used by pedestrians to cross the river to Clyde Street. All they made out was a shadowy figure in the bridge archway.

'Can you describe the man who beat you, hen?' enquired Constable Sharkey.

'He was a wee, messin' bastart, ah'm tellin ye, Constable Sharkey,' sobbed Mary. 'He tried to fuck aff wi' ma five pound!'

'Ah, business must have been good the night, Mary. But can you describe him or his clothes?' countered Sharkey with a grimace.

Meanwhile, the senior cop asked Angus to investigate the shady observer, across the road at the footbridge archway, as he continued questioning Mary. A tiny red fag glowed intermittently by the spot where the suspect hovered.

'The wanker wore a black donkey jaicket, a black woolly hat and white sannys,' said Mary, pausing, 'and, aye, he smokes Woodbines tae. Ah keeps ma money up ma juke in a wee red purse wi' Rothesay on it. He didna get it!'

Angus returned after ten minutes, breathless. He removed his helmet, brushing back his sweaty, sandy coloured hair and exclaimed disconsolately. 'The basket got away! By God, that bugger could move. He vanished into some close or dunny. I just couldnae find him, but I found his lit Woodbine dowt here.'

When questioned by his colleague, Angus mentioned that although it was dark, he could make out that the suspect was small, around five feet five, slight of build and wearing a dark jacket and woollen hat. He wore soft white shoes and 'could bloody move'.

'Why not go home, Mary,' said Angus gently, 'and put that bottle away; it'll do you no good.'

'Ah havnae ony hame since my bairn died, an ma bloody man ran off wi' a whoor frae the Calton, leavin' me sweet nothing,' said the pathetic figure.

'Come on, woman,' said Constable Sharkey sharply, 'If ye dinna leave, I'll have to arrest you for soliciting. Now away home with you!'

'Ah dinnae want tae go ower the river tae yon wumman's hostel. It's so bloody noisy an ye canna get ony peace,' sighed Mary with a resigned smile as she made off along Carlton Place towards the Glasgow Green.

The following night as he went on shift, Angus was stunned and saddened at the news. Poor Mary had been found in the rear court of the same close where the two cops had seen her the previous night. She had been savagely stabbed to death and her red purse with the money was missing. The pathetic soul had not returned to her hostel as she had promised the constables, but had continued to ply her trade. There she had met her nemesis. Two of Mary's pro pals, Fly Alison and Clatty Dot, last reported seeing her 'arguing wi' a guy wearing a black jacket and white sandshoes'.

Angus felt such pity as near made him weep. Mary had been a human being, someone's daughter, aye some wean's mother too! She had not merited such a cruel death in her fight for survival. If only he could lay his hands on the filth that had done such a thing, the blighter would swing for sure. Angus was learning about being a Policeman. He would encounter many more horrific experiences as a Cop on the tough Gorbals beat, and though he couldn't have envisaged it then, he would meet some pleasant ones too.

Angus Auchterlony was a 'Teuchter' from Campbeltown, half an inch off six feet in height with sandy coloured hair, going thin on top. A large ruddy face, weathered by countless seasons in the open, was beset by a pair of striking blue eyes which appeared gentle in repose but cold as steel in action.

At the Police Training School in Oxford Street, Angus and his colleagues were put through a tough course of physical instruction and drilling which reminded him of the army but with many extras. There were unarmed combats, writing reports, first-aid and learning the essentials of Scottish Criminal Law and Police procedures.

Angus readily made friends in the barrack-like surroundings of the Police dormitories, where discipline was tight and the new entrant had to live in during basic training. There were fellows like Jock MacAllister and Rab Sinton from Glasgow, Billy Armstrong, a 'Doonhamer' from Dumfries and Drew Cameron, a 'Teuchter' from Oban.

Although not academically nor physically top of the bunch, it was Cameron's star which was to rise above his fellows. During one of Cameron's interviews, a mature Highland Inspector had asked him about skills and interests.

'And do you play the football?'

'No,' Cameron had replied to the frowning Inspector.

'Do you have the Gaelic, Cameron?'

'Yes, pretty well,' replied Cameron smiling. A big smile came from the Inspector.

'And what about the pipes?' said the Inspector tentatively.

'I'm no plumber but, yes of course,' blurted Drew Cameron, 'I was a piper wi' the Cameron Highlanders during the War.'

The Inspector liked the little joke and said, 'Och, yes, yes. I knew you were one of our people,' announcing, 'you will go far in the Glasgow Police Pipe band, there's no doubt, no doubt.'

After a month's basic training, Angus would be out on the beat under the guidance of a Senior Cop as his two year probation commenced, and it was with Senior Constable Horace Sharkey, the Fox, that he had encountered the unfortunate prostitute, Laughing Mary.

Angus and his pals soon learned about the pecking order in the canteen when they were rudely told by some senior cops to 'Bugger off, this is our regular table, and don't you sprogs forget it!'

As Constable D93 of the Southern Division, Angus found his mentor, Sharkey, the Fox, to be cold and uncommunicative at first. After his first week on the beat one of the shift sergeants at the Gorbals Police Station had enquired as to how he was making out. Angus had replied that he felt like resigning there and then.

'Don't fret, Auchterlony,' replied the Sergeant knowingly with a laugh, 'Ye'll be all right when the Fox stops for a smoke and asks where you are from. Say you like Millport on the Clyde and you're home and dry.'

One night at a street corner, the Fox stood in a close-mouth scanning the reflections of passers-by in an adjacent plate glass window, as he smoked a fag-end in his cupped hand. Suddenly Sharkey asked Angus if he liked the Clyde coast area, and where was he from? He answered from Campbeltown, and aye, he loved riding the hired bikes around the Big Cumbrae and having a pint in Millport. A big smoke puff from a smiling mouth showed he was now in with the Fox.

Suddenly, without warning, as a result of his plate glass observations, Constable Sharkey had extinguished his fag and was up and off, in hot pursuit of a shady figure nipping behind a shop's rear entrance.

'Quick, Auchterlony. Looks like a weasel is on the prowl.'

As Angus came off night shift, he made his way along Norfolk Street to Charlie's the barber for a haircut. Later he would return to his spartan accommodation in the Police Training School, praying for the day he could have his own pad.

After a sleep, he would call in to see Kathy MacDonald and her mother Nan, who ran the the Fruit Box shop in Norfolk Street. He was needing to buy some fruit, and besides, the owners of the Fruit Box, Nan and Kathy MacDonald, had family connections in his hometown of Campbeltown, and Angus enjoyed their 'crack' over a cup of tea in the back-shop when passing on his beat. His particular interest was Kathy, the petite redhead in her early twenties with the turned-up nose and sparkling blue eyes, a younger version of her mother Nan. Angus really fancied the Dinah Shore look-alike with the great figure, and terrific pair of legs. Kathy would, he hoped, make the Gorbals a more bearable duty.

And Angus Auchterlony was soon to learn, even in the tough and grimy atmosphere of the much maligned Gorbals, amongst grim and barbaric conditions which ordinary folk were forced to bear, the milk of human kindness endured still.

CHAPTER 2

Angus had managed to find a comfortable room and kitchen with inside toilet in Merkland Street, Partick, two up and near main shops. This suited the radius rules and allowed easy underground travel to Bridge Street and his Gorbals work station. Compared to his earlier spartan accommodation in the training college the privacy and freedom was heavenly but he missed the cheery company of his colleagues.

Angus was very comfortable in his small flat, warmed by a shiny black Alexander range with roaring coal fire and hot oven including a small gas cooker for preparing his favourite diet of mince and tatties, alternated by fried fish and chips. Below the kitchen window was the sink ('jawbox') with cold water tap and, in the corner, a sparse larder with shelves for his dishes, pans and foodstuffs but Angus usually ate at the Police canteen or bought a fish supper coming off back shift.

He had inherited a square solid kitchen table and four chairs, an old settee and a table for his Bush wireless which made his lonely hours bearable. All in all, he managed quite nicely on his four pound ten shillings and his weekly ten bob rent allowance and looked forward to inviting Kathy one evening for a specially prepared meal, with candles and wine. Angus had even bought a portable electric gramophone from Bach's in Eglinton Street along with Kathy's two musical favourites, Frank Sinatra and Glenn Miller records, as he planned many a cosy evening with the attractive redhead. But Angus would find he was in for a lot of competition from Sean Robb and American Joe Cherkowski.

'You know, Angus, big Sean has been talking about us getting engaged,' Kathy had told him one night as they talked in her close after a night at the pictures.

'Did you say yes?'

'I never said yes or no.'

She must be pretty close to Robb for him to pop the question, thought Angus, who quipped, 'So what about me and your friend, Joe whats-is-name?'

'Cherkowski's the name, it's Polish you know,' Kathy replied, grinning. 'It's still a three horse race, Angus, so don't fret yerself.'

One night as Angus sat drinking hot Bovril, listening to Scottish dance music on his Bush wireless, the tune of 'Campbeltown Loch' came tripping over the airwaves, taking him back to the first time he laid eyes on Kathy MacDonald.

Angus remembered the scene well. It was on the West Coast bus from Glasgow to Campbeltown as he returned home from his Police entrance test that he had first caught sight of the attractive redhead. Not unlike Dinah Shore, the film star, Angus thought as he eyed the petite figure with sparkling blue eyes, radiant smile and peaches and cream complexion. Maybe the eye colour was different, didn't Dinah Shore have brown eyes? Angus mused. He didn't care, she looked good enough to light his light.

Seated behind, frequently peeping over the top of his *Glasgow Herald*, Angus was entranced by the attractive young woman who chatted animatedly with another woman who was an older version of herself, obviously her mother, he thought. At one stage, the enthralled Angus let his defences down as his paper fell about his lap, and the wonderful creature had actually smiled at him! Was it his imagination? No, she did it again some minutes later. Not only that, she was casting flitting glances in his direction every so often. Angus recalled the rhyme:

'It's easy to spy; she's giving me the eye.'

At Inverary the bold Angus decided, his heart palpitating, that he would make his move. That was the convenience stop when passengers would be relieved to stretch, have a bite to eat and chat with their fellow passengers.

It was a pleasant summer's day as Kathy and her mother, Nan, stood feeding the gulls. As Kathy held aloft a piece of her sandwich to a particularly adventurous gull, her red hair flowing in the gentle breeze, Angus sidled up beside her and remarked, 'Take care or he'll be away with yer hand!'

'It could be a she, of course, and it makes no difference when they're famished,' replied Kathy with a grin.

'Well, they do say the female of the species is the deadlier.'

'Aye, so they say. Are you going right on?'

Angus replied, 'Yes, to Campbeltown.'

'Well, maybe we'll meet again, Mr . . . er . . . er?'

'Sorry. Angus Auchterlony. I should have introduced myself.'

'I'm Kathy MacDonald from Glasgow. Me and my mum are visiting relatives in the Wee Toon for a few days.'

'Perhaps we'll bump into each other again, who knows?' smiled Angus hopefully.

Angus explained that he was hoping to join the Police, having just been down to the Training College in Oxford Street for tests. Kathy replied excitedly, what a coincidence, as they ran a fruit shop nearby in Norfolk Street so again, their paths could easily cross.

Some days later on the following Saturday, after a couple of whisky and beers in the Royal Arms overlooking the harbour, Angus and his cousin, the small Ally MacIntyre, made their way up the Main Street to the Town Hall where the local dance had already started. Both cousins walked with a purpose as the dark, dapper fisherman planned to meet his girlfriend, Ella Oman, there and Angus was keen to cast an eye over some of the local talent.

No sooner had they entered the dance floor than a woman's voice cried out: 'Ally, over here.'

An attractive petite brunette came across the floor from where she had been chatting to a group of girls and planted a huge smacker full on Ally's lips.

'Ella meet Angus Auchterlony, my cousin,' announced Ally proudly.

'Oh, I know this fellah, Ally. Mind, he used to pull my plaits at primary school!'

Angus laughed hugely and asked Ella for the pleasure of the first dance, glancing at Ally who deferred gracefully with a bow.

As Ella and Angus danced to a waltz, Angus spied a figure across the floor. What a surprise and delight. It was Kathy MacDonald. As his partner Ella rattled on about Ally buying his own fishing boat the following year, Angus's attention was elsewhere.

'Sorry, Ella, I was watching the lassie across yonder. I met her on the bus,' replied Angus, nodding in the direction of Kathy.

'Nice. But she doesnae look too happy,' replied a frowning Ella Oman.

Ella was right. Kathy MacDonald's face and demeanour was one of distress as she was being danced by a tall, rough looking character whom Ella knew well. It was none other than Tom MacFadyen, a local building labourer and bully, who was accompanied by his habitual drinking cronies whom he always addressed as Calum and Fergie. Calum was a tall, vinegary character; the other a broad individual with the face and hair of a warthog. Even in the soft light of a romantic slow fox-trot, it was obvious that the drunken MacFadyen was holding Kathy very close, nuzzling her cheek. She was held vice-like across his barrel chest, a reluctant captive trying to wrest free from his unwelcomed advances and liquor reeking breath. Her mother Nan was totally unaware of her daughter's predicament as she danced with an old friend.

Big Tam, as MacFadyen was known locally, and his two cronies had eliminated any competition by their posturing and quietly mumbled threats to any male who dared invade the area where Kathy sat. Nan popped over every so often to chat briefly, and Kathy said nothing of her discomfiture, not wishing to spoil her mother's evening out.

Angus quickly sussed the situation when an Excuse Me waltz was announced, telling Ally: 'You and Ella join me at the end of the next dance. There might be fireworks.'

As Big Tam lumbered around the floor, fired by Calum and Fergie's encouragement, a swooning Kathy recoiled from his whisky laden breath. She had made up her mind, she was leaving when the music stopped. Then an unexpected miracle happened. Suddenly, to her relief and surprise, a tall, good looking man had broken in, strong arms seizing her around the waist, ignoring McFadyen's warning to 'bugger off', as the apparition whisked her off to the opposite end of the hall.

'Angus Auchterlony. I'm right glad to see you this minute!'

'I know all about your problem. I've been watching him. You don't need to worry any longer.'

16

'I didn't know you were here, Angus, but you're welcome as good news.'

For the rest of the evening, Big Tam and his ugly duo stood glaring resentfully from the opposite end of the hall, as Kathy tried hard to ignore them. From then Kathy felt secure in the company of Angus, Ally and Ella, as the dance drew to a close.

Just before midnight, the happy party collected their coats, having taken their leave of Nan and her partner earlier. As the two couples linked arms and made their way down the Main Street towards the Harbour, heading for Kathy's relations in Low Askomill, across the Loch, three figures emerged furtively from Shore Street and followed behind them.

Kathy had just been saying how her evening was spoiled by MacFadyen's presence at the dance: 'He of the wandering palms and whisky breath.'

Angus cautioned the group to ignore the louts and their comments and walk quickly on, but Big Tam and his two cronies followed behind, with quickening pace and even louder abuse and swearing. As they reached the low wall alongside the lochside at the Esplanade, Tam MacFadyen made a sore mistake when he yelled a remark about Angus's companion being 'one o' those cows frae Glasgow'. Turning smartly Angus made a bee-line for MacFadyen, seized him by the lapels and gave him a punch on the jaw of such force as sent the recipient headfirst over the wall into the loch.

'Jesus, Joseph and Mary!' screamed the lanky Calum, leaping over the wall. 'Ah hope the tide's no in. Tam'll be drowned.'

Bulky Fergie Warthog followed his crony shouting, 'Ye bloody Glasgow hooligans. I'll have the Polis on yous!'

Luckily Big Tam lay over the wall with his head inches away from the waterline, his limp figure resting on the stones' protective apron, out for the count, chin on chest.

'Is he all right?' cried a worried Kathy to Calum.

'Aye, no thanks to you lot. He's comin' round.'

Ally grabbed Angus by the arm, pulling him away. 'Hurry, Angus, for Christsakes. You'll be done for, if you get into a stramash wi' the local Polis – especially after yer recent application! Keep a low profile. You'll be going home in a few days.'

Angus and Ally hurried the girls home, but not before Kathy insisted on stopping on the way at a local phone booth to make an anonymous ambulance call.

As Angus sat there listening to the wireless and drinking Bovril in his Partick flat, he smiled when he recalled the hullaballoo at his first ever dance with the attractive Kathy MacDonald.

Sergeant Ratley, the beat Sergeant, was a tall ascetic man from Lanarkshire who rarely smiled. With thinly fleshed face, his head resembled a balding skull with grey eyes and habitually downturned thin lips. The only time he smiled was invariably at someone's misfortune or whenever he managed to catch any of the young Cops out for whatever reason, smoking on duty, lateness, dress, writing reports or whatever trivial matter caught his attention. At such times he was a martinet, and became widely disliked by new recruits. Ratley had taken an immediate dislike to Angus when as a new recruit he became allocated to the Gorbals Police Office as part of the Southern Division. Perhaps the question of Angus's boots had something to do with it.

At the outset of his commencement on the beat, after completion of the month at the Training School in Oxford Street, Angus had soon complained to Sergeant Ratley that his new boots were making his feet bleed.

'Can I have permission to excuse boots for shoes, Sergeant?" asked Angus one night as he hobbled around his beat.

'What in the hell for, Auchterlony, are ye going to walk about in yer bare feet?' replied Ratley derisively.

'My heels and ankles are rubbed raw and bleeding, Sergeant, with these bloody rawhide boots. I can hardly walk,' retorted Angus testily.

'Well, you know what to do if ye cannae take it. We dinnae want a lot of nancy boys in the Force. Away and get some Carnation corn plasters.' With that quip, Sergeant Ratley turned and walked away.

'Jesus, corn plasters! Where do I get corn plasters at midnight? It's not corns, it's the rubbing of leather on skin. Silly scunner,' murmured

Angus to himself after Ratley had left.

Luckily for Angus, the appearance of his Senior Cop, Sharkey, the Fox, solved his predicament. 'Right, Auchterlony, come along with me and we'll put you straight.' Without further ado, Constable Sharkey was soon knocking on the door of his friend, a local midwife in Gorbals Street. Used to being summoned at all kinds of hours, the kindly woman bathed Angus's feet with disinfectant and applied bandages and linament.Miraculously she produced a pair of woollen socks, saying, 'These will protect your ankles, my mannie.'

Constable Sharkey went away with a smile on his lips, in order to keep an eye on the beat, arranging to rendezvous later with Auchterlony. As he departed, the Fox shouted: 'You'll need to get some Vaseline or dubbin to soften up that hard boot leather, Auchterlony,' adding, 'We old cops used to chew new boots in the tough old days. By the bye, don't forget to visit the Out-Patients at the Western tomorrow for yer feet.'

At an early shift muster, Sergeant Rat Ratley allocated Angus to a local school crossing and also alerted him to complaints about the early morning crowing of a cockerel in the vicinity of Nicholson Street. Angry citizens were being disturbed in their dawn slumbers by full blooded 'cock-a doodle-dooing' and Auchterlony was warned to be especially vigilant, as the Glasgow Police motto said: *Semper Vigilo.*

Sergeant Ratley had informed Angus that an extra Cop would assist him during his time at the school crossing, as they had to locate the source of the crowing. The individual, Ratley had announced with a malicious grin, was to be none other than Constable Thomas Cahill. Holy Moses, thought Angus, it's like the funny films – cock crowing at dawn, in deepest Gorbals, investigated by the Keystone Cops of Southern Division. What's more? His colleague was the famous Tam the Bam who, when once informed by his Inspector that he never forgot a face, but in Tam's case would make an exception, was thanked profusely for his kind remarks!

When Angus had made an indiscreet remark about Ratley's lack of compassion over his boot problem, whilst coming off duty in the locker room, the words 'unfeeling rat' were instantly picked up by the alert ear of PC Snakey Flockhart and passed to his master within the hour. Soon the nickname would stick to Sergeant Rat Ratley like plaster – and so would his dislike for the man from Argyll.

Like all Policemen, Angus was forced to become a social misfit because of shifts and standby regulations, least of all never having a Saturday off as a serving Police Officer. Angus did have time off on a Saturday afternoon to play in the Police rugby team but had to conform to shift rosters in the normal manner.

Angus saw Kathy and her mother Nan in the fruit shop on his regular early and back shifts, when he stopped to have a cup of tea, a chat and enquire if there were any problems. Most times the answer was no.

Angus was very disappointed, knowing he was due a Friday off, when he asked Kathy some days before if she would accompany him to a fun show for a laugh with Dave Willis and his Crazy Gang at the Empire, or the alternative of going to the La Scala to see 'A Thousand and One Nights' starring Evelyn Keyes and Cornell Wilde. All Kathy said was she was really sorry but she had a prior date with big Sean Robb at the Locarno dance hall where Carl Barriteau and his orchestra were playing. Maybe another time.

Kathy had a number of men friends of whom Sean Robb and Angus were part. She did not treat any of them as a special case but Kathy knew for sure that Sean Robb, the tall, dark rugby playing potato merchant who supplied their fruit shop, was crazy over her. She also knew that Sean resented any other male competition. With the build of an ox, no one ever messed with big Sean Robb. Robb made no bones to Kathy of his opinion of her association with Policemen and Yanks.

One morning the paths of Angus and Sean crossed as the Policeman entered the back-shop of the Fruit Box to find big Sean sitting with a roll and mug of tea, chatting heartily to Kathy and Nan after heaving a load of tatties off his Albion lorry.

'So this is the Polis Teuchter ye told me about,' smirked Robb without rising to extend a hand. Angus just stared, reddening but effecting a fixed grin.

'Ah hear you play wi' the oval ball,' said Robb markedly.

'Aye, I play for the Glasgow Police, in the pack,' replied Angus.

'Well, well. Ah'm a lock forward and play for Cartha RFC, at Dumbreck yonder. Ah know we have a game wi' the Polis in a month's time. Look forward tae locking horns with ye,' said Robb without smiling or extending a hand.

'Sit, Angus, here's a roll and tea,' quipped Nan cheerily.

'Ah'm off, cannae gossip all day, like some folks,' said Robb, putting on his cap. I'll wipe that smile off his face, grinned Angus, as Sean Robb took his leave, relishing the coming encounter.

Jock Grant was a veteran of the Great War. He had enlisted in 1914 at the age of seventeen years into the 9th HLI, the Glasgow Highlanders, and had lost a leg in the brave attack on High Wood in 1916 in the bloody horror of the Somme. He still suffered from the effects of an earlier gas attack.

Jock had lost his wife, Agnes, who was knocked down and killed by a lorry, crossing Crown Street as she returned from her work in the local UCBS bakery. His daughter, Lilly, was then only ten years old and Jock brought her up with loving care in their single end. Jock was both mother and father to his sad little girl, cooking her meals, washing and bleaching her school blouse with Oxydol and then ironing it till it shone pristine white. He nursed Lilly fondly like a mother hen when she became ill. Jock, pandering to Lilly's every wish, even put himself into hock for her new bike from Young's store in Stockwell Street for over a year.

Now aged sixteen years, Lilly was a beautiful slim girl with long fair hair, blue eyes and a peaches and cream complexion like her mother which invariably drew all the males into her company.

Jock was pleased with Lilly and said, 'That was really great, hen, you managing to get a job at Twomax fashions. The McClures are good employers.'

'Aye, Dad, and they do a lot o' knitwear for good shops like Marks and C & A's too.'

'Ah've been looking at a ground floor flat, a room and kitchen in Bedford Street, Lil,' announced her father. 'With yer extra money, my pension and the burroo money, we'll manage fine. An' you can have a room to yerself.'

21

For Gorbals folk this was indeed luxury, as many poorer families were overcrowded, half a dozen to a single room, with children of mixed sexes, all sharing a single landing toilet with three or four other families. Neither the 'sanny men' (sanitary) from Glasgow Corporation, nor their circular metal plate 'tickets' fixed to entrance doors, denoting the number of persons permitted to each dwelling, managed to alleviate the plight of the overcrowded poor, nor prevented the exploitation of rapacious landlords.

It was one sunny day as Jock was having 'a hing oot o' the windae' that he was greeted by a cheerful voice.

'Hello there, see you're enjoying the fine weather,' said Angus cheerily.

'Och yes, it's good to see the world go by, Constable,' replied Jock, extending his hand

Both being old Army men it didn't take long for Jock and Angus to find common ground, exchanging war stories and amusing events. Jock soon got to know the times of Angus's shifts, day and night, and Angus would pop in to Jock's flat regularly for a brief chat and a hot cup of tea. Other times, on cold damp evenings, it would be something a little stronger to keep out the cold, but only a nip, and Angus only lingered briefly as the Beat Sergeant, or his Senior Cop, were always on the prowl. Besides, Angus was a sober and conscientious type who was eager to prove himself in his new calling, but he liked people on the whole and had a deep antipathy for those who broke the law.

As Lilly turned seventeen she started to go dancing, attending the National Halls in Gorbals Street, and the Diamonds in South Portland Street where she had taken dancing lessons. Angus learned of her father's concern.

'Lilly's developed into a fine young woman, Angus. She goes to the pictures, you know the Coliseum or the Collie as she calls it, and the Bedford and the Palace with her workmates.'

'Well, I call that great,' said Angus enthusiastically.

'Yes, OK,' replied Jock with a crestfallen look, 'But now she's graduating to places like the Barrowland and Locarno. I'm no so happy about that, Angus.'

'Can you explain?' enquired Angus pointedly.

'She's liable to meet trouble there. Those scoundrels Con Dougal and his henchman, Bull Bakley, frequent those dancehalls looking for innocent young girls.'

'Oh yes, we all know about those bastards,' said Angus, adding with emphasis, 'Don't worry, Jock, I'll keep an eye open for your Lilly. You can count on me.'

Little did Angus know then, this would prove easier said than done.

CHAPTER 3

Con Dougal was the vain, ruthless leader of the local criminal gang engaged in all manner of shady activities: theft, loansharking, Blackmarket, illicit booze, shebeens, prostitution and illegal bookmaking. Anything with easy money in it was fair game, Dougal was a successful predator who attracted his victims, especially if they were attractive and naive teenage girls, with gifts of nylons, baubles and clothes – like an exotic plant luring butterflies to its deadly attraction. His camouflage comprised his bonny face, azure eyes, neatly combed blond hair and fixed smile which gave him the air of a friendly mister nice-guy. But nothing could be further from the truth. He was a frequenter of the Barrowland and Locarno dancehalls, looking for a 'click' with some likely doll.

Dougal had never served in the War on account of a perforated ear drum, or some such problem, but had worked as a storeman and later gave it up to concentrate on the Blackmarket. His special lieutenant, and chief Heavy, was Bull Bakley, his former school pal. Bakley had avoided military service with flat feet and poor eyesight, earning a living by working on and off as a labourer on building projects where he finally got his books for punching a foreman. It was soon afterwards that he took up with his alter-ego, Con Dougal and his Blackmarket activities.

Bakley, around six feet tall, with dark hair and a blue-black 'four-o'clock' shadow chin, had the blackest set of rodent-like eyes set in a human face. His lower thick lip habitually hung loose, slavering whenever he ate, or drank his favourite cheap VP or Eldorado wines and especially when he saw an attractive girl in the street or at the dancing. His manner was of a huge lumbering bull, and he always reeked of stale wine and body odour. Con Dougal, his antithesis with his

25

aftershave and body lotion, was always repelled by Bakley's personal hygiene but careful not to inflame his disciple's violent temper with a misplaced remark. Bakley was his creature, a valuable gang member, ready and willing to execute his every order.

Another valuable associate of Dougal's was the middle aged, greying, fat and selfish individual named James Kane from Govanhill. Kane had been dismissed as a lawyer with the Corporation for bribery and corruption, and involvement with a clique of shady councillors regarding building contracts, not forgetting his Police record which he had kept secret. Kane's wife had left him, taking her two young daughters with her, to stay with her widowed mother in Langside after she learned of charges against him involving two ten year old girls in a park. Her older daughter, twelve year old June, had complained to her mother of 'Dad touching my legs when I was in bed' on several occasions. Mrs Kane knew he had often bathed the girls in the tin bath, and so thought nothing of it.

But Kane still had a good knowledge of the law, and the extra money he got from Con Dougal augmented his income as a clerk in a lawyer's office, where they were unaware of his past record.

Kathy had promised to attend the rugby match in which her two men friends were to face each other, while her mother looked after the Fruit Box. That day had now arrived as Kathy stood on the sidelines of Cartha Athletic's ground shouting alternate encouragement.

'Come on, Cartha; Robb, get stuck in!' or alternatively in the scrum downs, 'Polis, Polis, Polis. Auchterlony heel, heel, heel!'

As Sean had passed Angus coming out of the dressing rooms, prior to the match, the twelve and a half stone muscular Cartha forward looked menacing in his dark scrum cap – a lean machine, thought Angus. In the pre-match warm up, both men waved at Kathy who grinned, returning their greetings by blowing kisses.

'To the winner goes the spoils,' shouted Sean Robb grimly.

'No quarter, then, Robb,' replied Angus mock heroically.

The day was damp with a heavy pitch as the game progressed, a day for forward battles with a heavy greasy ball, not one for the light cavalry of the threequarter lines. Weak cheers rose from the small group of supporters who lined the pitch: girlfriends, family members, children, old men and a barking terrier who insisted in participating in the game, to the irritation of the players, until expelled by the irate referee. Outraged barking from the expelled four legged player, now securely tied to a fence post, brought forth spectators' protestations. Kathy shouted, 'Oh what a liberty, ref!'

As Angus ran with the ball, he was heavily tackled from behind. Rising, he heard Sean's voice uttering, 'Well if it's no the Teuchter, himself!' Minutes later Angus launched himself at Sean as he descended with the ball from a lineout, ten yards from the Police line, bringing him crashing down like an oak.

'No you again,' smirked Angus.

At half time Kathy came over to say a brief word to both players as they sucked their orange slices after which the second half started with the sleek haired referee blowing his whistle for a Cartha drop-out. The awaiting captain of the Police team urged his men on with a grim and determined visage, as the lighter and faster Cartha backs bore down on them. The second half seemed to be all Sean Robb, hitting the Police scrum-half before he could release to his stand-off. The sleek haired referee was not slow in noticing that Sean was late tackling Angus on two occasions, after the latter had released the ball and arisen rubbing his shoulder. Sean was given a referee's warning, and even the supposedly neutral Kathy was surprised to find herself roaring, 'Foul, ref!'

When Angus was held by the jersey as he jumped for the ball in the lineout, Angus responded with an elbow in Robb's eye and the culprit-potato-playing merchant went down like a sack of Kerr's Pink tatties. Strangely the lynx-eyed referee failed to notice the incident!

The game ended with a ten points to six win for Cartha as the home team clapped their Police visitors into the pavilion, the pitch like brown porridge.

'Well, Teuchter, old boy, the best team won,' taunted Sean.

'Ach away, Robb,' retorted Angus, adding with a sting, 'You Cartha buggers train all the time. We poor buggers are too busy chasing crooks!'

'Ah, poor loser, Auchterlony,' riposted Sean. 'Sorry you canna join us the night. Me and Kathy are off tae the Half Past Eight Show after a meal at the Rogano. See you, sport.'

Kathy waited in the club bar as the players bathed and got changed. Angus was going to be stiff on night shift after the bruising game.

'As the G & S operetta said, Angus, a Policeman's Lot is Not a Happy One,' quipped Kathy as she gave him a peck on the cheek. 'Never mind, it's your treat next Friday.'

Angus felt much better as he looked forward to accompanying her to the Green's Playhouse ballroom, dancing to Joe Loss and his band.

Con Dougal fancied himself as a ballroom dancer, frequenting the Barrowland dance hall where he won over impressionable young girls with his patter and free spending ways. There before him was a covey of four young partridges, all ready for the plucking, and his eagle eye alighted on the youngest and prettiest.

'Well, hello there, young yin?' purred Dougal smilingly. 'Are you enjoying yerself this cheery night?'

'Oh yes, it's smashing, especially Billy Mac's band,' replied Lilly, surprised at the stranger's sudden self introduction. Little did Lilly realize that fresh young seventeen year olds were always choice of the day on Con Dougal's menu.

'So what's yer name, hen, and what do you do? Would you like to dance?'

'My name's Lilly, and yes, I wouldn't mind dancing,' said Lilly, adding, 'let me tell my pals first.'

Lilly, who had been for a drink before the dance with her pals from the work, had consumed two Pimms Number One, thus putting her in the mood to face the music. She soon found the fair stranger sweeping her off her feet with his skilful dancing technique and amusing conversation. She told the stranger that her name was Lilly, she worked at Twomax's knitwear and was at the Barrowland with her workmates for a night out. He told Lilly his name was Connor Dougal and he was in selling. When she asked what line he was in, Dougal had answered vaguely: 'Oh just this and that, you know,' and suddenly, 'You must come round to one of my houses in Warwick Street and meet the gang.'

'That's not far from where I live, in the Gorbals,' replied Lilly excitedly.

'Good, Lilly. Can I see you home? I've got a car, it's no problem.'

Lilly was really impressed. This man has his own car. No ordinary working lassie ever meets a lumber with his own transport. Lilly smiled. Little could she know that the man she had just met would turn out to be one of the worst crooks, brothel keepers and inveterate womanizers in the whole of the Gorbals, along with his alter ego, the loathsome Bull Bakley.

Back at the Gorbals Police office, Sergeant Rat Ratley had been castigating Angus for not solving the case of the crowing cockerel. And there were break-ins at cafés and wholesalers as the crooks (Con Dougal's gang) sought clothes, drink and cigarettes for the flourishing Blackmarket. Tenants were complaining about the noisy cockerel, business men were complaining about the thefts, Sergeant Ratley was complaining to Auchterlony and his colleagues about both, and local councillors were pressing the Chief Constable himself.

In one case, that of the crowing rooster, the time had come for the plucking of the troublesome fowl's tail. Mrs Rafferty, who resided in Nicholson Street above a certain Bahadur Ali, was sure that the crowing was coming from Ali's flat below. She was sure, and even her next door neighbour, big Ina with the varicose veins, agreed, for she had the keenest pair of ears in the close, except when you asked her for a loan.

The sound of chanticleer always broke at dawn and ceased as daylight grew.

'Do ye hear that bliddy cratur crowing now,' said Mrs Rafferty. 'Ah rose early tae be here wi' yous Constables, as a witness.'

'Ach yes, missus, it would waken the dead,' replied Angus.

His companion, Constable Rab Haw Dingley, the Southern's biggest glutton (he had eaten three full dinners at the canteen, complete with three puddings, and then had a sausage roll and tea afterwards) piped up. 'Why the hell does this Ali fellow keep a bloody cock? Is it a pet or something?'

Angus shrugged his shoulders sheepishly and said, 'Right, we're going in,' as if it was an attack. Without further ado, the two sturdy Policemen hammered on the door of the flat below with the faded brass plate announcing 'B. Ali'.

'Mr Ali, open up, Police!' cried Constable Dingley.

After a long pause, a further hammering brought forth the sound of a male voice uttering in what sounded like gibberish.

'Who is there, please, tank you?' came a voice in broken English.

'Police, open up!' came the sharp reply.

There followed the sound of rattling of chains and the turning of locks with the exhortation, 'Please be waiting, tank you.'

The door opened on a small brown gentleman with white hair and white stubbly chin, and to the aroma of stale curry. The wee Indian stood before the door holding the leg of a chair, dressed in a woolly singlet, grey longjohns and faded leather slippers.

'You can put the club away now, sir,' said Angus gently.

Constable Dingley enquired officiously, 'Are you the tenant of this property?'

The nervous oriental gentleman replied that yes, he was Bahadur Ali, the tenant of the flat. He lived with his Scotch wife, Maggie, now sleeping, and was a pedlar to trade.

'Do you, Mr Ali, have fowls on the premises,' enquired Angus pointedly.

'Fowl. Fowl?' stuttered Mr Ali, his dark eyes rolling in yellow sockets. 'Is fowl not for players of the football? You are wanting to discuss the football so early in morning?'

'Whit the hell is he on aboot, Auchterlony?' cried Dingley. 'Does he think we're here to discuss last Saturday's old firm game at Celtic Park?'

To the amazement of both Constables, Mr Ali piped up, smiling broadly. 'Ah yes, sirs, Celtic 4 Ranger 3 in scorings of the goals. My wife ees very keen fan!'

Both constables grinned widely in amusement as they realised the conversation was turning into farce.

'Do you have a cockerel in your house, Mr Ali?' enquired an almost exasperated Dingley bluntly.

'Oh, the cockerel. He's make too much singing, cock-doodle-doo early morning, I thinking,' sighed Mr Ali.

Questioned as to whether he was harbouring a male fowl of the species, namely a cockerel, Mr Ali freely admitted it – the obvious din was proof enough, and Mrs Rafferty nearby was uttering, 'Whit a bliddy heathen thing to be keeping in a shuman hoose!'

When the constables were invited into the dimly lit hall, the shuffling and dispirited Mr Ali led them to a cupboard and threw open the door. There, on a sawdust floor, stood the biggest cockerel that Man had ever laid eyes on. It stood as tall as an Irish wolfhound, its malevolent yellow eyes set in a large head topped by an impressive red cockscomb! The gigantic cockerel stood resolutely with glistenening brown plumage, its black tail arching jauntily, its yellow eyes blinking menacingly, and let out the most ear-shattering crowing the constables had ever heard. 'Co-ack-a-doodle doo. Co-ack-a-doodle doo!' There followed the protesting sounds of neighbours hammering on walls and ceilings, from all points of the compass in general.

'Very nice *murghee*, no?' smiled Mr Ali proudly. 'I keep him for Ramadan feast, soon near weekend.'

'*Murghee*?' queried Angus.

'Yes sir, *murghee* is fowl in my language, Urdu.'

To the question as to whether he realised he was contravening the law and sanitary regulations by keeping a fowl in domestic dwellings, Mr Ali just smiled and raised his hands. He was Mussalman and just fattening up the *murghee* for the Eid feast at the end of the holy month of Ramadan.

'I fasting all Ramadan. Very hungry. So hard carry heavy case all over Scotland in cold weather. But cockerel not making best curry. Big hen murghee, much better. I got cockerel for good price.'

'To get to the point, Mr Ali, our Sergeant and Inspector both have issued orders about the noise your – er . . . *murghee*, or whitever ye call it, has been making. You have to get rid of it,' shouted an excited Dingley.

'Savez,' said Angus. 'Get rid of it, let it fly away. If it doesnae – blow it up!'

'*Sumjee*' [understood], said a crestfallen Ali. 'Such a lovely *murghee* also.'

On the way back to the station, Angus remarked he didn't look like a muscular type to him, Mr Ali saying he was a 'muscle man'.

'He is a Mussalman, ye nutter, Auchterlony. He's a Moslem. I met them in the Army out in India. They make good soldiers, like Sikhs, Pathans and Johnny Gurkhas,' replied Dingley, shaking his head.

On a more serious matter, Angus had been called into Sweeney's pub in Eglinton Street to investigate a disturbance. Angus arrived just before the ambulance to find a man lying on the floor of the bar, surrounded by chards of glass, his hands and face drenched in blood and barely conscious.

'What happened here, pal?' whispered Angus into his ear.

'It wis they Brigton boys. The Billys that chibbed me. Mah ribs is broke tae,' came the faint reply. He had passed out by the time the ambulance men arrived to whisk him away to the Victoria Infirmary, and Angus had been unable to obtain his name.

Angus questioned several patrons including Big Sam, the barman, who revealed the victim was a young man by the name of Michael Patrick Feeney.

'Whit a damn cheek for those blue nose so-and-so's to invade a Sou'side bar!' cried Big Sam with obvious outrage. 'Wait till the Cumbie Boys find out. There's sure to be a raid.'

'Aye, honour I take it,' replied Angus disapprovingly.

The arrival of DC Ed Moran and the CID, along with Sergeant Ratley, led to further questioning of patrons and staff.

'Ye better make your report, as soon as possible, Auchterlony,' said Sergeant Ratley. 'Liaise with DC Moran here of CID.'

Angus had known Detective Constable Ed Moran from the time he had assumed one of his famed disguises as an Irish navvy, complete with brogues, dungarees and clay pipe, as he dug a hole in the road opposite the Portugal Street lodging-house. Erecting a Water Board sign to give his cover an authentic look, Ed had paused often on his pick and shovel as he kept watch on the illegal activities of a street bookie in a nearby close.

'Good day, Mr Moran,' smiled several of the local underworld as they passed by, smirking. 'Hiv ye taken up a new line of work?'

However, like the Mounties, DC Moran always got his man.

'Angus, I obtained a tip-off about the victim, Michael Patrick Feeney,' said Moran quietly.

'Well, maybe we can check Feeney out. He's recovered fit to talk, according to the Victoria,' replied Angus.

'It seems the motive for the attack was the two Billy Boys were out "to claim" Feeny for what he did to their sister. Seemingly the two brothers "chibbed" Feeney, shouting "Fenian bastard" at the time of the attack,' announced Moran.

'And the reason?'

'The unfortunate Mr Feeney had put their sister "in the club",' said Moran.

'Oh, I see it now. Respectable Proddy lass got in the family way, and the Fenian bass buggers off,' laughed Angus grimly.

Subsequent questioning of Feeny in hospital proved the above case to be true.

Another outstanding problem plaguing his beat was a pack of unruly dogs. The Sergeant had been on his back and Angus had always seemed to be one step behind the trail of the canine hooligans. Murderers were probably nearer the mark.

'These bloody curs have torn a woman's cat to pieces. Not only that, they ran off wi' a full leg of lamb from a local butcher,' Sergeant Ratley had shrieked and continued. 'They also attacked an old drunk from the model lodging-house. Finally they chased a bitch on heat into Dr Berkeley's busy waiting room, in Norfolk Street, caused such a shindy that scattered his patients. They're still running yet I hear.'

Angus would have to be on his toes on this one. The Council dog catchers had failed so far to effect a capture but Angus had a plan. But first he would have to pay a visit to Alex Munro's butcher's shop in Cumberland Street when he had a minute.

The saga of the tribe of 'hooligan dugs', as one old cove described them, remained unsolved. Like a tribe of marauding Apaches, pursued by the Glasgow Police and City dog catcher cavalry, the ubiquitous canines were never where they were expected to be. The leader of the seven dogs, which Angus had observed from time to time, was a big dark Alsatian whom he named Geronimo, whilst his dominant female consort was a tan half-breed Labrador whom Angus named Princess. The other members of the tribe were mongrels of varying hues, sizes and dispositions including a particularly waspish character – a black Scottie named Mac whom Angus had warmed to. Mac was always at the tail-end of the pack, his wee legs working like pistons to keep up with his larger mates.

'Here boy,' Angus would cry to the Alsatian pack-leader as he managed to talk to the band of free spirits. They always kept their distance, barking in unison, before making off with little Mac in the rear. The latter, stopping and turning last in line, barked extra loud as if to say that goes twice for me too, before vanishing into the grim canyons of the South Side.

'OK, OK. I hear you!' cried Angus petulantly.

One sunny afternoon, on his two-to-ten shift, Angus had been carrying a number of bones wrapped in brown paper which Munro the butcher had given him. He also carried a handkerchief soaked in essence of aniseed, which his friend Frazer the chemist in Eglinton Street had provided him with.

Angus was becoming concerned with the odour which these bizarre objects gave off as he rested between rounds of his beat in a police-box in Cumberland Street. Knock, knock and the voice of Sergeant Ratley wakened him from a brief cat-nap.

'Skiving again, Auchterlony?' announced Ratley, adding with a sour expression, 'The place smells like a knocking shop!'

Angus wondered how such an upright individual as Sergeant Ratley could know such a thing as that? With a brief enquiry about the dogs, Sergeant Ratley was soon gone, to Angus's relief.

At the corner of Cavendish Street, not far from the school, Angus spied Geronimo and his six braves resting in an untidy tenement front garden, taking in the sun. Advancing cannily, Angus took off his helmet, and spoke gently to the dogs. 'Hello, friends. Gently now. I'm not going to hurt ye.'

Geronimo stood up and walked over to Angus unaggressively. Angus gingerly withdrew a bone from his parcel, offering it to Geronimo as he came closer, and amazed that the pack had not made off barking as they formerly did. Little Mac rose, stretched himself, yapped at Angus, then ambled over to receive the small bone being held out to him. The other dogs moved closer, obviously hungry, and Angus shared out the remainder although there was a brief dispute over the largest bone which Geronimo secured with ease.

Miraculously, Little Mac sniffed Angus's aniseed soaked handkerchief, his bone still gripped in his tiny mouth, and listened to Angus purring, 'Awright, wee fellah. Just calm down now,' as he allowed the dogs to sniff his hands and handkerchief. Soon the whole pack was trotting behind Angus down Abbotsford Place, as he held the mesmerized Little Mac in his arms, before the amused local population. At the Gorbals Police Office, it wasn't long before Angus was leading his band of docile doggies into the dog pound as half a dozen cops, an Inspector and Sergeant Ratley stood gobsmacked witnesses to the remarkable scene.

Like John Wayne leading the surrendering Injuns into Fort Apache, Auchterlony announced to a bemused Sergeant Rat Ratley. 'Seven hostile dog soldiers for the pound, Sergeant!'

It would be many months later that Angus, to his delight, received the sum of seventeen shillings and sixpence from the Excise people for apprehending unlicensed dogs running free. The windfall would help to pay for an evening at the pictures with Kathy, viewing Alan Ladd and Veronica Lake in 'The Blue Dahlia'.

Privately, Angus felt like a Judas. He fervently prayed that some kind person would come forward to claim the seven individualistic free-spirited souls who now lay in the Dog and Cat Home in Cardonald.

CHAPTER 4

The cry of 'R-e-cor-r-r-r-d ... Ti-i-i-mes ... Ce-e-e-e-e-tizen' broke from wee Phil's raucous voice as he stood at his usual spot on the corner of Eglinton and Norfolk Streets selling papers to the punters coming off shift or returning from late night dances.

'Hellaw rerr, ma wee china,' said Angus Auchterlony, imitating the usual Southside greeting, giving the diminutive figure a friendly slap across the shoulders. 'Are ye going to give us an Irish song, before I buy a paper?'

'Sure enough, Constable Auchterlony, no trouble at all,' came the prompt response,

'With a toot on the flute and a diddle on the fiddle,
Dancing in the middle like a herrin' on a griddle,'

And so on ... and so on, wee Phil O'Hara sang, dancing a jig as he dispensed his papers to grinning customers, simultaneously taking in and giving out loose change.

'Great how you do all that ... all at the one time,' exclaimed Angus, clapping his hands in unison with the rest of the bystanders.

'Aye, I'm just naturally gifted,' quipped the wee man, as he remarked seriously, 'I'll see ye, Mr Auchterlony, for your late paper.'

It was an hour later that Wee Phil caught sight of a black Austin 10 pulling up before him as the window wound down and a voice called, 'Citizen, wee man.'

The driver was Bull Bakley. On the backseat, to Phil's surprise, sat Con Dougal with his arm across Lilly Grant's shoulders. Jock Grant sure wouldn't like the sight of this, thought Wee Phil. He would run round after selling his papers and alert Lilly's father, Jock, about the lousy company she had fallen in with.

On his beat in Warwick Street Angus was approached by an elderly, distraught woman who ran up to him crying, 'Constable Auchterlony, hurry. Jock Grant's been beaten up!'

Within minutes the door of Grant's ground floor flat was opened by a neighbour and Angus was confronted by old Jock lying on his bed with bandaged head, a black eye and his body racked in pain.

'What in the name of heavens happened to you?' enquired Angus, adding with urgency, 'I'll away for an ambulance.'

'No, Angus, please. Just gie me another swig o' whisky, it'll dull the pain.'

'I'm no happy about this, Jock,' replied the Policeman.

Jock explained what had happened. He had heard from Phil that Lilly was seen in the car with those two sleezebags, Dougal and Bakley. Much later Jock had dragged himself round to their shebeen. Crawling on his knee up the stair, Jock had hammered on the door with his crutch, calling his daughter's name loudly. Jock described how a drunken Bull Bakley had said there was no one of that name there, and banged the door in his face. When Jock continued, Bakely came to the door, shouting, 'Right, you silly old fucker, you asked for it.' Jock described how he was hit full in the face and physically pushed down the stair by Bakley onto the landing. He tried to climb back up, but couldn't move. Luckily a kindly neighbour called Willie, now in the room, had helped him safely home. Jock described how inadequate he felt at that moment, saying:

'Nae use, wi' this bloody leg o' mine. And me who faced the Hun on the Somme wi' the bare bayonet. I feel so useless, Angus.'

'Dinnae fret, Jock. I'll sort that barrowload of filth out,' hissed Angus vehemently.

Unfortunately there had been no actual eye witness to the attack on Jock. By the time a search warrant could be got, the birds would have flown the coop.

Angus had made up his mind. His blood was on the boil as he hurried round to Con Dougal's house of disrepute. He was upset to see the brave old soldier in tears. Before he realised it, Angus was running up the stairs two at a time, hammering on the door.

'Police, Police. Open up!'

Presently the rattle of a lock revealed the huge dishevelled figure of a scowling Bull Bakley.

'Whit is it ye want, copper?' he snarled.

'I have reason to believe you are holding the young girl, Lilly Grant, here without her parent's permission!'

'Fuck off, fuzz. Where's yer search warrant?' shouted Bakley, raising his fists as if to deliver a punch.

Such threats, and such insults to a Kintyre man like Angus Auchterlony, could only be answered in kind – with the instant retribution of the steam hammer. In a thrice, big ugly Bull Bakley was propelled backwards into the hall by a whacking Joe Louis knock-out punch, as twittering yellow canaries flew round in his brain. Drawing his baton, Angus entered the kitchen through the hall, shouting, 'Police, Police. Police raid. Give way!' Tawdry men and women lay around, some comatose, others drunk as skunks as they regarded the apparation before them with disbelief. Wine and whisky bottles, beer bottles, glasses and cups lay in disarray on the kitchen table; others lay on the floor drained of their contents.

Angus quickly spied Lilly, skirt above her knees and blouse in disarray, seated on Con Dougal's knee, both asleep in a drunken torpor. Quickly securing his baton, Angus gently lifted Lilly across his broad shoulders from the sleeping knee of Con Dougal, simultaneously kicking his chair, sending it backwards onto the linoleum floor. Its occupant didn't move a hair but continued in his state of inebriated bliss. As Angus made his way to the front door, he brushed passed a couple preparing to enter.

'Holy Moses, Po-lice!' cried the sozzled American sailor to his Glasgow floosie.

'Gangway, Police business!' cried Angus brushing them aside, a pair of slim nylon clad legs dangling from his shoulders.

'You ain't gonna tell me, sweetie, the Po-lice are usin' dis place too?' cried the bemused Yank throwing down his white sailor's hat.

Angus all his days would never forget the look of gratitude on Jock's face when he brought Lilly home and laid her on her bed, still asleep from the effect of the drink poured into her at Dougal's shebeen. Jock was like a mother, crying, 'Oh, Lilly, ma wee lass. You're hame again safe, thank God. Angus I'll never forget ye, never.'

It reminded Angus of the time he rescued a sheepdog down a hole in Kintyre, how it licked his face, tail wagging and eyes beaming – just the gratitude of it. Little did Jock realise, in his euphoria, that Angus in rescuing his daughter the way he did had placed himself in jeopardy in the process.

But Angus had been upset at the thought of Lilly being in the grasp of Dougal and Bakley, as he imagined what might happen to her, an innocent and inexperienced young girl. Then there was her father, Jock, passionately looking after her welfare since the death of her mother. Surely a man who had spent four years in the Great War, at Ypres, in the mud of the Somme and at Passchendaele, fighting for his country, deserved better. Sergeant Ratley would undoubtedly relish the opportunity to destroy him, Angus mused. So be it. He had been fully prepared to take the risk for his friend !

As Kathy and her four friends entered the Locarno ballroom one Saturday after a meal and drink to celebrate one of their birthdays, they noticed the two Navy SPs (US Shore Patrol) clad in gleaming white helmets, fondly handling their long white batons, where they stood guard in the foyer.

'The Yanks are in, girls,' whispered a grinning usherette. 'Hang on to yer knickers.'

As they entered the dance-floor it looked as if the whole US fleet had come in: nothing but a sea of navy blue suits and bell bottoms everywhere, swamping the locals. This didn't bother the local women a bit, but it sure as hell did the local men, who found themselves competing with hordes of physical giants. Not only that. They had to contend with all these girl hungry, gum chewing Yankee sailors with swollen wallets and fistfuls of dollars after months at sea, giving the local dames a line on how they had friends in the movies and, if they played their cards right, they might be able to get them a part.

Kathy was not one of those gullible ones, to fall for a line like that as she danced with a series of partners, both Yanks and locals, but with no particular interest except passing conversation. Not, that is, till a tall handsome guy wearing a short sleeved Hawaiian shirt approached her. Kathy took an immediate shine to the guy with the smiling face and light grey eyes who purred, 'Would you like to dance, honey?'

'You're an American,' Kathy remarked as they danced a foxtrot to 'My Foolish Heart', saying, 'Are you a civvy?'

The big man laughed loudly. 'Oh no. I'm glad to be out of the uniform of the US Army Airforce for once. My name is Joe. Joe Cherkowski from Boontown, New Jersey to be precise. The name's Polish but I'm American as apple pie.'

'Well, Joe, I'm Kathy MacDonald from hereabouts. Glad to meet you.'

For the rest of the evening, Kathy had eyes for no one else, politely refusing dozens of invitations from men in uniforms and local guys. When the band had struck up with 'Anchors Aweigh', a fever descended on the sailors who accidently or deliberately shoved the Marines and their partners. Soon the concerted voices of the Marines broke out into 'From the Halls of Montezuma to the shores of Tripoli' and the song filled the hall as the band took up the strains. Soon men and women patrons were scattering as outbreaks of fighting erupted between Navy and Leathernecks.

'Right, Kathy, time to skedaddle. It's gonna get hot in here soon,' yelled Joe, grabbing Kathy's hand. Kathy was relieved to meet her pals out on the hall with Joe, as half a dozen SPs shot from a jeep, whistles blowing and white batons waving wildly as they rushed like mad firemen to a conflagration.

Joe explained that he had to meet his buddies on the Airforce bus back to Prestwick at midnight. Before parting Joe gave Kathy his base phone number and, generously hailing a taxi, told the cabbie to take them all back to the Southside. The driver beamed as Joe thrust a five pound note into his hand, shouting, 'Thanks, Yank.'

Meantime, with the vagaries of police shifts, leaves and exingencies, Angus managed to arrange a Friday evening date with Kathy.

'Can you never manage a Saturday off, Angus?' cried an irritated

Kathy on the many occasions he came into the Fruit Box for a brief chat.

'The only Saturday you get off in the Polis, dear, is when you're dead or win the Littlewoods and quit!' Angus replied with a grim smile. They had all laughed. One advantage of shifts, Kathy recalled Angus saying, was you could always use it for turning down unwanted invitations.

Kathy met Angus in Sauchiehall Street which suited them both, coming from opposite ends of the city. After a drink in the Rogano, Angus treated her to an enjoyable evening at the La Scala, at one of those tables serving tea and cakes, with a great view of the screen. The picture was called 'I Know Where I'm Going' with Wendy Hiller and their favourite Roger Livesey, an actor whose unmistakeable voice they found so magnetic. It included other fine actors like Finlay Currie and John Lawrie who together with the drama of the Corryvreckan whirlpool and the accompanying singing of the Glasgow Orpheus Choir, made it a thoroughly memorable evening for them both. They had held hands, the pulsing of the blood through their veins becoming as one.

They returned on a yellow number 3 Coronation tram to the Southside, alighting at Bridge Street, and were soon at Kathy's close in Norfolk Street.

'I really enjoyed the picture to-night, Angus,' said Kathy dreamily.

'Was that all ye enjoyed? What about me?' came the reply.

'Ach, you big teddy-bear, Angus, ye're just looking for some sympathy,' whispered Kathy kissing him on the cheek. To her surprise, Angus suddenly grabbed her tightly round the waist, kissing her impulsively.

'Take it easy, D93. What would the Chief Constable say about your conduct?'

'You know what he can do with himself,' replied Angus squeezing even tighter and then enquiring, 'What did the bold Mr Robb say about our date to-night?'

Kathy bit her lip, then answered, 'You know Sean. He said it was a waste of time going about with you. There's no future marrying a Cop – no life for a woman.'

'Och, he doesn't like me, fine I know it,' said Angus, shrugging his broad shoulders as if hurt, then adding, 'But the guy's got a point, a Cop's wife hasn't an easy life.'

Kathy smiled and said, 'It makes no difference what a man's job is if a woman loves him. And besides, I have no plans for getting hitched at present. I'm having too great a time being free.'

Kathy was really fond of Angus, saying nothing as they kissed and embraced. She was not about to tell him about her meeting with the handsome Yank she had recently met at the Locarno. That he was a Flight Sergeant in the US Army Airforce, that he was based in Prestwick, and that she was seeing him regularly on his regular flights between Germany and the States.

Angus was no fool. He sensed that Kathy was holding something back and asked her bluntly. 'Kathy, there's something on your mind. Don't hold back if you're wanting to tell me something.'

Kathy hesitated at first. She couldn't play games with Angus. She started to tell Angus of her meeting with Joe Cherkowski at the dancing, and how they planned to date regularly. 'I have always made it clear that you boys, Sean and yourself, are friends, that we all enjoy going out together. No complications, no commitments.'

What she said took the breath from him, but he didn't reveal a flicker of emotion. Kathy could detect in the gaslight, however, the veiled emotion in Angus's eyes as he said goodnight, pecking her on the cheek before making his way for the last subway back to Partick.

One day, as Angus walked up Abbotsford Place, savouring the lovely aroma of chicken soup issuing from Geneen's Jewish restaurant, he noticed the light flashing in the Police box as he turned into Cumberland Street. Angus quickened his step. When the call came you could never tell whether it would be tragedy or comedy – it usually meant trouble. The urgent message was to attend immediately at number 10 Abbotsford Place, one up, Mr Morris Bloch, structural damage. The fire brigade and local authority had been alerted too.

A small dishevelled man answered the door, his bald head and clothes covered in white plaster and what looked like coal dust, saying: 'The bloody ceilink ees fallink on me. A mann cannot make supe for his dinner without ceilink fallink down!'

Angus entered the hall and made his way into the kitchen, led by the apparent victim of some tragedy or other. Mr Bloch simply pointed up. As Angus looked up the sight left him gobsmacked. A large hole, about two feet square, glared at him in the ceiling of the flat above, coal hanging precariously around the edges.

'In the name of all that's holy!' cried Angus, continuing, 'What could have happened?'

Mr Bloch's gas cooker with his pan of soup lay under a large heap of coal and plaster. The offending coal had obviously come from the flat above. Bloch had been lucky, he was not injured, but he was upset – especially about his dinner. Angus enquired about the neighbour above, intending to pay him a visit.

'The mann above, kinder and frau is all friendship of mine. He is mine *Shabbos Goy*.'

'Shabbos what?' enquired Angus, scratching his chin.

'Jah, jah. He is mann who light fire for me on *Shabbos* – you call Shabbath, no?'

Angus understood right away. Jewish people paid their Christian neighbours a few coppers to light their gas or coal fires on their Sabbath in accordance with the strict religious code. Angus inspected the flat above where the door had been opened by a skinny, dark haired boy about twelve years old. He said, 'Ma name is Ronnie, and I'm off the school to see about the hole. My ma and da are away to the shop, and my wee sister's at school.'

'What happened here, son?' enquired the Constable.

'It was after the eighth bag that the coalbunker fell in,' said Ronnie. 'My dad makes me stand at the bunker door, and count the bags. He says the coalman sometimes misses a bag oot!'

'Is that a fact, son?' said Angus jotting down a few notes in his black book.

'Are ye putting down aboot the coalman missing oot the odd bag, constable?'

'Oh, aye, aye, Ronnie, that's very important, son,' replied Angus reassuringly and adding, 'Mr Bloch says you are a very helpful boy, helping to light his fire and run his messages.'

'He's a nice old man, Mr Bloch. At times I cannae make oot whit he says though. I mind I brought him a tin o' soup from Morrison's. It was soap he was wanting instead, it sounded like "soup" he was saying.'

Angus smiled and looked down the hole in the kitchen cupboard which had been turned into a coal bunker. A fireman's helmet appeared and shouted:

'In the name o' Bayne & Duckett's. Whit happened here, Constable?'

A subsequent visit by Angus and the Building Inspector of Glasgow Corporation to Ronnie's parents brought forth the answer. When Ronnie and his sister Kathleen came home from school they always made tea by heating up the pot on the gas ring. Against the instructions of their parents, who were out at business, the kids always emptied the old tea leaves into the coal bunker in order to keep the stour or dust down. They should have flushed the leaves down the sink but were too lazy. Just as the coal man was humping in the eighth bag, the floor joists and boards which had become infested by wet-rot collapsed under the load. Ronnie had said the black faced coalman's white eyes went round in circles like in the films and he screamed, 'Holy Christ! Ah've been doing this job fer years and ah've never seen the like o' it before in ma puff!'

The findings of the Building Inspector and Insurance Assessor found Ronnie's parents liable for Mr Bloch's damage which was all restored to its original condition. Ronnie had his rear end tanned by an irate parent, and never again emptied tea leaves into the nearby coal bunker. Mr Bloch continued having his kosher soup once again, but forever after wearing an old top hat and throwing frequent nervous glances at that spot in the ceiling above.

Mr Bahadur Ali, a Johnnie Pedlarman, was carrying his large leather case as he made his way home off the bus at around 6 p.m. His big case was a lot lighter than it had been when he set out in the early morning. Business had been good around the wee Lanarkshire mining towns and he had secured many orders from kind housewives who plied him with large mugs of hot tea and sausage rolls, which his eastern palate had great difficulty adjusting to after his normal diet of curry and chapatties.

Mr Ali, he of the infamous crowing cockerel case, solved by the intrepid D93 Police Constable Auchterlony, was looking decidedly down in the mouth when he bumped into Angus making his rounds.

'Mr Ali, is this you away home after yer day out? Where were you to-day?'

'I been Carluke to-day. Very busy. Case not so heavy now,' said Ali, thankfully laying down his big case. Then he added with a frown, 'I go Police affice see Inspector Ali. Now.'

'Is that about yer *murghee*, as ye called it?' enquired Angus.

Mr Ali nodded his head, and after saying farewell to Angus, made his way down to the Police Office in Nicholson Street.

As he entered, Mr Ali was confronted by the Bar Officer.

'Can I be of help, sir?' enquired the Policeman.

'I come see one Inspector wallah,' said Ali.

'What's it about, sir?' asked the Sergeant.

'Is about my *murghee*. Sorry, cockerel, you call him. Policeman name Aucheelony, number D93, tell me see Inspector Benjamoon Ali,' replied the Indian, adding, 'I am thinking he *burrah* [big] Indian Police wallah, in your estation.'

It was a while before the Bar Officer returned, having enquired about the whereabouts of an Indian Police Inspector name Benjamoon Ali. No one had ever heard of, let alone seen the person mentioned by the pedlar. It was the appearance of Inspector Benjamin MacAlee that finally settled the mystery, who confirmed he was the officer who was dealing with the cockerel business.

'Ah, *shabash*! [all right!]. So you are a *gorah wallah* [white man] not an Indian *logh* [man] with name of Benjamoon Ali?'

'My name is Benjamin MacAlee, sir. Not Benjamoon Ali!' emphasised the Inspector with a dead-pan, unamused expression.

Mr Ali confirmed the cockerel was now long dead. 'It make okay curry. Meat a bit tough.' He said it had taken himself, his wife and a neighbour to kill it, and it kicked like a donkey!

Inspector MacAlee finally warned the swarthy fellow. 'No more live cockerels, Mr Ali, before or after yer Ramadan. Ye need tae kill them first.'

'Yes, most impotent [important] personnage,' replied the wily Indian. 'I make no more problem with chicken. I am promising you.'

Before departing, Mr Ali had opened up his case and displayed his last remaining samples to the gaze of the intrigued cops behind the Bar. They were hooked. Before departing the station with a warning, Mr Ali had secured orders from half a dozen bemused officers for shirts, ties and two pairs of socks a-piece – with a promise of further orders!

Nevertheless, Inspector MacAlee would never fathom how the wily Oriental had sussed that he and his wife couldn't have children. He remarked to his friends later:

'Aye, the Indian must be some kind of fakir or mystic. He addressed me directly as "most impotent personnage" before he left. And the Bar Officer heard him too!'

When Mr Ali told Angus of his encounter with Inspector MacAlee later, Angus could hardly contain himself, especially the part about making the sales. The big fellow folded up in uncontrollable laughter as Ali finally departed, saying, 'I go home now, Mr Aucheelony, need rice and curry. You come my house, next week. I cook you nice Indian food.'

CHAPTER 5

Detective Constable Moran had mentioned earlier to Angus, back in the Gorbals police station, that the CID had received a tip-off from an informer. Supposedly one of Con Dougal's houses, the one in Surrey Street was stashed with stolen goods, such as watches, cigarettes, and booze including hooch. The CID were planning a raid. Angus commented to Moran that at the time of his foray into Dougal's other flat in Nicholson Street, to rescue Lilly, he had caught sight of a bottle of the clear liquid on the table. He hadn't got time to stop and investigate but the odour of hooch he knew well.

'Oh yes, Angus. You better be prepared for flak about the unauthorised entry into Dougal's place,' commented Moran, his face taking on a serious look. 'I hear Mr Con Dougal's lawyer has made a formal complaint.' Angus's reply was unrepeatable.

Nevertheless, Angus wasn't mistaken about the hooch or moonshine, or whatever you want to call it. He recalled an incident as a young man at a shepherd's bothy on the island of Islay, as he and some cronies had been imbibing the local 'firewater' around a roaring fireplace. They were all 'pretty full', as Seumas Macalpine recounted local tales of ghosts and queer happenings to young Angus, and half a dozen grizzly, old, drunken shepherds. Macalpine would take a swig of his own 'mountain dew' every so often, smacking his lips as he paused in the telling of his tales.

Angus remembered with a smile how Finn O'Shea, an ancient shepherd from Donegal, had produced a bottle from a smelly old sack, shaking it and holding it up to the light, causing little bubbles to rise. A smiling O'Shea purred, 'Ah see the wee darlin's rising now.' His face glowing in the heat of the fire, O'Shea had announced, 'That's the podgereen: the sign of true quality. Made it meself from praities and beets. And it's over bloody 150 proof!'

As O'Shea had bent over the open fireplace to light his pipe, he inadvertently let out a loud belch. Instantly everyone fell back alarmed as a huge tongue of flame shot out, singeing O'Shea's hair and beard. The latter cried out, 'Bejaysus. Ah thought old Nick had got me!' Angus and all present had burst into stitches at the sight of O'Shea's smoking hair and singed beard, his pipe still between clenched teeth.

Here and now, Angus had been informed by Sergeant Rat Ratley to be ready for a dawn raid with the CID next morning. He didn't reveal the target of the raid but Angus felt smug, knowing beforehand, courtesy of DC Moran. Angus's smugness was soon washed off as Ratley called him aside. 'Auchterlony, you're in trouble, boy. Con Dougal's solicitor has lodged a formal complaint to the Chief Constable about your harassment, and entering his property without an authorised search warrant.' Sergeant Ratley was clearly relishing Auchterlony's discomfort, finally adding, 'You will be called before Inspector MacAlee and the Divisional Superintendent in the near future.'

Angus did not say a word. As a final barb Sergeant Ratley announced, his voice dropping conspiratorially, 'The word on the street, Auchterlony, is that Con Dougal and Bull Bakley are as mad as meat cleavers with you taking the Grant girl away, and they're out to get ye. So watch out!'

Next morning, at three-thirty a.m. on a cold, grey and drizzling dawn, when the world was in deepest sleep, the Police raiding party was readied. The Inspector, Sergeant Ratley and six burly Constables including Auchterlony, alighted from the Police van following behind the unmarked car which contained the CID team, comprising DC Moran and three detectives. The party ran swiftly up the stairs to the third story flat in Surrey Street with a noise that would have awakened the dead, hammering loudly on the door. 'Open up, Police!' screamed the Inspector, repeatedly hammering on the door, his back-up squad crowding expectantly behind him like a primed fist.

Presently, a tired voice could be heard crying, 'Okay, okay, haud yer horses. Ah'm comin'.'

The door opened with the rattling of the lock to reveal a large fat face, dressed in a tatty nightshirt which looked as if it had been nicked from Paddy's Market. The fat man blinked into the Inspector's torch as the rest of the Police heavies brushed a gasping Fatty Brown effortlessly aside as he protested, 'Hey, hiv yous got a search warrant?'

The Inspector waved the search warrant under Fatty's nose shouting, 'Here's our authority. We have reason to believe you are harbouring stolen goods in here!'

'Be my guest, Inspector,' smirked Fatty Brown shouting, 'Edge-up, Police. And, bye the bye, Mr Dougal is not going to be happy aboot a' this.'

A thorough search revealed a foul-mouthed slut in the bedroom, shivering and holding a blanket to her chin, shouting, 'Hey Fatty, whit in fuck's name's goin' on?'

'Get up, missus,' shouted Sergeant Ratley roughly. Then he barked an order to Auchterlony and another cop.

'Search that mattress – and under the bed too!' Fatty's woman stood in a corner traumatised, with an old blanket wrapped around her, shielding her virtue – if ever it had existed. A young girl, clad only in a vest and knickers, materialised suddenly from under the bed to the amazement of the cops present.

'Looks like three-in-a-bed,' cried Angus to the delight of the other cops.

Inspector MacAlee exclaimed. 'Lucky Fatty Brown. A *ménage-à-trois*. Gie the lassie a cover for goodness sake!'

The kitchen recess bed revealed a drunken couple, arms entwined as they snored away their dreams, thanks to the empty beer bottles and drained Red Tape whisky bottle which lay on the untidy kitchen table. They were finally wakened from their comatose state, rubbing their sleepy eyes as a minor earthquake was taking place around them. Two cops up-ended their mattress, with Sergeant Ratley shouting like a mock Goldilocks, 'Wake up, you bears. Or you'll be nicked!'

A thorough search of every niche of the room and kitchen revealed nothing. Even floor boards had been lifted. The crestfallen Police squad departed, with Inspector MacAlee remarking, 'Yer clean this time, Brown. But we'll meet again.'

'Inspector, yer always welcome. Especially if ye have a warrant,' quipped the fat man.

'Aye, an let's hope yon wee lassie isn't under age, Brown. Otherwise you're in trouble. We have her home address,' replied Detective Moran, adding the parting shot, 'No doubt we'll see you, and your Mr Con Dougal again.'

Little did the Police know that the wily Con Dougal had transferred their haul of watches, booze and cigarettes the night before, tipped off by a bent copper.

One drizzling morning Angus was on school crossing duty in West Street, by special courtesy of Sergeant Ratley. Every morning Angus would guide the horse-drawn bread vans and grain carts through the crossing coming from local bakeries and mills, as he held back the exuberant school kids till they passed by. On this particular morning in question, Angus's senses were alerted by the approach of an unusually fast bread van. He soon realised that two driverless horses, reins trailing on the road, were runaways and shouted an alarm to the kids.

'Stand back on the pavement. Quickly, quickly and don't dare move!'

With his heart pounding, Angus stepped into the path of the oncoming horses and driverless van, his arms outstretched horizontally. He shouted 'Who . . . ah. Who . . . ah!' but it was obvious the two terrified horses had no intention of stopping in their distraught state. Angus visualised his flat, run-over body being lifted in the form of a cross. How fitting, he mused in this moment of jeopardy.

Recovering his wits, Angus sprinted alongside the maddened horses, frothing from their mouths, manes streaming wildly as steam issued from their extended nostrils, with the cacophony of screeching pupils yelling like impis of Zulu warriors in the background, 'Go on, Constable Auchterlony. On, on, Auchterlony. Auchterlony!' An oblivious Constable Auchterlony didn't hear a thing, as he ran and prayed that the runaway horses wouldn't collide with other vehicles or pedestrians on the busy thoroughfare.

By the time the runaways reached the low railway bridge just past Scotland Street, the frothing and neighing horses had slowed down.

They weren't the only ones that felt that way. By a combination of sheer tenacity and good fortune, Angus manged to pull level with the horses, and bending down as he ran seized a rein in desperation, crying, 'Who . . . oah. Who . . . oah, cuddies. Who . . . oah!'

Almost immediately, Angus felt himself being dragged along the hard tarmac road, his legs and rear end taking a hammering, his head bouncing painfully off the vibrating shafts of the van as he desperately heaved on the reins whilst at the same time trying to avoid the flying hooves. He miraculously managed to push himself across the nearest horse's neck, and finally mounted its broad back, as he had done on the farm in Kintyre when a lad. Exerting his full weight on the reins with continuous cries of 'Who . . . ah. Who . . . ah, cuddies,' Angus was immeasurably relieved when his efforts finally paid off. The momentum of the runaways lessened markedly, finally coming to a halt before Crawford Street near the mineral depot. Gently soothing the two stationary and whinnying horses in gentle tones, their muzzles flecked with foam, a thoroughly exhausted Angus Auchterlony dismounted and lay on the pavement still gripping their reins.

'Now there, it's all over, shush now,' repeated Angus over and over again, as if in a trance.

Soon an admiring crowd of kids and adults stood around the recumbent hero, patting him on the chest. Some were shouting, 'Hi-oh Silver, Cowboy!' Others cried, 'Gene Autry!'

A passing detective, whom he instantly recognised, announced, 'Jeeze, Auchterlony, that was pure, bloody magnificent. I'm sure you'll get the VC,' adding, 'And I'm yer witness. I'm phoning for an ambulance right away. Just rest awhile.' The detective tied the horses' reins to a lamp-post temporarily.

Angus was soon aware of an inebriated old tramp, clad in a ragged raincoat and black beret, standing over him, as he slowly opened his eyes from his recent exertions. The old tramp was holding a soggy brown carrier-bag and rattling the shards of glass with the overpowering stink of methylated spirits pervading the air. The old character was soon giving him laldy (scolding) as he shrieked, 'Ye and yer bliddy cuddies running wild. Ye made me drap ma kerry-oot as ah crossed the road!'

adding with further vehemence, 'Ah'll be suing ye Polis bastards tae. Imagine playing fuckin' Hopalong Cassidy – and you on duty tae!'

Angus was immediately convulsed in laughter which made all his sore parts tingle with pain. He didn't care, though, because he was enjoying the laugh. It relieved the pressure. 'Playing fuckin' Hopalong Cassidy, indeed!' Angus tittered at what the tramp had said. And the meth was his carry-out too. The tramp looked and left, muttering, 'Yon, Polis is aff his heid. Aff his heid!'

Angus was still in stitches as he waited for the ambulance to arrive and would no doubt be too when he reached the hospital.

In the meantime, as he waited, his mind went back to a time when as a youngster he used to help his father with the horses at a farm at Southend in Kintyre. He recalled Bess and Bob, the big Clydesdales which were so gentle and intelligent. Bess was the worker and Bob, the easy-going soul who loved to share his corn and oats with the sparrows who hung on his huge mane, whistling and peering into his big, brown eyes, as if to say thank you. Angus particularly remembered the amazing tale of Uncle Lachlan's big Clydesdale named Tam. Big, good natured Tam ploughed Lachlan's farm at Achmore, between Strome Ferry and Plockton. Angus recalled how big Tam was loaned out to a neighbouring farm across the loch to assist in the harvest. He well remembered his Uncle Lachie relating how, early one morning, the noise of a horse's hooves clomping on the cobblestones of the farmyard, accompanied by loud whinnying, awoke him and his wife. When Lachie looked out of the farmhouse window, he had screamed:

'Heather! Quick, Heather. It's big Tam. He's back, but how in heaven's name?'

When both farmer and wife went down in their night-clothes, sure enough big Tam came forward and nuzzled them fondly. The horse was soaked in salt water and covered with strands of seaweed and Uncle Lachie had cried out in tears, 'Tam, Tam, ma auld buddy. Ma auld frien', ye finally came home.'

What a feat and what a story, for big Tam had swam more than a mile across the stretch of the Strome Ferry – clear across Loch Carron ! And a tidal sea loch too! That is why Angus adored horses, especially the big work horses, whom he could always befriend by speaking into their muzzles, and offering a welcomed sugar lump or juicy carrot.

Soon the arrival of the ambulance brought Angus back to reality. A carter from the local bakery led the horses away, adding with gratitude, 'That was a great feat, Constable. The firm will be in touch with your office, thanks again.'

Several days recuperation had been grudgingly accepted by Sergeant Ratley upon the insistence of Inspector MacAlee who declared, 'Superb job, Auchterlony. A full report has been requested by the Chief Constable himself. The Divisional Super says the Chief has read all the newspapers about yer exploits too. Good for the Force, ye see.'

Sergeant Ratley stood silent, his stoney face reddening, and saying nothing, as if Angus's deed had never happened. All Ratley smirkingly said later was, 'Your Dougal harassment case – don't forget it's next week.'

Kathy MacDonald was enjoying the dinner dance at the Swan Hotel in Ayr. She had been invited there, all expenses paid, by Sean Robb to celebrate his nephew Joseph's twenty-first birthday. Joseph was a darkly handsome young man, similar in looks to his Uncle Sean but of a sunnier personality. Kathy enjoyed dancing with Joseph, laughing at his funny jokes and patter. She learned that his father, Sean's elder brother, had died a Japanese prisoner-of-war on the Siam Death Railway.

Sean's mother, Margaret, was a friendly Ayrshire woman in her late fifties, with blond hair and a love of dancing. She was up for every dance and never ceased talking of her Sean. 'He's a good boy, Sean. He'll mak' a good catch for some steady lass, ane day,' winking as she added, 'And he'll inherit the tattie business too when I go.'

Kathy's blue eyes darkened imperceptibly as she took in the hint. She smiled noncommitally, saying, 'Aye, Sean's a fair catch for a lass.' She couldn't add, especially when he wasn't in one of his dark moods, or when the drink wasn't in him. She always had reservations about Sean in a way that she didn't have with Angus or even with her new American friend Joe. But you never know someone till you've lived with them, and then it's too late when you're married. But that was the last thing on her mind at present so she had several gin and ginger beers to jolly herself. She chatted to Sean's two sisters, Alice and Lorna. Alice was a blonde and plump like her mum, Margaret, and friendly. Lorna was a different character, dark and distant. She gave Kathy the impression of not being family and only there on sufferance.

Sean's uncles were pleasant Ayrshire farming and country folk whom she took to immediately. Sean introduced her to a big fat, happy faced man.

'This is Alfie, the manager of this den of iniquity. He and I were at school together,' laughed Sean, slapping Alfie on the back. Alfie responded by bringing a bottle of champagne over to their group's table. Sean's mum, his sisters, Joseph, and Kathy all shouted excitedly as Alfie, with a knowing wink at Sean, popped the cork. 'Here's tae us all. Wha's like us. Here's to a good night, Sean.'

Sean Robb laughed with a knowing smile at Alfie which puzzled Kathy, but she would only fathom the meaning later.

It was just past midnight when the quartet, which had provided a great selection of current hits as well as tunes of yesteryear, struck up 'Auld Lang Syne'. Kathy held hands with Sean on her right and Margaret on her left, as they sang:

'Should auld acquaintance be forgot,
And never brought to mind?
Should auld acquaintance be forgot,
And auld lang syne.'

There were tears in Sean's mother's eyes as the song ended.

'Auld Rabbie gave the world a truly universal sang there,' Margaret said, recalling her deceased husband, Jack, who had been born in Ayr. 'Aye, as Rabbie said, "Auld Ayr, wham ne'er a town surpasses, For honest men and bonnie lasses".'

'Aye, mither,' said Sean, slurring his speech after countless whiskies. 'You were the bonnie Ayrshire lass, and my da' was ane honest Ayrshire man.'

'There's nae mony o' them left,' laughed one of Sean's favourite uncles, but the others all cried in mock derision, 'Ach away wi' ye, mon, they're all here.'

The dance broke up with family and friends kissing and hugging, some departing homewards with a song on their lips. Sean's mother gave Kathy a big hug, saying, 'Now mind, Kathy, yer always welcome to our hame like ane o' the family.'

Collecting their keys from Alfie at the desk in the foyer, the latter remarked, 'You two are neighbours. Yours is number seventeen, Sean, hers is number eighteen.'

'He looks as if he'll need some help,' said Kathy, 'I doubt if he'll find his room.' Alfie said he'd take care of his old pal Sean, and wished Kathy sweet dreams.

Kathy entered her room which was clean and basic, and changed into her nightdress in a kind of a fog. She noticed that the door to the adjoining room had a swivel lock on it but thought no more of it. Before descending into sleep, she smiled. She had won one of the raffles, a bright red and yellow garter. They all insisted she roll up her blue cocktail dress, to slip her garter over a shapely nylon leg, to the hoots and whistles of all males present. It was all good clean fun, she thought, and was soon asleep.

Kathy awakened as if in a dream to something beside her. Heavy breathing, and hands under her nightdress caressing her breasts and private parts, gave her a pleasant yet unreal sensation. Was this an erotic dream brought on by the effects of imbibing too many gins?

Soon a heavy weight pressing on her body, and the strong smell of alcohol stifled her breathing, leaving her in no doubt. In the dark, all Kathy was aware of was that a male was in her bed, and she was about to be raped. She switched on a rickety bedside light and there, to her surprise, was Sean, eyes half closed, panting like a dog on heat. The open door to Sean's bedroom left no doubt how he had entered. Suddenly Kathy was wide awake, pushing Sean roughly off her.

'Sean, what the hell ye playing at?' hissed Kathy like a tigress. 'Get out of here right this minute. You randy, drunken bugger!'

'Kaa . . . Kaathy,' mumbled the inebriated Sean as he slurred, 'A haaard a real need for yer company.'

'Ye'll have a medical need in yer crutch if ye dinnae get out of here,' whispered Kathy, trying not to scream. She felt like a tart. What would

Sean's mother Margaret and all his family think of her ? This fast city girl using her wiles to snare their precious Sean?

'Kaaathy, I loves ye,' slurred Sean, trying to climb on her again.

With one great shove, and a cry of 'Get to hell off me,' Kathy was out of the bed standing with her shoe raised ready to strike.

Sean Robb lay on his front, snoring loudly and out for the count.

Kathy wondered what to do, then had a brainwave. She turned Sean over on his back, loosened his collar, then placing a pillow under his head, covered him over with a blanket. Collecting Sean's things from the neighbouring room, Kathy gathered her own belongings and fled to Sean's room, swivelling the lock tightly shut and placing a chair against the knob for additional security. Sean's bed was unused so Kathy would have a place to sleep without giving cause for scandal. She would waken Sean next morning when he became *compos mentis* and ask for an explanation. More importantly she'd save him any embarrassment.

Early next morning, a surprised and humble Sean Robb was acquainted with his nefarious wandering by an irate Kathy.

'Kathy, Kathy. What can I say, apologise or anything.'

'Get yerself into yer own room and get ready for breakfast. You're lucky yer mother and sisters didn't find out about this. They'd think me a right tart, too,' hissed Kathy. 'You're lucky I'm understanding. But nothing like this better happen again!'

As they went down for breakfast, Alfie the manager gave Sean a knowing wink and quipped, 'Did ye have a comfortable night, Sean old bean?'

Sean said nothing but hung his head, his face reddening. Kathy thought, yes, I bet you pair were the undoubted authors of the tawdry interconnecting door escapade. Kathy stared steely-eyed at Alfie, saying nothing.

The time was at hand for PC D93, Angus Auchterlony, Probationary Constable of the Southern Division, to face the music at Craigie Street Police Station over the Con Dougal unauthorised entry charge. Standing with Sergeant Ratley, Angus faced a battery of seated officers. An Assistant Chief Constable, the Divisional Superintendent 'Toffy Legs' and Inspector MacAlee faced him like a battery of loaded cannon.

'You have committed a serious breach of Police procedure, entering a public dwelling without proper authorisation,' announced 'Toffy Legs' severely. 'What have you to say, Constable?'

'Sir, I acted to save a defenceless young girl, at the mercy of known criminals and exploiters of young women,' replied Angus straightforwardly.

'How did you know she was in there to act so?' enquired the Assistant Chief Constable.

'I learned from the witness stated, the newspaper man, that she was seen in their company. Lilly's father was distraught and had been attacked by Bull Bakley.'

'There are elements of doubt in this case which will need to be handled by the lawyers,' replied the Assistant Chief Constable. 'But the Chief Constable has been very impressed by your valiant action with the runaways. You are to be recommended for the Corporation Police Medal for bravery.' A pause ensued. 'Nevertheless, Auchterlony, you are formally cautioned that the Dougal unauthorised entry case will be entered against you. So be careful in future. Dismiss!' concluded Divisional Superintendent 'Toffy Legs'.

'You are one lucky bastard, Auchterlony,' snarled Sergeant Ratley afterwards.

Angus gave a great sigh of relief. He was off the hook, and with a medal to follow as well. He resolved to rush over to the Fruit Box right away, with a bottle of wine, to share the good news with Kathy and Nan.

CHAPTER 6

Police Constable Angus Auchterlony patrolled his night beat down Bridge Street, Gorbals, checking premises such as the Café del Sole and John Bach's, the music shop where he frequently bought his Crosby and Sinatra gramophone records. The chill mist from the nearby River Clyde swirled along the dank streets, like a street scene from a Jack-the-Ripper film.

Angus had been warned by the CID that the big furniture store at the corner of Bridge Street and Carlton Court might be hit. The office safe was to be targeted, so the word said. This information, combined with recent warnings from Sergeant Rat Ratley, made Angus edgy and alert. He concluded that if any personal threat was imminent it had to come from Messrs Dougal and Bakley, particulary after his forced entry into their Nicholson Street sheeben to carry young Lilly Grant away.

As Angus turned into dimly lit Carlton Court, directing the narrow beam of his flashlight on the rear doors of the big furniture store, he was entering one of those dark regions of danger and uncertainty which Policemen the world over had to face daily. That particular night Angus became aware of a tall male figure standing at a close-mouth, silhouetted against the dim rays of the gas-light. As he approached Angus observed that the figure appeared drunk as he muttered to himself, his black donkey jacket collar drawn up, obscuring his face.

'Hello, Constibule,' the man slurred. 'Ah've been waitin' for a feckin taxi for the last hauf-hoor.'

'Where you going, sir?' enquired Angus shining his flashlight into flickering eyes.

'Brigton Cross's whaur ah stay. Just been tae a party up the close here,' said the man hoarsely.

Angus's suspicions were aroused. Why was this character shielding his face? And why was he hanging around on such a dark, wet night – and near the rear entrance of the furniture store? Angus decided to question the suspect; after all he had to watch out for a possible break-in at this location.

'Can I ask your name and address, sir?' questioned Angus taking out his black book.

McCabe, Constibule,' slurred the man, asking another question in return. 'Can you tell us the right time?'

Angus pushed up his sleeve and shone his flashlight onto his wristwatch, as the rain pattered off his heavy raincoat and helmet. He was brushing away the raindrops from the face of his watch when it happened: a sudden flash as a heavy blow struck the back of his head. Strangely, Angus felt the torch slipping from his hand. All he could remember, as if in slow motion, was himself answering, 'One-thirty-in-th . . . ee-moo . . . rr . . . ning!'

Although not aware of an ambush, two more thugs emerged swiftly from behind the fake drunk in the donkey jacket. They set about Angus with a will. Soon the dark figure's confederates were belaying the helmetless and defenceless Policeman with kicks to his legs, and punches and coshes to his head, face, chest, arms and sides. Angus went down, and the kicks continued with curses like 'Fuzz bastard,' and 'Fucking Polis scumbag!'

As Angus lay dazed, half-conscious, eyes barely open, he was just able to make out the figure in the dark donkey jacket bark, 'OK, OK, fellahs. That's enough. We don't want a murder on oor hands. Beat it!'

Angus seemed to be gliding, snake-like, along a long dark tunnel. Then came darkness and unconsciousness, and no more pain. A bloody and bruised Angus lay in the rain, on the bare tarmac, like a rag doll crushed by the sudden and vicious attack. His proud helmet and badge lay in the gutter, the fading light from his flashlight casting shadows across his pale and bruised face, the shards of glass from its smashed cover gleaming in the darkness. It was thus that an early morning workman found the unconsciousness Bobby and immediately phoned for an emergency ambulance which was soon speeding to the Royal

Infirmary with its battered patient.

It was a full day before Angus recovered consciousness and mumbled to a smiling young nurse, 'What am I doing in bloody hospital? My God, I feel as if I've been through a meat grinder!'

'Welcome back to the land of the living,' smiled the young nurse. She replied he was in the Royal Infirmary, and was just recovering from an attack.

Angus nodded slowly, saying, 'Ah, yes, I remember now. Carlton Court.' Then rubbing his bandaged head he quipped, 'Nurse, I'm starving, Can I have a mug o' tea wi' a roll and sausage?'

'I'll go down to the kitchen, and see what I can do, Mr Auchterlony,' replied the nurse. 'I think ye deserve it, Mr Auchterlony. But I'll need to mind the matron.'

'Just call me, Angus, lass,' replied Angus smiling, still rubbing his bandaged head.

It was not long before impatient CID Detectives were at Angus's bedside, with doctors informing them that the patient had not long recovered from surgery and not to be too long with their patient. Ed Moran and his colleagues had waited while Angus had lain unconscious, eager to grasp clues which would lead them to the perpetrators of the vicious attack on a fellow Police Officer. It was twenty-four hours, after a blood transfusion, with drips inserted into him, that Angus's eyes had first flickered open, and he suddenly desired his roll and sausage!

It was clear from the doctors' reports at the Royal that Constable Auchterlony was very fortunate not to have suffered serious brain damage in the attack which could have either killed him or left him a vegetable. It must have been Angus's thick Hielan' skull that saved him; his twenty odd head stitches were healing nicely, according to Mr Shaw, his consultant surgeon, His hazy vision was beginning to improve, although the intermittent headaches persisted. These would fade away but Angus would need a period of rest and recuperation stated Mr Shaw.

Meanwhile, Angus was being spoiled with get-well cards from Kathy and Nan, and from his colleagues in the Gorbals Police Office, with Inspector MacAlee's name to the fore. The signatures of Messrs Ratley and Flockhart were markedly missing. Ordinary members of the public and shopkeepers sent cards and flowers to their favourite beat Cop, wishing him a speedy return. Grace and Dan, from their fish restaurant in Norfolk Street, paid Angus a visit with a large bunch of grapes and bottles of his favourite Barr's Irn Bru.

Kathy and Nan were never away, coming with smiles and large baskets of fruit and flowers, saying, 'These will cheer up the ward, Angus, and ye can share them out wi' the nurses, hard working lassies.'

A signal event which raised a stir with the hospital and his local station was a brief visit from Chief Constable McCulloch who strode in with an executive aide from the hospital management.

'How are you, son?' enquired the Chief, pulling up a chair. 'Are they treating you all right?'

Angus replied, 'Very well, sir, couldn't be better.'

The Chief smiled broadly at the aide as if well satisfied, then spoke in a loud voice, for effect. 'Oh, aye, Auchterlony. That was a brave effort with those runaway cuddies [horses] in West Street. You're being recommended for a medal. You'll be hearing from us.'

'Thank you, sir,' replied Angus, not knowing whether to salute or raise himself to sitting attention.

'Get well soon, son,' announced the Chief Constable, picking up his black leather gloves. 'You'll be hearing from me.'

With that, the smiling Chief departed with a friendly wave of his hand.

Life went on as usual in the Gorbals without Angus's presence, for individual human beings are not indispensible. The Gorbals Police Office kept chasing criminals; Jock Grant still did his 'hing out of the windae' though missing Angus's chat; Kathy and Nan kept to their daily routine with the tatties and veg; and at number 40 Abbotsford Place, Mrs Golda Fineman kept fussing her husband, Louis.

The reason was the imminent Bar Mitzvah ceremony for their son Myer, who had just turned thirteen. Golda harped on. 'You've arranged with Rabbi Goldblum the time at the Synagogue?'

'Yes, dear, everything is organised,' adding as if for assurance, 'we got Myer a nice tallith [prayer shawl]. Silk too, best quality.'

'Good about the quality. I prefer silk to wool. After all he'll be buried in it one day, and silk is more comfortable,' replied Golda thoughtfully. 'I've also given the Rabbi the Siddur [prayer book] for Myer's presentation too.'

'Cheer up, Golda, the boy won't be worrying about comfort then, for goodness sake. It's for Myer's Bar Mitzvah – not his funeral!' quipped Louis lightly, placing a comforting arm aroung his plump Yiddishe wife.

The ceremony of Myer's Bar Mitzvah would take place several Saturdays later, on Shabat, the Jewish sabbath. Shabat really started on Friday evening and closed on Saturday evening. Louis and Golda Fineman had two children, Myer aged thirteen and Sarah aged eleven years and about to take her eleven-plus in nearby Abbotsford Primary. Sarah hoped to join her brother's secondary school in Govanhill. Sarah was still receiving religious instruction from Rabbi Goldblum at the South Portland Street Synagogue in Hebrew language as she would be inducted into the Bath Mitzvah, the corresponding female ceremony, in a few years time.

Angus knew Rabbi Goldblum too, when he came to investigate the squabble between some local drunks and the young Maccabi footballers, going home after a training session at the social club in South Portland Street.

Angus knew the Finemans from the time they had reported a break-in at their wholesale women's garment business in Clyde Place. He learned they had fled from Germany before the Nazis took control, having lost many relatives and friends in the horror of the concentration camps. Then another time, Angus had come to the rescue of crying little Sarah when she had somehow got her head stuck in her school railings, and soothed the little girl who had taken a 'dare' from her pals. Louis and Golda had even invited Angus to Myer's Bar Mitzvah party later in nearby Geneen's Restaurant. Even though Angus was a 'goy' (non Jewish) little Sarah had specially asked for him to be invited, and the Finemans were glad to invite him.

'Sorry, Mr Fineman,' Angus had said smiling, 'but a beat Cop never gets a Saturday off – less'n it's for his own funeral. I'm truly sorry.'

Angus was still in the Royal Infirmary, recovering slowly from his horrific attack, and was about to receive a surprise. Angus had not been able to attend Myer's party, so what did the Finemans do? They would take the party to Angus! The Fineman family would go up the hill by taxi to the very Royal itself. They arrived before a startled Angus and nursing staff, loaded with bags of cheese-cakes, apple-strudel, cream sponges, bagels and cinnamon cakes from Myer's celebration party the night before in Geneen's. Angus's eyes popped from his head as he beheld the smiling Finemans with their kosher bounty.

'That'll keep your belly filled for a few days, Mr Auchterlony,' cried Golda happily.

A wide-eyed Angus exclaimed, 'Mercy me, that'll keep the whole ward going for a week.' Then he quipped, 'Aye, and doctors and nurses too!'

Angus was right. He was not alone that night as night staff, doctors, nurses, night porters, patients – and even matron herself – indulged their faces in pure kosher delight.

Around six o' clock, one winter's evening, two cold and tired Indian Pedlar Johnnies alighted from their respective buses near the corner of Norfolk and Nicholson Street. They laid their large cases down with ease on the pavement, as business had been good that day and their cases were not as heavy as when they had first set off.

Mohan Singh, a Sikh man who resided in Portugal Street, greeted his friend Bahadur Ali with '*Salaam-al-aikum*, Ali. Where was you to-day?'

'I been Newmains to-day, Singh. Business very good. I selling many lady jumpers, under-knickers, socks, dresses and few shirts,' announced Ali proudly.

'*Teek-hai*' [good], replied Singh smiling. 'I been Shotts myself. Big sell of lady skirts, blouses, kiddy dresses and few shirts. Good peoples. Mostly mining of coal. Very nice people, having big heart. They give me *gurram chai* [hot tea] with roll and beef of corn inside, every time. If I not walking with case, I soon be very fat wallah,' guffawed the tall Sikh, adjusting his blue turban, his pearl teeth highlighted by a handsome bearded face.

'*Shabash, gee*' [good man], said Ali laughing. 'Yes, people of much kindness. One old lady was very sad when ask if I wishing bacon sandwich. She not understand I am Mussalman, cannot eat pig meat.'

'What she thinking then?' enquired Singh.

Ali replied, 'She thinking bacon not agreeing with my stomach. Allergee? . . . or something like that. She told to me, go see doctor about Mussalman problem'

'She not understanding, *gee*, Muslim cannot eat pig for religion reason,' laughed Singh. 'She thinking you having pain in muscles!'

'They rule all Empire but not understanding Indian people's custom,' replied Ali shaking his head in disbelief.

'You no believe me, Ali sahib. One *gorah* [white] lady give me tea and one thing called scone with jam,' said Singh conspiratorily, adding, 'She then trying on lady bloomer underpants in front of fire. She say me – how is looking then?'

'What you saying, *gee*?' quizzed Ali.

Singh replied with emphasis. 'I say, sorry missus, I need go now. I take case and running – *bought jheldi* [very quickly]!'

'Yes, one woman asking to me question. I am very embarrassing,' said Ali looking sheepish and continuing, 'Something like you darkie fellah being well endowed?'

'Why she ask about such business? This is private business,' retorted Singh disapprovingly.

Ali replied, scratching his head. 'I say no, missus. I am having no endowment. Only contents and buildings cover. By Prudential Insurance. Good company!'

'What woman is saying then about insurance?' questioned a puzzled Singh.

'She then looking at me as if me crazy man. She start laughing, then afterwards take order,' concluded Ali.

'Why she want discuss insurance business with Indian pedlar-man. Is very strange?' answered Singh, scratching his beard.

The two friends shook hands in the traditional Eastern fashion, as Singh said, 'Come my house, Ali, next Saturday. I make you some chicken curry, *munghi dall* and nice chupatties, my brother.' Singh smiled and added, 'Don't worry, Ali, no *dharroo* [drink] and everything will be hillal [Muslim style].'

'*Teek hai* [OK], you can drink, Singh. After all you are Sikh,' replied a laughing Ali.

Not streets away, in a first floor room and kitchen in Apsley Place, a domestic drama of the Gorbals mozaic was unfolding. It was just one of the many conflicts of culture. Danny Desai, a young Glasgow Corporation driver of mixed Indian and Irish blood, was seated by his girl-friend Annie McKinstry, a slim blonde girl with smiling blue eyes. The pair faced Annie's family across the kitchen table, hostility in the air.

Danny was a handsome twenty-four year old, dark with brown eyes and sleek black hair which belied his origins. With his colouring he was often taken for Italian or Spanish but his father was an Indian ex seaman who had settled down with his mother, a kindly woman of Irish Catholic antecedents. Young Danny, an only child, had joined the Paras at eighteen years of age. He had fought bravely in the War, being wounded at Arnhem.

He had always laughed, 'Here's me fighting for freedom against Hitler, for King and Country. In India, Mr Gandhi is fighting for freedom against the same King and Country?'

Equally puzzling was his mother's father, who had fought with Michael Collins for Irish Freedom against the British Army. Then two of her younger brothers and three cousins from the Irish Republic, fought and died with Monty in Libya and with Slim in Burma.

Meanwhile across the table, like hostile chessmen, were Annie's mum, Senga McKinstry, and her inebriated husband, forty year old Thomas. The terrible twins, Tom and Billy, in their late teens, flanked their parents like supportive bookends.

'Look, Mr and Mrs McKinstry,' pleaded Danny earnestly, focusing on Annie's sympathetic mother Senga. 'I love your Annie very much. We'd like to get engaged. Later when we've worked and saved, we can rent a good place of our own.'

The father, Thomas – he was never called Tom – just grinned with a blank smirk. Then he spoke, spitting out, 'I am a true blue. A Protestant. My family is pure bred Scottish, through and through. An ah'm a member of the Orange Lodge – upholder of oor way o' life!'

'You're damn right, da!' roared the twins. 'True Blues!'

Thomas continued as he slurred, 'We are Scottish and proud o' it. Sorry, I want nae mongrels in mah family.'

Danny remained cool, Annie holding his hand in support. This is worse than facing the German Panzers at Arnhem, Danny agonized.

'Oh, for God's sake, Thomas. Gie the laddie a chance!' screamed Senga, rising from her chair. 'This is the second time Danny has asked you!'

'Well ah'm away tae the pub. Ah'm no gonna let ma wee lassie marry some bliddy darkie wi' a coolie faither and a Fenian mother.' Thomas rose unsteadily from the table and left with a parting shot. 'Oor family is white and Protestant, and always will be. Do ye hear? Tom, Billy, let's get oota here. I don't want tae see Sambo here again, understand?'

Danny tightened his fists, his eyes filling as he felt the humiliation, the injustice of it all. Annie put her arms across his shoulders and pleaded, 'Don't pay ony heed to him, he's drunk and ignorant.'

Danny, ready to explode, closed his eyes, recalling the horrors of war. Was this the brave new world he and his mates had fought and died for against the Nazis? That man, Thomas, wouldn't be out of place in the Gestapo. What had it all been for?

Annie simply addressed her mother. 'Look, ma, we're gonna marry even if ah've tae leave hame. Danny and I love each other very much, an I'm not aboot to let that drunken faither of mine, or they stupid brithers, stop me.'

'Well, hen, you're my ain wee baby, an I'm on both yer sides,' said Senga smiling through her tears. 'You'll aye have ma support. Even if that stupid old fool says to the contrary.'

'Ah know you have to stick by him an' the twins. But thanks, ma,' replied Annie, kissing and hugging her mother. 'Pity, Danny's a real nice guy, ye know.'

Angus was released from the Royal Infirmary with strict instructions to take at least one month's sick leave, to rest and recuperate. He would have to attend the local out-patients' department at the Cottage Hospital in Campbeltown, for that is where it was best to go, rather than remain cooped up in Partick. He wanted the fresh Kintyre air and sea breezes, and clear mountains of home set amidst the sea views, with family and old friends about him.

That would surely help bind his battered tissues and heal the trauma of his scarred mind. Sergeant Ratley had been po-faced when he departed but Inspector MacAlee had shaken his hand and wished him an early recovery and return to duty. That was the difference. Ratley's mean spirit always sapped Angus's morale, making his daily routine a type of purgatory where one is condemned to eternal Hell. Surely the Police deserved officers imbued with positive leadership and morale boosting qualities, he thought. I would certainly try if ever I was promoted, mused Angus.

One of Kathy's cousins, Ross, who drove a van regularly between Glasgow and Campbeltown, would collect Angus together with his case at the Merkland Street flat. Ross had fitted the seat with cushions and foot rest to make Angus more comfortable, and leaving Angus's flat in the West End was very handy for travelling north.

It was a lovely run up Loch Lomondside, with a grand view of Ben Lomond and the mountains as they sped over the Rest And Be Thankful, thankfully clear of snow for a change. After a short convenience stop at Inverary where they had sandwiches and hot tea, they were soon turning left for the long scenic run along the sea to Campbeltown – or the Wee Toon as the locals called it. As they sped along the coast road, Angus breathed the bracing, salty air of home once again and felt in a state of bliss. All the tensions of the Police and city life were melting from his shoulders, like snow off the hills in summer.

His heart stirred instinctively with a welcoming feeling as he spied the panoramic sea views on his right, across to Gigha, God's Island in the Gaelic, and to the misty Isles of Islay and Jura. 'Welcome home, son,' they seemed to whisper, like enchanted islands. As they passed Bellochantuy, the Pass of the Fairies, Ross gave Angus a gentle nudge, the sea air having put him to sleep. 'Wake up Angus. You're nearly there. Home sweet home!'

CHAPTER 7

With Angus's absence on sick-leave in Campbeltown, his duties were temporarily taken over by a new Constable named Gerry Armstrong or Smiler as he was known locally. Constable Armstrong checked in on Kathy and Nan, as he had promised Angus, and always brought cheer which lightened up their day. Smiler invariably departed with his deep pockets stuffed with apples and oranges, courtesy of the Fruit Box's owners.

Kathy was seeing more of big Sean Robb, enjoying nights dancing at the Locarno, or enjoying a picture show at the nearby Bedford or Coliseum cinemas. Sean always bought a box of her favourite milk chocolates from nearby Birrell's, a veritable Aladdin's cave of goodies. Later Sean would see Kathy home to her close in Norfolk Street where they would linger by the flickering gas mantle. It was here that Sean would put his arms round Kathy's waist. 'Did you enjoy the show the night, hen?'

'Aye, it was fine. Especially at the interval when the ice-cream girl came round.'

Sean laughed out loud. 'You and your chocolate vanilla. Ye're like an overgrown schoolgirl, Kathy.'

'Not really,' replied Kathy impishly. 'Otherwise you wouldn't be taking me out.'

Sean smiled, a serious look coming into his dark eyes, and said simply, 'You wee tease.' With that Kathy was seized in his strong arms, his breathing heavy with desire as he pressed his lips close to hers.

'Stop, Sean. I canna breathe, for goodness sakes!' Kathy cried in mild admonishment.

Often their lips had met, with Sean whispering his feelings for her,

73

but Kathy was always in control, pushing Sean away when his passionate advances went beyond the mark. She was quite content to let him hold her with the occasional kiss but that was all. Her feelings of attraction for Sean were a puzzle to her. There was a raw physical animal quality in Sean which attracted her, and she was very wary of her capacity to resist his prolonged efforts. Angus was different though, more controlled, more of the gentleman. Joe Cherkowski she was still getting to know, but he really was the most attractive of the three. But as the saying goes, you cannot always judge a book by its cover.

Kathy's reverie in the arms of Sean was broken by an embarrassed neighbour's voice, apologising as she passed the courting couple.

'Hello, Kathy. Sorry, hen.'

Sean suddenly made an enquiry which surprised her. 'How's yer friend Auchterlony getting on?' he said with furrowed brow.

Kathy explained he was recuperating back in Kintyre. Sean said nothing at first, then looking knowingly into her eyes, remarked. 'Ach, Kathy hen. Ye dinnae want tae bother yerself wi' the likes of Auchterlony and that Yank, whitever his name is!'

'There's nothing wrong with either Angus or Joe,' retorted Kathy gamely, breaking free of his embrace.

'Ye'll hae nothing but worry aboot his safety, whenever he goes on duty, wondering will he come back in one piece,' exclaimed Sean heatedly. 'I know, my cousin married a Cop.'

'It should make no difference, Sean, if a wife loves her man,' replied Kathy.

'Ach, Kathy. Then there's the shifts. You'll no have ony social life at all.'

Kathy regarded him coldly, not deigning a reply.

Sean continued, fulminating further. 'And as for they bloody, randy Yanks. They're a load o' . . . !'

'That's enough, Sean. I have no plans to marry anybody at present,' exploded an incensed Kathy. 'Thanks for a great night which, up to now, has been enjoyable. I'll away up to my bed – it's up early for work for us both to-morrow.'

Sean wished her goodnight, apologising coldly for his behaviour. As he made his way home on the bus, he hardened perceptibly. He had meant every word he'd uttered to Kathy. It was going to be either him or them – simple as that!

Angus was truly glad to be back home in Kintyre, lodging with his sister Fiona, her husband Murdo Mackenzie and their three children. He loved living on the big dairy farm at Glenbarr, north of Campbeltown. Angus adored the sweeping views from his upper bedroom over to the islands of Gigha and Islay, within clear sight of the Paps of Jura.

Although not fully fit, Angus could nevertheless play outrageous piggy-back and hide-and-seek games with his adoring nephews and niece: Andrew and Donald, aged nine and eight respectively, and bonny wee Jean, aged six, who Uncle Angus nick-named 'Goldilocks' for her golden tresses and violet eyes. With plenty of fresh food, fresh air and gentle walking, Angus was rapidly returning to good health and fitness. His medical condition was monitored by his weekly visit to the cottage hospital in Campbeltown, accompanied by Fiona, in Murdo's battered old Morris.

Angus's old Aunt Julie, a retired school teacher, often accompanied Angus to places of local nostalgia with comments such as, 'Do you remember when you and your school pals went over to Davaar Island, Angus, and the tide came in over the the Dhorlinn [tidal causeway] and you were stranded?'

'Aye, Aunt Julie. Old Seumas came out in his row boat to take the four o' us home,' laughed Angus, relishing old times when the bounty of loving parents was bestowed to overflowing. They had long since gone, his mother first with cancer, followed by his father drowned at sea.

At weekends, Fiona with the kids, Angus and Aunt Julie, would drive to Carradale. Angus was enthralled by his favourite views – the panoramic view over the Sound of Kilbrannan with views to the mountains of Arran and the Ayrshire Coast. On a clear day his favourite, Ailsa Craig, was visible over to the right. Further on at Carradale, the family stopped at the hotel on the right going towards the harbour for a fine lunch of fresh salmon, during a meeting with Aunt Julie's friend

Vicky, who recounted amazing stories about the local author, Naomi Mitchison. Naomi, then in her late forties, had written numerous books, enjoying a liberal marriage which allowed her the attention of a goodly number of lovers.

After lunch, taking leave of Vicky, Angus and his relations continued past Saddell Abbey in the hollow, then up the narrow and twisting road to Claonaig where the Macbraynes's ferry ran across to Lochranza on Arran. Angus enjoyed a visit to Skipness, and stood before a small cottage, saying ruefully, 'I once courted a local lassie who lived here. She now lives in America: Chicago I think. She is married to a banker with a whole tribe of kids, last time I heard!' Angus returned to reality with the kids crying, 'Hurry up, Uncle Angus, we're going for ice-cream.'

Meanwhile back in the Gorbals, unknown to Angus, events were taking place which would impact on Police enquiries into Angus's attackers.

Kitty, a friend and workmate of Lilly Grant, had related some startling news to her friend in confidence. Kitty had sworn Lilly to utter secrecy, confiding: 'My life depends on it, Lil. Don't breathe a word of it, for Christsakes!'

Kitty then revealed that she had found out that her boyfriend, Bull Bakley, had been two-timing her with a barmaid at a local pub in Gorbals Street, without mentioning its name. During a confrontation about the barmaid with the drunken Bakley, in the Nicholson Street house, he had lost the head and savagely beaten her. She ended up with a bruised face and a black eye. Holding his razor, or 'malky' as he called it, Bakley growled into her ear. 'If you mention this tae anybody, or go tae the Polis, ah'll carve yer pretty mug into little pieces. Ah'll claim ye for sure!'

Kitty lay down and closed her eyes; it was safer for her not to antagonise him. She heard Bakley boasting to his gang members as he knocked back a whisky. 'That's how tae treat the wummin – show's them who's boss.'

'Yer right, Bull,' cried one of his lackeys. 'Show 'em all.'

'Aye, just like "Teuchter" Auchterlony. The meddlin Polis bastart. He got some of oor special medecine last month. Eh, boys?'

Even in her faked comotose state, Kitty explained to Lilly. 'I was nearly gonna scream out loud. I felt like bursting and hoped they wouldn't see my face going red with rage.'

'You were lucky, Kitty. But it looks like you're saying that Bull Bakley was involved in the attack on Constable Auchterlony?' said Lilly in shock.

Kitty explained nervously that she found it hard to contain her fear and revulsion of the creature who now threatened her. She wanted to flee as far away from the Gorbals as possible, to rid her nostrils of the stink of Bull Bakley and his hold over her – once and for all!

Lilly was appalled and horrified at what she was hearing as she tried to comfort her friend, cuddling Kitty's head on her shoulder. Presently, Lilly said in motherly fashion, gazing into her friend's tearful eyes, 'Kitty, we need to speak to ma dad. Jock'll advise you, hen.'

'Oh God no. No, I canna,' wailed Kitty. 'The Bull is a plain out and out nutter. He'll do me in, for sure!'

'We canna let those bloody cretins that did for poor Constable Auchterlony get away wi' it, hen,' replied Lilly, taking her arm. 'Mr Auchterlony is a fine, helpful man.'

After a while Kitty's sobbing subsided and Lilly handed her a towel to dry away the tears. Kitty suddenly looked directly into her friend's eye and said softly:

'Ye're right, Lil. We canna let those bastards get away wi' beating people up. Me, Mr Auchterlony and yer dad too. Let's see old Jock, yer faither. He'll know what tae do.'

Jock Grant was shaken but not entirely surprised by what Kitty and his daughter Lilly were telling him. Jock remained calm in order to give the two excited girls some assurance and comfort. It was like in the trenches before an attack, putting on a wee smile, putting on a brave face to reassure your comrades, even though you were shitting your breeks.

Jock regretted Angus's absence at this time, but suggested that they go with him to the police. He would seek out Dectective Constable Ed Moran, Auchterlony's friend – he would be sure to help and protect Kitty. Kitty nodded in agreement.

'We'll both go the whole way wi' you, Kitty. Ye can depend on us both, Lilly and me,' said Jock softly.

And Lilly's smiling gaze and nodding head boosted Kitty's confidence.

As Angus had to attend a final examination at the Royal a week on Tuesday, it then being Thursday, Kathy had phoned to say that Ross was driving her up on the Friday morning. She would spend a weekend staying with relatives in Campbeltown. Ross would be glad to drive them all back on Sunday. Angus was as excited as a child and eagerly looked forward to Kathy's visit. He wanted to see that smiling face, the sparkling blue eyes, to take hold of her, catching the scent of her perfumed hair. Kathy had phoned regularly over the past three weeks, but he had not beheld her physical presence. Yes, absence does make the heart grow fonder, Angus had learned.

It was an ecstatic Angus who welcomed Kathy and her cousin Ross, as they stopped to say hello at Glenbarr on their way to Campbeltown. Kathy was delighted to see how well Angus looked, the tall figure alert, his earlier pale face now ruddied by the bracing sea air of Kintyre and showing the effect of Fiona's wholesome Scotch feeding, kept in check by regular walks along the numerous local beaches. She was pleased when Angus invited her to join him and his friend Hector at Tarbert for a sail up Loch Fyne to Lochgilphead in Hector's motor launch. Angus exclaimed, like an excited schoolboy, that they would be able to trawl on the way, adding, 'Hector's a retired ship's cook. And makes great sandwiches too . . . with a dram to keep out the chill.' They would pick Kathy up next morning in Hector's old Alvis.

Meanwhile in Glasgow's Craigie Street headquarters, Kitty, accompanied by Jock and Lilly Grant, was being interviewed by two detectives. The one, Ed Moran, with the dark hair and sunny smile, was known to Jock Grant as a true friend of Angus. The other, a severe balding man with the rank of Detective Inspector, sat listening, saying nothing.

'Just take your time, lass,' comforted DC Moran, addressing Kitty. 'Just tell us what happened in your own words. Later we will ask you to sign a statement, OK?' Kitty nodded in agreement as a shorthand typist readied to take her statement.

Later, as Kitty and the Grants departed, Detective Moran and his severe looking superior regarded each other knowingly. Moran's boss said, 'That story fits perfectly with Toffyleg's witness too.'

The nickname referred to the head of the Southern uniformed branch at Craigie Street, a tough officer so named because of his gait, who had grilled an ex-boxer named Slogger Struth. Struth – his deceased father had been a former middleweight Army boxing champion – was once a fanatic razor wielding member of the Cumbie Mob in his younger days, battling against the Billy Boys, the Calton Entry and the San Toy and other gangs. But the attack on Jock Grant had brought on Slogger Struth's understandable outrage. For one thing, Jock Grant had been an old comrade of Struth's father in the Great War, serving in the same regimental company. Later, when he learned of Bakley's attack on Kitty he became incensed as Kitty and he had been at school together. Slogger was overheard saying, 'Ah'll claim the bastarts that did they things tae Jock and Kitty.'

To that end, Slogger had revealed a bombshell when he had voluntarily called into to see the Police in Craigie Street. He claimed he had been approached by Bull Bakley in a local pub in the South Side.

'Bakley said he needed someone to claim a punter who'd been givin' them bother,' related Slogger Struth.

'Who was the punter?' asked DC Moran.

'All that the Bull would say was that it was one of the local fuzz who was giving them loads of aggro,' replied Slogger.

'He didn't mention any name?' quizzed Toffylegs who was present at the interview.

Struth said, 'It was not till later he mentioned Auchterlony's name, and that it was worth a century to me [hundred pounds].'

'Nothing about dates. Or locations?' questioned Detective Moran.

Slogger quoted chapter and verse on the date and location. This caused a flurry of note taking on the part of the Police Officers. The gang leader was to be none other than Cosh Evans, who was well known for his use of the black-jack.

'When I heard it was a fuzz, and that Cosh Evans wis involved, ah told Bakley tae count me oot. I wanted no part,' replied Struth markedly.

'So what was his reaction,' quizzed DC Moran eagerly.

'Reaction! The Bull turned and walked away, his face like a burst sofa!' roared Slogger Struth.

It was not generally known that the Police had recovered a small black cosh from the scene of Angus's attack in Carlton Court. If the fingerprints on it could be positively identified with those of Cosh Evans, then Slogger's additional testimony would prove a double whammy. But Cosh often wore black gloves in his work. Toffylegs and the CID were well pleased. Kitty's evidence against Bull Bakley would ensure the second string in the bow of the Prosecution's case.

Back in Argyll, Angus had no inkling of the dramatic developments taking place. Kathy and he had enjoyed a wonderful day's sailing on Loch Fyne from Tarbert to Lochgilphead, made all the more enjoyable by Hector's company and the mild spring weather.

Hector announced, 'Now, Kathy, we have salmon sandwiches, or a choice of beef and pickles. Then again there's Campbeltown cheese ones – it's braw strong cheese. Now for beverages there's flasks of tea and coffee, sweet, without, black or white. Whitever takes your fancy.'

'Aye, an what's for afters, Hector?' enquired Angus with a sly wink.

'Well, after the homemade scones and strawberry jam, and if yee's have ony space left – there'll be a generous dispensation of the *Usquebaugh*,' reeled off Hector knowingly.

'*Usque* . . . what!' exclaimed Kathy laughingly.

'*Usquebaugh*. Gaelic for water-of-life, lassie. Whisky you know,' retorted Hector in mock surprise, as he continued. 'We have a fine local Springbank, a double malt, and Angus's favourite whisky too.'

'Oh, I'll need to share that with Mr Auchterlony,' laughed Kathy happily. Soon the trio were transformed into a happy band of 'drouthy cronies', as Rabbie Burns would have described them.

On the return journey, Angus had unhooked yet another fleshy mackerel from Kathy's trawling line, plopping it into a large metal bucket after knocking its head expertly on the boat rail.

'Look, Kathy, ye have a full bucket of mackerel for your Aunty's cat,' cried Angus like a kid on a school outing. Kathy was taken aback as Angus planted a whopping kiss fully on her surprised lips, shouting, 'It was the motion of the boat, I slipped.'

'Angus Auchterlony,' shrieked Kathy loudly, feigning outrage. 'Too much fire-water's turning your head!' Angus blushed unashamedly, like a big cuddly bear.

'Och, he's crazy for ye, Kathy. Dinna ye know it!' cried Hector as he reeled in another full line, exclaiming, 'Mercy me. We have more o' the silver darlings – fine fat "Glasgow Magistrates"!'

Kathy blushed like a beetroot but questioned him, '"Glasgow Magistrates"?'

'Aye, that's the local name fer the big fat Loch Fyne herring hereaboots,' cried Hector, smacking his lips. 'Very juicy. We'll grill ye some later, Angus and I.'

As the *Jenny* chugged into East Loch Tarbert Harbour, Kathy pointed enquiringly to an old ruined castle on the hill to the left.

'Aye, lass, that's Tarbert Castle there. Ye ken Robert the Bruce built or repaired it or something,' replied Hector briskly. 'Then there was a Norwegian King named Magnus who dragged his longship bodily across the narrow neck of land, from West Loch Tarbert to East Loch Tarbert in full sail to win control of Kintyre.'

'Aye, it was a wager with the Scots King, Edgar Canmore, to prove Kintyre was an island. We got that in history at the High School,' replied Angus, showing off.

'Holy Moses. What a feat,' exclaimed a gobsmacked Kathy.

'Well, Kathy, I'm for Southend on Sunday for a wee visit to the beach and Dunaverty Castle. Do ye fancy a jaunt?' offered Angus, knowing she would say yes. Kathy said dreamily that she would like to see the Christ Cave painting too on Davaar Island. Angus said the high spring tides would make it very difficult to cross the shingly beach of the Dhorlinn, especially with the limit of time available to them in Campbeltown. Another time, assured Angus.

'Yes, sure, Angus. We can see Columba's Well in Southend, though,' replied Kathy cheerily. 'I need to get some holy water for my mum, or she'll roast me for sure!'

'Ye see, Kathy, Angus enjoys yer company,' said the voice emanating from a supposedly snoozing Hector, whose right eyelid suddenly opened, scanning the couple like an inquisitor.

'Ach, Hector, ye old reprobate,' cried Angus. 'Behave yerself!'

All of a sudden laughter shook the wee boat from stem to stern.

CHAPTER 8

Kathy and Angus were sadly unable to visit the cave painting on Davaar Island owing to the constraints of tide and time which, as they say, wait for no man, nor woman. Fiona and her kids were off to friends in Campbeltown, after church, and so she dropped Angus and Kathy at the entrance to Southend, near the small kirk opposite the manse.

Angus and Kathy walked hand-in-hand along the golden sands before climbing up to the desolate ruins of Dunaverty Castle, within sight of Sanda Island around whose terrible waters lay the graves of so many stricken ships. Peering cannily over the precipitous Dunaverty Crag to the sea below, Angus said grimly, 'You know, Kathy, here Argyll's men massacred over three hundred MacDonalds and their supporters, in the old Covenanting days. Many others died jumping over the cliffs.'

'God. How horrible,' sobbed Kathy. 'The Lord rest their poor souls.'

'One poor woman with her wee bairn was taken and hidden in yonder caves, saved by a pitying Campbell soldier, they do say,' remarked Angus, pointing across the bay past the ancient church of Kilcolmkill, where St Columba first landed from Ireland and not far from the burnt out remains of the old Keil School.

'Can we go to St Columba's Well now, Angus? I've a wee bottle which Mum asked me to fill,' said Kathy sadly, obviously affected by the aura of the place.

As Kathy filled her bottle from Columba's Well, she said, 'This is for the christening of one of our customers who's expecting. She's from hereabouts.'

They stood silent, influenced by the ambience of the place, with the water trickling from the rock marked with the ancient sign of the cross into the cress-lined pool. Presently, as they stood on the footprints in a large rock, reputedly made by St Columba himself, Angus felt an urge to tell Kathy his feelings. Maybe it was the setting, the sea and seals in the foreground with the soothing ripple of the waves.

'There's the coast of the Emerald Isle over there,' shouted Kathy pointing like an excited schoolgirl on an outing.

To her amazement, Angus was close and whispering, 'Kathy, I want you to know I think an awful lot about you. Would you be my girl?'

Kathy replied, gently parting Angus's arms from around her waist. 'Ach, Angus man, behave yourself. You know I'm very fond of you, but I am no' the marrying kind – at least not at the moment. Now how about that lunch you promised me up at the hotel?'

Although Kathy hadn't shown it, she was deeply touched by Angus's gesture. She was confused by the images of the three men crowding her life, Angus, Sean and Joe. They were all separate, yet part of the whole. Just like fingers on a hand, but there were only three and not four fingers on this hand. Thank goodness! Even though four men would have flattered her ego, three were just bearable; four would have sent her over the edge. Four? No thanks!

It was a pleasant journey home on Sunday evening as Ross drove Kathy and Angus back to Glasgow, their baggage safely stowed in the back of the van. Back to the big city and work. Back to Sergeant Ratley. Back to the old pressures!

After the customary convenience stop at Inverary for hot drinks and sandwiches, the happy, chattering trio were soon entering the West End, and Angus was dropped off at his lodgings in Merkland Street with his baggage and some groceries which Kathy had procured for him. With cheery shouts from Kathy and Ross of 'Be seeing you, Angus,' the van soon sped out of sight.

Angus was feeling fit and glad to be back on his beat. Friendly greetings came from his colleagues, from shopkeepers and the good citizens of his Gorbals beat. Exceptions were the likes of Dougal and Bakley, and the other local crooks, followed by his so-called fellow officers, Sergeant Ratley and his minion, Senior Constable Flockhart. All Ratley said was, 'Ah see yer back frae your skive, Auchterlony!' He continued with,

'Well, ah've a few nice jobs that'll be needing your immediate attention.' Not even welcome, or how are you feeling. Even a dog gets a pat on the head and a greeting.

Angus was known as 'The Teuchter' by the public or as 'Angus Og' by his colleagues in the Police, just as Sergeant Ratley and Constable Flockhart were nicknamed BAB and WAB by the other Cops: Big Arrogant Bastard and Wee Arrogant Bastard, respectively; but not respected if you know what is meant? There were Cops on the beat with names like Robb and Steel, Curry and Rice, and Hyde and Seacombe in the CID. The Traffic Department had their duo Speedwell and Horn – those inseparable twins nicknamed 'Simmit and Drawers'. As Cops loved nicknames Sergeant Ratley, because of his manner, soon became Rat Ratley.

When Sergeant Ratley had welcomed Angus back with, 'Ah see you're back tae plague me again, Auchterlony,' he also added, 'We've had some developments on your attackers. Inspector MacAlee will soon be filling you in about it.' Then it was suddenly end of story. Nevertheless Angus felt elated by this news.

Back at work in the Fruit Box after her idyllic sojourn in Kintyre with Angus, Kathy was giving serious consideration to the three men in her life. The pressure from two of them, Angus and Sean, was growing a bit more intense. She had made it clear, though, to each of the three men, that their relationship was 'platonic' – like they said in the films – but each had laughed as if it was all a big joke, Kathy thought. Here she was in her late twenties and clearly attractive. She'd better not blow her chances and end up an old maid with a house full of cats! There's nothing wrong with cats, she chided herself, but concluded she was a doggy person – cats were too independent for her. She had nearly had a canary at Southend when Angus was about to pledge his troth. Then, as Sean Robb never failed to warn her, what future was there being a Policeman's wife? No life at all! Worrying about Angus's safety every time he went on duty, living all those unsocial hours, with no Saturdays off, with pay that didn't reflect putting your daily life at risk. But so what if you love the man, she agonised inwardly. Kathy felt a sense of self denigration as she weighed out her thoughts in such a mercenary fashion, as if weighing out tatties for a customer. But it was her life at stake, not some old tatties, and she wanted to make the best choice. Warm feelings stirred in her for Angus, and others more lukewarm for Sean, though the latter had a raw physical presence which Angus's gentlier mien was without.

Now as regards her other man friend, Joe Cherkowski, there was a definite attraction there. Maybe it was because the dark, handsome guy came from another world, a land of make-believe, like Holywood films such as 'Gone with the Wind', with pretty women like Scarlett O'Hara and handsome men like Rhett Butler and Ashley Wilkes. Her heart missed a beat whenever she beheld Joe, tall and dashing in his well-cut American Army Airforce uniform, replete with his Sergeant's stripes and shining wings as he greeted her with a kiss, saying in that soft American accent, 'Hi there, Kathy, honey. Nice to see you again.'

Joe was always so generous to her, entertaining her to theatres and dancing at the Green's Playhouse, which he preferred to the Locarno, after the sailors' brawl. Then there were dinner-dances at the Dutch Barn near his base at Prestwick or fine meals at the Whitehall or the Rogano, with the super seafood – made you forget the post-war greyness and rationing for once!

Both Kathy and Joe indulged in innocent smooching at friends' parties, held in homes of Americans married to Scots lassies.Other times, when Joe had the jeep, they would drive out to one of the beaches at Prestwick or Ayr and sit and chat. At such times Kathy would allow Joe to kiss her but that was as far as it went.

Joe didn't say much about the war, but Kathy eventually wheedled it out of him.

'Did you know, Kathy, before my Mom married Pop Cherkowski, she nearly ran off with a Skatch merchant sailor from Aberdeen?'

'Was that before she was married?' queried Kathy eagerly.

'Oh Jeeze, yes,' cried Joe. 'She met the Skatchman at a dance in New York. His name was Willy Dunn, I recall her saying, with pure ginger hair an all. You know, my Pop hates ginger haired men to this day.'

'Especially if they are Scotsmen, I bet!' replied Kathy in fits of laughter.

'You got it, honey,' quipped Joe.

Some Saturdays, Kathy would stay overnight in a local hotel near Prestwick. It was in the bar lounge she would get to know Joe better, over several nightcaps. Kathy learned that Joe, a navigator, had flown more than the average number of sorties in a B17 Superfortress with the Eighth Airforce over Germany. He had lost many dear comrades, and at one stage was grounded for a short period owing to battle fatigue. He really never discussed his wartime experiences, but when pressed by Kathy he said simply, 'I just did my jab, honey, like those brave boys. Just a simple guy from New Jersey.'

Kathy was strongly attracted to Joe Cherkowski – he had real charisma! Whenever he held and kissed her, she felt those same sensations radiating to every fibre of her being, like watching Ronald Coleman kissing Madelaine Carroll. She had never experienced such intensity of sexual stirring before. Certainly never with Angus and to a lesser degree with Sean, yes, but not the same as with Joe. She would always enjoy Sean's company, especially when he wasn't high on drink. She became irate when he made denigrating remarks about the 'Yanks being overpaid, oversexed and over here.' This was usually followed by, 'You're wasting yer life wi' a bluddy Polisman. It's nae life at all fer a woman!'

However Kathy was not going to rock the boat. They would remain what she intended them to remain – good male friends whose company she enjoyed. She had no plans for marriage at present.

Angus was now back in harness. At the late shift muster, Sergeant Ratley was reciting complaints about a local, Tim Heaney, recently released from prison and up to his old tricks of emerging blotto from the Mally Arms and challenging local passers-by to fisticuffs or else, as he stood in the middle of busy Eglinton Street! Then there was a small man on a miniature, unlit motorcycle driving recklessly about areas like Norfolk and Nicholson Streets, threatening life and limb and scaring the hell out of the locals.

Sergeant Ratley's final statement made Angus's ears prick up.

'There's been reports of Count Dracula on the prowl,' announced

Ratley in mock solemnity. 'The nutter's dressed all in black, wi' a cape and iron teeth.' A sudden howl of laughter broke from the ranks, immediately suppressed as the Sergeant said, 'This is nae laughing matter. This maddy is frightening old folks, women with babies and children in general. Inspector MacAlee wants him nicked right away!'

Ratley concluded that the Central Division had many reports of sightings, particularly in the Old Gorbals Burial Ground in Rutherglen Road, as well as in the Southern Necropolis in Caledonia Road. All the cops were told to liaise with their colleagues in Central in the event of pursuit across divisional boundaries.

Angus was mesmerised. He believed he had once seen a small drunken joker wearing gleaming metal teeth in Gorbals Street. The man was small, dark and light of foot, not dressed in his official garb, naturally, but in 'civvies' then. Angus thought it was just a joke at the time. Iron Teeth was later to become a real terror locally.

That Saturday night after pub closing time, Angus was approached by a breathless youth as he stood at the corner of Eglinton Street near the British Linen Bank with Constable Thomas Cahill, known locally as Tam the Bam, as they doubled up on their weekend beats.

'Constable D93, come quick, they're fighting ootside the Robin Bar. Givin' it laldy [thrashings] tae!' screamed the youth excitedly.

Immediately the two constables hot-footed it to the Robin Bar in Norfolk Street owned by Joe Dodds, the Celtic player. Arriving on the scene, they focused immediately on two battling contestants, shirt sleeves rolled up, their faces, arms and fists covered in blood.

'Jesus Christ, it's a real bloody donnybrook we've got here!' shouted Tam as he followed Angus into the fray.

Meanwhile the motley crowd which surrounded the combatants shrieked obscene encouragement such as 'Kill the messin bastart!' One old woman, in tartan headscarf and slippers with a dog on a rope, screamed, 'Gie it tae him in the balls, Cammy, the pig!' as her mongrel strained on the rope, nipping at the brawlers' exposed ankles.

Surging in like a couple of bulls with shouts of 'Make way, Police!', the mob of men, women and kids reluctantly gave way as the two Bobbies rushed forward, the battle maintaining its ferocity. As both

Constables strove to physically separate the bloodied contestants, their efforts met with considerable resistance. Angus was violently punched on the jaw by Owney Durnin and immediately fell backwards like a sack of potatoes, striking his head on the pavement which made him dazed and seeing stars.

Both brawlers, cursing loudly, instantly set about Tam the Bam with a will, landing a series of concentrated punches to his body and face, roaring, 'Fuck off, ye lousy Busies. This is a private fight!'

Tam, in deep trouble and down on his knees, screamed for help. 'Auchterlony, get up for Christ sake, I'm out of the game!'

A man wearing a flat 'doolander' bunnet (pigeon's landing strip) shouted, 'Late fight results! Cammy an' Owney 2. Glesga' Polis – Nothin'!'

The dazed Angus rose slowly vertical as Tam fell horizontally. Tam's cries of jeopardy infused Angus with a sudden burst of energy and determination, like Popeye after his spinach. Leaping forward with baton drawn, Angus roared like a bull. 'Out of the way, Tam, roll away. I'll sort this pair of chancers out!' With swinging baton, like a warrior of old, Angus was in among them, beating down on flesh, muscle and bone, aiming for the back of the neck. Owen Durnin and his opponent Billy Cameron went down from a flurry of baton blows across their necks and shoulders, with some bouncing off their thick heads, 'accidentally' of course, from the mighty arm of the valorous Kintyre warrior, Angus Auchterlony, his wrath fully aroused by drunken disturbers of the peace.

It wasn't long before the two hard-men lay prostrate and bloodied on the pavement, arms shielding their battered heads, crying, 'Stop. Stop. Murder, Polis. Ye're killin' us, stop, for Jesus sake!'

Angus came round from his state of bloody rage. He shouted peremptorily, 'Ye're both nicked. Get up, you pair of wasters. Put your hands together. Now!'

Tam, who had recovered, came across to assist Angus in cuffing the two recalcitrants, announcing with a wide beam, 'Bloody magnificent, Auchterlony. Just like John Wayne in the movies!'

Hurrahs broke from the crowd as Angus and Tam finished the cuffing of the two broken gladiators, reading them their rights, both cops showing facial weals on cheeks and below their eyes.

Both constables were surprised when one of the brawlers, Billy Cameron, spoke to his former opponent. 'Are ye all right, Owney? Ye Mick chanty-wrastler.'

'Yes, Billy-me-Bucko, 'Tis really nuttin at all. Just a bliddy broken nose!' replied Owney, adding further, 'I still say agin – your Rangers are a load of whoring Blatherskites!'

'Ach, Owney, we dinna want tae start all that again. We've baith worked too long togither for a' this bliddy crap. Mind ah fell doon that deep bastart excavation? Who was first doon tae help me?'

''Twas meeself, no less,' quipped Owney meekly. ''Twas on the hydro-dams wi' McAlpines. And sure, I'd do the same agin fer ye, Billy me darlin'.'

'Ach awa ye big Mick safty,' said Billy with a grin.

So, to the utter amazement of their custodians, the two old friends who had earlier been knocking seven bells from their hides, now hugged each other, their eyes flowing like rivulets.

Angus had been informed by Inspector MacAlee that they had arrested Bull Bakley in connection with the attack on him, explaining that the Crown Prosecutor now had a strong case with the evidence from their two witnesses, Kitty, friend of Lilly Grant and the formidable Slogger Struth. Inspector MacAlee added, 'You had better be prepared for the High Court appearance, Auchterlony. You'll be called to give testimony, no doubt.' Before he departed, Inspector MacAlee quipped, 'Good job, Constable, with those two drunks last week. Cahill reported you were truly formidable!'

One day on his day beat, Angus caught sight of an American jeep with USAAF marked in white letters and a big white star emblazoned on the bonnet. Sergeant Joe Cherkowski, thought Angus, it could be no-one else. As Angus was on the opposite side of Norfolk Street, near the library, he hesitated to look into a drysalter's window to observe the jeep from a discreet distance. Angus began to feel like a spy in one of those second-rate pictures. Presently, he observed a tall handsome Yank climb aboard the jeep as he waved to a smiling Kathy before roaring off towards Gorbals Cross. Angus suddenly felt a tide of rising resentment. What was that Yank doing waving to my girl, mused Angus to himself. Then the voice of reason broke in and pointed out that Kathy wasn't 'his girl'. She was simply his friend. Nothing more, nothing less!

As he crossed over and breezed into the Fruit Box, Angus was greeted with a cheery, 'Hello, PC Auchterlony. See you're back in harness,' from a smiling Nan. Kathy, who was serving a customer, looked up and gave him a big grin. During his accustomed cup of tea in the backshop, Nan did all the talking, explaining, 'We just had a flying visit from Kathy's friend, the Yank flier from Prestwick.'

Kathy came in for her tea, and Nan gave up her seat opposite Angus at the small coal fire. Nan went to serve in the shop, leaving the couple alone.

'Joe just dropped in to see us. He was picking something up from a friend at the Abbotsinch Naval Air Station,' said Kathy in a seemingly withdrawn and cool tone of voice as she continued. 'He has invited me down to London, to see some of his buddies and to take in a couple of shows. Mum said OK, she'll take care of things.'

Angus reddened, holding back his resentment, but piped up, 'Great, Kathy. Don't worry about Nan. I'll keep an eye on her.'

Kathy smiled. She wasn't fooled as she read Angus like a book. He was hurting. The cry of 'shop' from Nan meant things were busy out front so Kathy rose.

'Well, it's time I was on my way, folks. The Sergeant'll be on my back otherwise,' said Angus leaving. 'Have a nice time in London, Kathy.'

Kathy blushed and said, 'Cheerio, D93. See you soon.'

CHAPTER 9

Complaints were still coming in fast and furious about the mad miniature motor-cyclist terrorising locals and their pets with his outrageous and erratic driving. Some of the witnesses described the vehicle as more of a motor-scooter, like the type the Airborne used.

Sergeant Ratley had been taking flak from Inspector MacAlee and was passing it on to his Cops with interest. An unusually niggly Ratley announced, 'This pest's got to be stopped as soon as possible. We know the mad-skull must be local.' His head turned towards Auchterlony and the others with a sharp glance as he continued. 'Then we have that other maddy, Iron Teeth, giving it laldy too hereabouts!'

A voice rang out, 'Central Division's patch, Sergeant. With respect!'

Sergeant Ratley's face reddened, not enquiring about the comment's source, as he replied with control. 'Not strictly true. Iron Teeth has been shitting in our back yard too. Keep your eyes and ears alert. Your local crows [narks] should know something, they just need a bit of coaxing.'

All Angus knew from reports was that the small motorcyclist figure habitually wore a red beret and drove a miniature motor scooter. This gave Angus an idea and he would need to seek out Popeye without delay. Popeye was a local street-wise character and he usually knew the score.

After coming off the early shift, before making his way back to Partick, Angus decided to pop in to see the owner of the Café del Sole in Bridge Street, not too far from the subway station he used to travel home. The owner Emilio Lombardi, had recently been experiencing hooligan trouble from a local gang of youths in his café, and Angus was about to give him some information.

'Ah, Constable Auchterlony,' beamed Emilio. '*Come sta?* How are you?'

Angus who had learned a few words with the army in Italy replied, '*Bene, grazie.*'

'Francesca, it's Mr Auchterlony,' cried Emilio happily and soon a pretty Italian woman appeared. Francesca, although a little plump, had raven hair and invariably wore a bright hair band which gave her an exotic aura, a ray of sunny Italy in these grey northern climes. 'How nice to see you, Mr Auchterlony. Wait you see. I make you nice macaroni and cheese. Specially for you.'

Angus smiled and replied, 'Great, Mrs Lombardi. Sounds great.'

Then turning to Emilio, Angus explained that they had arrested five neds who had been causing similar trouble in other cafés and chippies. When Angus asked Emilio if he would be prepared to identify them, in order to corroborate that the hooligans had also given him trouble, there was silence. Emilio said slowly. 'We don't wanna any trouble, Mr Auchterlony. But if it's got to be then, OK. We give evidence.'

'Good, Emilio.' said Angus firmly. 'We'll look after you, don't fear.'

Emilio just shrugged with a wry smile, and said. '*Deo volente* [God willing].'

Soon Angus was tucking into a delicious plate of Francesca's macaroni and cheese, as Emilio sipped a cup of his favourite espresso coffee.

Emilio asked Angus if he had time to listen to a story he simply had to tell. Could he spend time and listen?

Angus replied, 'I'm just off duty, Emilio, and I've plenty of time.'

'Come into the back-shop. Francesca will look after business out front,' announced Emilio gravely.

He said he had just received news from the War Department that a body had been found in Italy which they believed was that of his son Franco, who had fought with the 8th Army. The Lombardis had been informed at the time that Franco was believed to have been captured by the Germans at the Gustave Line. What the Lombardis were not to know was that Franco had later managed to escape, fighting with the Italian Resistance behind the enemy lines and sabotaging German communication and supply lines.

After thirty Germans had been blown up by partisans, the Germans had pounced, with information provided by a traitor, and Franco and others had fallen into their net. Over three hundred prisoners had been rounded up and executed at the Fosse Ardeatine prison near Rome in reprisal for the dead Germans.

With tear-filled eyes, Emilio, simply said. 'Our Franco was one of them.' Angus put a comforting arm on the grieving father's shoulder, unable to find words.

'You know, Mr Auchterlony, my younger son, Alberto, joined the RAF aged eighteen years old and serviced fighters during the War,' Emilio cried, wiping away tears with a large handkerchief. 'I am going to Italy, you know. Going to bury Franco. *Deo volente.*'

Emilio, in sad and reminiscent vein, explained how he had arrived as a baby with his poor immigrant parents from Italy at the turn of the century. His parents, Angelo and Maria Lombardi, had originated near Bologna and had taken months to walk all the way from Dover to Glasgow on foot. They had made the journey by hitching rides from kind farmers and carters. They slept in barns and outhouses. One unfortunate Italian woman had even given birth by the roadside.

On a brighter note, Emilio announced that his parents' home was in the Emilia Romagna region, the culinary capital of Italy and the home of Dante and Plutarch. Angus raised his eyebrows as if trying to recall ancient history from his days at Campbeltown High School, then simply said. 'Dante and Plutarch. Yes, of course.'

'Thank God my parents died before the War started,' sighed Emilio with head bowed. He went on, 'You know, Mr Auchterlony, many older Italians were interned on the Isle of Man. While all this was happening, their sons, my sons too were fighting and dying for their country, Great Britain, in the Army, Navy, and Air Force. Would you believe it?'

Angus replied gravely. 'Yes, Emilio, I know it. I saw the pictures of their sons and daughters in the cafés and chip-shops, along with pictures of the King and Queen!'

'Many Italians, including my uncle were labelled "Enemy Aliens" and sent to Australia and Canada and were drowned when their ship was torpedoed by the Germans,' continued Emilio, shaking his head sadly. 'Some came from here, with broad Glasgow accents, and their boys fighting in the British forces. Some even winning medals too!'

Angus let Emilio go on. What could he say? The madness of war was beyond him. He had experienced it first hand. Just craziness and waste.

Emilio explained how he had taken his wife and young *bambini* on a visit back to Italy before the war in 1933. They had travelled by ferry and train to Bologna where his young sons had met their cousins, Angela, Vittorio and Augusto who were of similar ages. The family had enjoyed the sunshine, the fruity cassata ice-cream, iced drinks, pizzas and delicious spaghetti Bolognese, all the kids revelling on the sun-drenched beach at Rimini on the Adriatic which was quiet then. The only thing which spoiled it were the Blackshirts; they were everywhere you went, said Emilio.

'And you know, Mr Auchterlony, the family story ends sadly,' sighed Emilio, as he exhaled a puff from his cigarette. 'At the Battle of El Alemein we had a tragic battle going on. There Franco, my son, with the 51st Highland Division under Monty was facing his two cousins on the other side in the Bologna Division.'

'God Almighty,' uttered Angus, rubbing his hand over his hair.

'Yes. It was the same small cousins who played so happily on the sunny beach at Rimini that wonderful day. So Augusto died at Alemein and Franco was shot in Italy.'

By this time Emilio was weeping unashamedly. Angus got up and comforted his distraught friend, saying, 'It was started by all those power mad bastards like Hitler and Mussolini. And I was through it all with the Argylls, ye know, Emilio.'

Presently, Emilio calmed down as he lit another cigarette and said philosophically. 'You know, my friend, most Italians were not interested in war with Britain and America – we had family living there. It was the likes of Mussolini and his damned Fascisti who caused the War. All we wish for is the *dolce vita.*'

'Aye, as we all do,' said Angus, pointing out, 'You Italians weren't always like that. Remember the Roman legions and Caesar conquering the world?'

'Yes, the good old days,' laughed Emilio lightly.

'Mind though,' replied Angus. 'Even wi' all your legions, you still couldn't finish off the Caledonians!'

The two friends broke into a fit of laughter.

As they parted company, Emilio said cheerfully. 'Soon, when you are off duty, you must come to our house in Abbotsford Place. Me and Francesca will make you nice Italian food, specially for you. Minestrone soup with mozzarella cheese, spaghetti Bolognese, lasagna, chicken risotto, followed by cassata ice-cream. Then we finish with red or white Italian vino, eh?'

Gracious me, thought Angus. In post war Glasgow, laden down by rationing, coupons and scarcity, this was akin to plundering Aladdin's cave. He replied smiling, 'Thank you, Emilio. I'd be delighted and honoured.'

Emilio said seriously. 'Mr Auchterlony, I'll be away to Italy soon to see about Franco's burial. I know you'll keep an eye on Francesca and the shop.'

Angus took Emilio by the arm and said softly. 'Call me Angus, Emilio. Remember, I'm your friend. You can count on me.'

What a crazy world, Angus thought as he travelled home on the subway. All those German and Italian Americans, including those in Britain, knocking blue blazes out of their cousins in the War, just as Emilio's family had done. What a bloody, crying waste!

A strange and scary phenomenon had arisen in the South Side. He, or whatever it was, took the dark form of a hooded figure who suddenly appeared like Count Dracula, terrorising women and children, old people and courting couples. Most frightening of all was the way the Dracula figure confronted his victims, with beady black eyes and gleaming metal teeth which flashed menacingly in the moonlight. He, or it, became known locally as 'Iron Teeth' or sometimes 'Dracula'.

Iron Teeth's favouring stamping ground was in the old Gorbals Burial Ground in Rutherglen Road, and the Southern Necropolis, in Caledonia Road, amongst the moss strewn graves and sombre tombestones of the

City of the Dead. In this gloomy necropolis Iron Teeth would appear suddenly and silently.

'It vanished into thin air,' swore one courting couple, whose horror-stricken faces had convinced the reporting Constable of their veracity. Another witness, an old wino sleeping off his excesses near the tomb of Sir Thomas Lipton swore blind, 'The bluid-thirsty creature was aboot to sink its gleamin' teeth intae ma gullet, when ah made the sign of the cross – wi' two empty beer bottles.'

'And what did it do?' enquired a quizzical Cop.

'The bluiddy thing opened its wings an' flew like a bat oota Hell. Up intae the sky. It wis a full moon. Aye, ah saw it all. Ah swear!'

'Holy Mother o' God. It's like Bela Lugosi!' reported the wide-eyed Hielan' Cop, hurriedly taking out his black notebook.

One pair of terror-stricken winchers (courting couples) in the Southern Necropolis reported seeing Dracula's iron teeth gleaming as he stood in the reflected glow of Dixon's Blaze's furnaces nearby. Just like the Devil from Hell with flames behind him! Other sightings of the monster had been reported along the Clyde in Adelphi Street, and near the school at the tidal weir. One old soul who related her brief encounter with the dreaded Iron Teeth had sprinted home like a spring lamb, breathlessly telling her tale to her grumpy old man who replied, 'Awa' wi' ye, Mary. Ye've been on the hooch again, hen!'

Angus had once mentioned to Sergeant Ratley that he might have seen Iron Teeth in human form, but receiving the usual derogatory responses, let things drop. Only later, as things worsened, was Angus surprised to find himself summoned before the local Inspector.

'Sergeant Ratley reported you've seen this Dracula. Is this true, Auchterlony?' quizzed Inspector MacAlee, with a po-faced Ratley standing in attendance.

Angus replied cautiously. 'I don't know him, sir. Directly that is.'

'Either you know him or you don't. Which is it!' snapped MacAlee testily.

'I think I saw him coming out of a pub, sir, in Gorbals Street one Saturday afternoon,' answered Angus with emphasis.

Inspector MacAlee blew a gasp. 'You think? And what made you think it was Dracula? Don't you know vampires can't stand the daylight!'

Angus explained it was the description of the menace as being small, with dark staring eyes, adding with emphasis, 'He snarled at me, drawing back his lips. It was then I saw the shiny metal teeth. It shocked me!' He explained that as he stepped forward to question the small dapper man, the latter hissed the word 'Dracula' then speedily made off across Gorbals Street.

'Why didn't you pursue him across into Central's area?' quizzed the Inspector sharply.

'The culprit had committed no offence, sir. I just took him to be another drunken Saturday nutter,' stated Angus.

Inspector MacAlee asked Auchterlony to wait outside for a few minutes whilst he conferred with Sergeant Ratley. Some minutes later Sergeant Ratley informed Angus, 'Auchterlony, as you are the only one able to identify this character, Iron Teeth, arrangements will be made for you to do some plain clothes work with our CID at the Clydeside, along Adelphi Street. You'll liaise with the Central boys too till this nutter's been caged,' announced a smug Sergeant Ratley.

'What difference does it make about identification, Sergeant?' queried Angus.

'Surely if he's apprehended that's proof enough. He'll be in his crazy disguise?'

'Maybe, true. But some clever bloody lawyer will argue differently. He'll say it was not his client. Or his client was going to a fancy dress party, or some such,' replied Sergeant Ratley.

Anyway that was how the Inspector wanted it handled. And that was that, but it was unusual. Angus's secondment would be temporary, in plain clothes but would be part of his overall course training.

Jock Grant regularly held a get-together with some of his cronies for a blether and a game of dominoes and cards. Hoping to brighten Angus's lonely bachelor's existence Jock had invited Angus to join them for a little bevvy and fellowship. Fortunately Angus's shifts allowed him to attend, and he would bring along the accustomed half-bottle of whisky and some screw-tops which Jock had suggested. He had no intention of having too much to drink, as a Policeman was always on call.

Jock introduced Angus to his small group of friends. There was Tug Wilson, a retired, boozy sailor who had been with Jellicoe at the Battle of Jutland. In the corner sat Jock's wily old comrade from the Great War, Sammy Gorman. The sallow skinned old soldier was very canny at cards but had the 'Doolally tap' (malaria shakes) from his time out in India.

Finally, and most interestingly, was the fairhaired Sandy MacLeish, born in the depth of the Gorbals, in Cavendish Street. Sandy, the son of one of Jock's comrades killed in the Great War, was a lecturer in History at Glasgow University.

Jock remarked cheerfully to Angus. 'Sandy's dad was our battalion's centre-forward when we won the regimental cup.'

After many eagerly contested games of dominoes, fed by generous free-flowing bottles, the happy band of friends were soon feeling 'friendly fu', a warm cosy feeling pervading the little kitchen with its cheery glowing fire.

Sandy suggested a game to see how many famous Gorbals names they could come up with. Angus, an outsider, found it impossible to contemplate that such famous men could originate from such a dump, though he would never have used such a word in this proud company for fear of being strung up.

Jock mentioned that he had known wee Benny Lynch from Florence Street. 'The first World Champion boxing produced frae Scotland. Flyweight Champion. An' he used to sell papers ootside the Mally Arms as a kid. My favourite pub, tae.'

'Whit aboot Sir Thomas Lipton, born in Crown Street, millionaire grocer and friend of kings and presidents,' quipped Tug Wilson, continuing, 'He's buried in the Southern Necropolis in Caledonia Road.'

Sammy pointed out notable Gorbals boxers like Johnnie McGrory, former Featherweight Champ of Great Britain. Then there was Elky Clark from Mathieson Street, then John Cowboy McCormack who lived in Florence Street, not forgetting Jim Campbell, former Scottish Flyweight Champ, born in Cumberland Street.

Jock chirped in with footballers like Pat Crerand born in Thistle Street and Charlie Gallagher from Cumberland Street.

Even Angus had heard of Alan Pinkerton who had founded the famous Pinkerton Detective Agency in America.

'Aye,' commented Sandy the Historian.' Pinkerton was born in nearby Muirhead Street near Ballater Street. He was a confidant of President Lincoln, and his agents hunted the James Gang. A simple couper laddie from the Gorbals too.'

Sammy pointed out that Ballater Street had once been Govan Street, and Nicholson Street was formerly Apsley Street. Jock laughed and shouted. 'Hey, Sammy, that's no fair. They're streets, not famous characters. 'You're no on!'

Sandy pointed out. 'John Buchan lived in Bedford Street. You know, the author of *The Thirty Nine Steps* and *Greenmantle*. He later became Governor General of Canada.' And so the battle for names continued, as Tug Wilson stated, 'The man who designed the engine for the Comet, the first steam boat, is buried in the Southern Necropolis – by the name of John Robertson.'

Jock tabled a motion an adjournment for tea and sandwiches which was carried unanimously.

Sammy Gorman came up with the name Robert McLeish, the writer of *The Gorbals Story*. Someone mentioned the name of the blind Reverend George Matheson from Abbotsford Place, who wrote the hymn 'Oh Love That Will Not Let Me Go'.

Jock added triumphantly, 'An' there was the founder of the Great Universal Stores, later Sir Isaac Woolfson, son of an immigrant Russian Jew, from nearby Hospital Street.' Jock continued in full flow, 'And Sir Hugh Roberton, founder of the famous Glasgow Orpheus Choir was born up the road in Wellcroft Street and attended Abbotsford Primary.'

Sandy, being an historian, gave out so many other interesting facts. Sir John Moore, the famous British general of Corunna fame, had lived in Crown Street; Bonny Prince Charlie's Army had marched through the Gorbals, finally camping in what is now the Glasgow Green; and Rabbie Burns often passed through the Gorbals from Ayrshire on his way to the Black Bull in Argyle Street. Sandy exclaimed exuberantly, 'Did you know that Kirkpatrick, the inventor of the bicycle, was arrested in Bridgend around 1839 or 1840 when he made his way on his new contraption. He'd knocked over a wee lassie and after a few shillings fine was allowed on his way.'

Sandy went on, as if with students at the University, 'You know the original name for the Gorbals was Bridgend until late into the eighteenth century. The name Gorbals is derived from the Gaelic, *garbh baile* meaning rough from *garbh* pertaining to the moorland and *baile* meaning village or hamlet.' All were attentive, save for the snoring Sammy Gorman who had gently dozed off under Sandy's hypnotic tones.

'Gorbals meaning rough village. I can vouch for that as a Policeman,' laughed Angus impishly. 'Especially on a Saturday night!'

'Aye, the Gorbals is no place for the faint-hearted on a Saturday night,' commented Jock, laughing. 'Can you gie us a story, Angus?'

Angus paused in thought for several moments, then went on, 'Well, there is an amusing tale about the flapping tracks [unregistered tracks] which my uncle Alec used to recount, when he retired from the Glasgow Police.'

Angus described how his Uncle Alec was on duty outside a local unregistered track when he noticed a punter coming out of a close with a white greyhound on a lead. He noted that it had black markings and immediately suspected the owner had been up to some skull-duggery, like feeding it pies or drugs. Slipping in to his wife, Alec asked her to place a bet for him – but on no account on the white dog, number six in the black and white stripes.

The outcome was that the white dog won the race at 8 to 1, its five competitors, including the favourite, following far behind. Number six was the only one which had not been stuffed with steak pies, rice pudding and condensed milk to slow it down.

'My aunt Claire and her old dad never let Alec ever live that one down,' cried Angus. 'He was forevermore excluded from their joint stakes.'

'A very amusing story, Angus,' cried Jock raising his glass, quoting from Pearson.

'Let Glasgow flourish in remodelled homes,
Not heaped and piled like cells in honey-combs,

Your fields are broad and free on every side,
Why jam your dwellings like a pent-up tide?'
'Gents, ah'm sure we've had a great night. You've all been most welcomed. Here's a toast, in the words of the immortal Sir Walter Scott himself – "To the Good People of the Gorbals".'

CHAPTER 10

One afternoon Kathy MacDonald was in for a surprise. Suddenly two well dressed figures entered her mundane workplace where she sold vegetables and flowers. It was Sean Robb and an attractive woman who entered, their dress evidently announcing they were either coming from or going to a wedding.

'Kathy, surprise, surprise!' cried Sean, laughing and looking so attractively dark and handsome in his tails and white shirt. But it was the woman who immediately caught Kathy's attention. She was raven haired, oval faced with long patrician nose and deep grey eyes which retained that faraway look, even when she regarded you.

'Kathy, it's my pleasure to introduce Sybil Barr,' announced Sean proudly. He continued, 'Sybil's father and my dad were raised on farms in Ayrshire and attended school together. He's the big noise in Barr Enterprises – you know the dairies, the fruit and vegetable wholesalers?'

Sybil, so striking in long black dress and fur stole, her long golden earrings dangling attractively, answered impeccably, 'So pleased to meet you, Kathy. Sean and I have known each other since childhood. He never stops mentioning you.' Her manner and accent spoke volumes she was private school and privilege. Her accent belied her looks, thought Kathy. Sybil, with her dark looks, seemed every inch a Spaniard – a dark señorita, out of place here in the Gorbals, misplaced from her castles in Spain!

'Is that a new car, Sean?' queried Kathy, pointing to the big silver car out front.

'God, no!' cried Sean. 'That's one of Sybil's dad's cars. The Alvis – a real smasher, eh?'

Sybil laughed. 'You know, Kathy, he thinks more of that car than he does of me.'

'Her dad uses it for business. He lent it to us for the wedding we were at yesterday. Remember I said a friend was getting married in the Cathedral, Kathy?'

Kathy nodded. She remembered he said he was staying in the Grand Hotel at Charing Cross. But he hadn't mentioned a woman.

'Yes, we both enjoyed the hotel, good meals and service,' said Sybil. Seeing Kathy's changing expression, she added hurriedly, 'Separate rooms though!'

Kathy just laughed, saying nothing but thinking plenty. Is Sean trying to tell me something, bringing this woman friend here? The word 'friend' struck home in her mind. After all, Kathy had always made it clear to her three men 'friends', Angus, Sean and Joe, that they were just that. That is 'friends' – nothing more. She was only wanting cheery companionship, a little flirtation but nothing serious. Who was this attractive woman, Sybil, with her alluring Spanish looks? What were her designs on Sean? In spite of what she had preached, Kathy felt uneasy in the pit of her stomach. Was Sean giving her a taste of her own medicine? What was sauce for the goose was sauce for the gander? To her disbelief, a feeling of resentment was creeping in, a touch of the 'green eyed monster'.

Some days later after heaving in her order of potatoes and vegetables, an ebullient Sean had quipped, 'Well, Kathy, what did you think of Sybil? Great looker, eh?'

'Yes, really,' replied Kathy casually, trying not to show envy, 'she certainly has style.'

'An' loads of money,' came the reply.

Nan came in from the back shop and said. 'Hello, Sean. Pity I wasn't in when you and your lady friend came in. Would you like a cuppa?'

Sean thanked Nan, but declined, having an extra heavy delivery schedule that morning. As Sean departed, Kathy stood silently weighing Sean's comments about his 'friend' Sybil. She instinctively felt there was more in this than met the eye. Kathy was right, although she didn't know it.

What Kathy couldn't have known was the past association of Sybil's family with Sean's. Sean's and Sybil's dads were old school friends from neighbouring farms near Ayr. Their kids, Sean and Sybil, played happily together as youngsters before the once simple country girl went to private boarding school and was transformed into a toffee-nosed little spoil sport. Anyway that was a lifetime away, but now Sybil's father, Andrew Barr, was a very wealthy man, some said a millionaire. Before Sean's father had died, Barr had announced that nothing would have pleased him more than seeing his daughter Sybil and young Sean happily married. Andrew Barr had stated openly to Sean and his dad, 'I have nae other kids, so everything would go to Sybil and Sean. Think on it, young Sean.'

Young Sean had thought on it. He loved Sybil like a sister. They'd played in the fields, searching for birds' eggs together, playing hide-and-seek with their pals and later kissing on the bales in the barn. He couldn't feel for, nor love Sybil the way he felt about Kathy, for instance. Nevertheless the thought of Barr's fortune hadn't been dismissed from Sean's mind. He was too much of a pragmatist. Perhaps he could have his cake and eat it. Sean was a great play-actor when it suited him, especially where women were concerned.

Sybil felt differently. She truly loved Sean – always did – and she would have married him at a moment's notice. But Sybil would never reveal her true feelings openly for fear of being rejected, or even worse, of being immeasurably wounded by such a rejection. She continued to play the little girl's game with Sean. He would always be the leader of the gang, she the pliant follower.

A plain-clothes Angus finally located Popeye in the Seaforth Bar, in Gorbals Street. Popeye was at his usual ploy of winning a drink. As he sat at the bar, unaware of Angus's presence, Popeye surreptitiously allowed his glass eye to fall out onto the counter as he was talking about the war. The small grey-haired man, thin faced and unshaven, spoke in staccato bursts. Looking at the eye, which had landed in a small pool of beer on the bartop, the wee man said accusingly, 'Aw gie us peace. Ye'll never let me forget, will ye?' Promptly picking up the beer soaked eye, Popeye slid it into his mouth, savouring the flavour.

One of the neighbouring punters, heavily under the influence, falling off his bar-stool, cried out, 'Holy hairy haggises. Did you's see that!' Picking himself off the floor, the drunk enquired, 'Jeese. How did . . . ye . . . do . . . that?'

'Ah, got that at Dunkirk, pal,' replied Popeye loudly, so all could hear. 'Aye, shielding my comrades from a bloody strafing Messerschmitt Me. 109!'

'Here bar . . . man. A . . . drink . . . for ma brave comrade,' cried the impressed inebriate.

The big barman, knowing Popeye well, smiled. 'Is it the usual, sir? A half and a half-pint [quarter gill of whisky and half pint of beer]?'

'Aye, aye. That'll be just fine,' announced the one-eyed rogue. 'Thanks, pal.'

Just as Popeye raised his whisky glass, rolling the rotgut in his mouth, he felt an iron grip on his upraised arm. Swivelling round to give the offender a piece of his mind, he focused on the big man in the cap and shoddy old jacket and trousers.

'Auchterlony, is that you?' whispered Popeye. Angus dragged him to a corner table as the victim complained about his drink being spilled.

'Never mind about your bevvy,' hissed Angus, intent on prizing information out of the old rogue. 'Yes, I'm in plain clothes for the business in hand.' Angus explained they needed to nab the menace known as Iron Teeth who was plaguing the area, as he no doubt was aware.

'Oh aye, we all ken him,' said Popeye grimacing. 'Whoever he is, he's no the full shillin', that's for bloody sure.'

'Look, Willy,' said Angus, using Popeye's real name. 'I need to find this joker, pronto. Understand?'

'Call me Popeye, Auchterlony. It's better for business,' said Willy, rocking his empty whisky glass knowingly from side to side.

Angus took the hint. Reaching into his pocket he slipped the wee fellow a pound note, saying, 'There'll be plenty more if you can nail this nutter for me.'

'Gie me a couple o' days, Auchterlony. Ah'll have a shuftie round,' replied the cocky little fellow. 'Meet me here.'

Until Angus could secure evidence as to the identity or whereabouts of the so called Dracula figure, he had no option but to continue patrolling along the south-bank of the river Clyde, up and down Laurieston Place and Adelphi Street, during the long dark hours of the late shift. These two streets ran at right angles to a host of thoroughfares which led to the Old Gorbals and Southern Necropolis graveyards, so beloved by Iron Teeth. Significantly, the toothed menace had frightened the locals in the area now being patrolled by Angus with special co-operation by Central and Southern Divisions.

Being dressed like a nondescript local, Angus was able to observe all manner of incidents which would have normally brought retribution had he been in uniform, like drunks urinating in public, women plying their trade, two blotto men fighting and a couple entering bushes for no good reasons. All he could do was to alert the local Cop on the beat. Once he awoke on a bench to something panting and gripping his leg.

'Away ye go, ye bloody randy dog. Goose my leg would ye!' shouted an outraged Auchterlony. Nevertheless, the damned mongrel followed him about all night as if he was a bitch on heat! He puzzled. Was his body scent of the doggy kind?

One night before midnight, Angus heard screams as he lingered in Adelphi Street, opposite the tidal weir. As he raced towards the source of the cries, two males and their female companions were standing on the tree-lined public footpath which ran parallel to the bank of the river Clyde. They appeared dishevelled and excited.

'What happened here?' questioned Angus sharply.

'It was yon Dracula thing,' screeched the demented woman. Her partner, a weedy looking character, replied excitedly. 'Holy God, it had flashin' teeth, so it had!'

'Where did it go?' cried Angus, looking about.'I'm a detective.'

They all cried in unison, pointing along the unlit footpath, 'Doon towards the Co-operative Bakery direction.'

As Angus sped along the unlit footpath, he drew his baton, just in case, thinking why couldn't they issue torches with more powerful beams. This nutter, Dracula or Iron Teeth, was becoming more adventuresome, straying further west away from his cemetery stamping grounds. Maybe it was because everyone was frightened stiff of entering his normal lairs, so denying him the satisfaction of the scare and chase.

After a breathless pursuit Angus suddenly stopped. Pole-axed with fright would be a better description. For there, at a distance of some couple of hundred yards, stood the dark clad figure of Iron Teeth, his face indistinct, his beady black eyes sparkling menacingly. The dark figure stood with commanding authority, his hand held like a traffic cop. A harsh voice hissed, 'Shss. Stop!' Angus was mesmerized, like a rabbit before a stoat as the Thing's teeth gleamed by the reflected light of the solitary street-lamp at nearby Commercial Road. Angus's arms and legs were paralysed. He was scared. As he summoned up his courage and resolve to move forward, baton clenched in right hand, Angus couldn't believe his eyes. Iron Teeth was gone! Vanished into mid-air! No amount of searching revealed any sign of the 'Vampire'. Perhaps he had flown up one of the many streets to the Old Gorbals Burial Ground or the Western Necropolis. Thank goodness, thought Angus to himself. 'I had no wooden stakes wi' me anyhow!' But all the night's happenings would go in his report. It was, at least, something more positive than the past two fruitless weeks of wild goose chases.

Some nights later, before resuming his watch along the Clyde, Angus met an impatient Popeye in the Seaforth pub, as he sipped a half pint of MacEwan's pale ale.

'Well, what have ye got, wee man?' quipped Angus expectantly.

'Boy oh boy, have ah got news for ye, Auchterlony!' announced Popeye in a low voice, like a conspirator in a bad melodrama.

Angus asked what he'd like to drink and Popeye laughed. 'This'll cost you. Ah'll have a double Red Hackle and a pint of pale ale.' Then he smirked. 'To be getting on wi', that is.'

Angus settled down with his mineral water, as he was on duty, and announced, 'I'm all ears, wee man.'

'Aye, ah noticed. Have ye ever thought of the operation?' laughed Popeye mischievously. Angus, ignoring the humour, just fixed him with a grin.

After several sips of his drinks, and shrugs of his shoulders, like a kid being coaxed to tell you something, Popeye said suddenly, 'Ah think we have a lead on this Dracula fellow.' Another few sips, and he continued, 'Seems he could be a character who used to work in the Paragon Picture House.'

'Really,' replied Angus, trying to control his excitement as he blurted, 'Drink up, wee man. There's plenty more this end.'

'Well, this guy used to work as an attendant in the Paragon cinema. You know, in Cumberland Street. A bit o' a flea-pit?' continued Popeye hesitatingly.

'Yes, yes. Get on with it,' chided Angus, thinking, 'is this wee bugger trying to spin this out till closing time?'

'His name was Kovic. His faither was some sort of a foreigner, frae the Balkans or some such. But he went funny when his wife died, so that old reprobate Charlie Williams told me. An' he knows, ye know,' uttered Popeye, his vocal chords lubricated by his host's generous libation.

'Funny. How do ye mean exactly?' queried Angus in detective style.

His little companion replied, 'Aye, he started to act funny when his wife died. He used to frighten patrons, those winchin' in the back rows, during horror films wi' false metal teeth. There were complaints. Naebody knows where he stays now.'

Popeye went on, after a further refill, that this Kovic fellow was finally sacked after ten years in the job at the Paragon Picture House, and was seen wandering about the streets wild eyed. Probably all those horror and Dracula pictures had gone to his head. Further CID enquiries revealed that Kovic had indeed been dismissed for strange behaviour, frightening patrons. And yes, these happenings occurred after his wife's death. Up to then, the Paragon's owner said Kovic had been a model employee. He had no idea where Kovic now lived, or whether he was still in the area.

During the next week a surprising series of disturbances broke out in the area of Iron Teeth's domain, to the alarm of many of the local residents, especially old people, as hundreds of children rampaged through Rutherglen Road into the Old Gorbals Burial Ground, and along Caledonia Road into Southern Necropolis. Armed with an assortment of wooden swords, bicycle chains, iron bars, dustbin lids, link chains and poles, the mob howled like wolves, rattling their weapons, and clashed their bin lids unceasingly, all the while screaming, 'Kovic, come oot, come oot. Iron Teeth come oot. We're gonna kill ye. Dracula come oot. Ye're deid when we get ye!'

The local newspapers were full of the news, The *Glasgow Herald* declared 'Police Clear Hysterical Vampire Hunters'. 'Horror Film Blamed for The Vampire' screamed the headlines of the *Daily Record*. Police drafted in to disperse the hordes of hysterical children were overwhelmed by cries of 'The vampire with the iron teeth is running about killing folks!'

The Police soon had the area under control, and calm returned to the dismal streets once again. Many sources believed the Vampire had been brought on by a combination of horror films like 'Dracula', 'The Wolf Man' and 'The Mummy' which played on public hysteria. However, many Gorbals folk knew they had seen Iron Teeth and so did the Police themselves. That Thing which Angus saw on the footpath that night was not a figment of his imagination. How could he ever forget those eyes, those teeth!

A week later, Angus was summoned before Sergeant Ratley in the Gorbals Police office.

'Well, Auchterlony, you'll be glad to know you're back in uniform. The Vampire case we believe is now solved,' announced a triumphant Ratley.

'How do you mean, Sergeant?' quizzed Angus, hardly concealing his eagerness.

'Iron Teeth was fished out of the Clyde by Ben Parsonage at the Glasgow Green, day before yesterday.'

'We're sure enough,' continued Ratley. 'It was a man called Kovic, who was known to wear the iron teeth, frightening people too. Poor chap went bonkers after his wife died. Used to work in the Paragon Picture House too, as your nark reported.'

'What about his address?' asked Angus, eager for the information.

Sergeant Ratley replied simply. 'He lived in an old single-end near the Southern Necropolis. He cooked soup on an old primus stove. The steel teeth and the cape were found there too. We found a picture of

Kovic's wife clenched tightly in his hand when his body was retrieved from the Clyde.'

'God rest his soul,' said Angus sadly. 'The poor, sick bugger.'

Back on the beat was a relief to Angus and many of the locals enquired. 'Been on holiday again, Constable? Must be great being a Polis wi' all that leave?'

Kathy and Nan knew that Angus had been on special duty so there were no questions from that source, except relief that the case of the Gorbals Vampire was now solved.

One afternoon Angus was talking to Constable Tam 'The Bam' Cahill at Gorbals Cross when they received a request to investigate the theft of a horse and cart outside a pub in Portugal Street. Arriving at the pub, the two cops were confronted by a distraught diminutive man who cried, 'Someone has half-inched ma horse and cairt. The ball's on the slates noo. They even took the cuddy's bag o' oats. Hislop'll murder me!'

The victim was quickly recognised by Constable Cahill as Wee Foley, the local rag-and-bone man. Foley was known to tie his horse to the lighting pole outside O'Neill's pub when he habitually stopped for his lunch. The horse had his bag of oats and Foley had the usual pie and a pint. However, on this particular day, his horse and cart were not there when he came out after his lunch. This was serious because it was not only his livelihood, but the horse and cart belonged to Hislop from whom he had hired them.

From investigations inside O'Neill's pub, the smirks and general demeanour of some of the locals led Cahill to suspect something suspicious was going on. 'I think there's some monkey-business here, Auchterlony.' Everyone in the pub had looked as serious as participants at an undertakers' convention, stifling their humour as they had tried to answer the cops' questioning without exploding.

'Sorry, officers, we have nae idea what could have happened to Mr Foley's horse an' cairt. We've been in here the whole time,' said a big docker with a beard. 'Is that not so, lads?'

The response was a unanimous 'Aye' from all the punters.

The two Policemen decided to conduct further immediate

investigations in the vicinity. Surely no one was going to get away with hi-jacking a horse and cart in broad daylight, they concluded. They had just stepped outside the bar, Tam saying, 'You go down that way, Angus. I'll search up to Bedford Street direction. Maybe the horse got loose and wandered off?'

They had only gone a short distance when a woman carrying a washing basket shouted after them. 'Polis, haw, Polis. There's a bloody horse oot back o' the close!' The sound of two pairs of size ten boots running through the dank close revealed a sight to behold. There, as large as life, was a horse's head staring them in the face. The animal was chewing contentedly into its bag of oats, facing forwards and linked to its cart.

'Sufferin' jeely pieces!' exclaimed Tam the Bam, scratching his head.

Angus simply said, 'This is impossible. The close is too narrow for the cart to pass through. It's just no' possible.'

Tam had removed his helmet and was scratching his head as he took in every detail of the back court, until finally nonplussed, the big Irishman stood gazing skywards towards the roof.

Angus could hardly stifle his guffaw as he exclaimed, 'For goodness sake. Don't be daft, Tam. Horses canna fly! Let's go in and see the boys in O'Neill's. I'm sure they'll dig up a way to get the cuddy and cart back.'

Back in the pub, Angus announced to a relieved Wee Foley, 'We've found your horse and cart. It must have strayed into the adjacent close.'

'How the hell could ma cart get through such a narrow close. It's no possible!' replied the rag-and-bone man.

'Oh miracles can happen,' piped up the big docker with the beard. 'Can me and the lads gie you a hand?' A sudden burst of guffaws broke loose from the pub patrons.

'A little joke, perhaps, at Mr Foley's expense?' said Constable Cahill out loud, to no one in particular.

'Yes, and a waste of valuable Police time and public expense,' said Angus to the barman loudly, glancing briefly at the big docker with the beard. The cart was soon brought out sideways through the close and hitched to the pony still chewing his oats by many willing and giggling hands.

Angus was just back over a week on the uniform beat when he was summoned by a man in Warwick Street who announced his concern. 'Constable, ma old neighbour Danny hasn't answered my knocks for the past three days. He's no away, ah'm sure.' The man who said his name was Kincaid mentioned that he had strung up a black thread across Danny's door between two penknife nicks (an old trick he'd learned out East).

Angus accompanied by Kincaid made his way to the ground floor single end. Knocking on the door loudly several times, and calling out Danny's surname brought no answer. All Mr Kincaid said was, 'You know Danny hasnae been well this last year. He's got growths inside of him.'

After several further attempts of knocking and shouting failed to bring forth any response, Angus said suddenly, 'Stand back, Mr Kincaid. Your thread shows he's not been out. I'm going to break the door in.'

It took half a dozen full kicks along with as many shoulder charges to force the door, because the chain was on with the Yale. As he entered the small hall, Angus spotted the door to the kitchen, He called the man's name. There was no answer. As he opened the door a scene and smell of horror assailed their senses. There lay Danny, his head in the gas oven. The smell of gas still lingered. Clouds of dead and living bluebottles flew in their faces and infested the victim's face and body. The window similarly was covered by them, the dead and living.

'Quick, open the window, Mr Kincaid, and the front door. Looks as if the meter emptied a while ago and cut off the gas, thank God,' cried Angus.

A note was found which said he couldn't stand the pain any longer, and decided to end it. He knew it was cancer.

Angus phoned for the ambulance, CID and Sanitary Department. Finding Danny like that was a shock for both Policeman and neighbour. It would take a long time for Angus to get the scene from his memory. It was all part of the big city life which any ordinary Cop on the beat had to take in his stride. Whenever he left to go on duty, a Cop would never know what he'd meet. If he dwelt on it, it was time to get out.

You had to face each day at a time, relying on your comrades and the Force, not forgetting the support and goodwill of the Public, whom you invariably protected with your life.

CHAPTER 11

Inspector MacAlee had been on to Sergeant Ratley. Sergeant Ratley had been onto Constables Auchterlony and Cahill about the local nuisance on their beats. That was the never ending saga of the phantom scooter rider with the red beret who plagued their areas abounding Eglinton and Gorbals Street and Bedford Street and Clyde Place. In the case of the crazy scooterist who continued to terrorise the local people: women with prams, old modellers from around Portugal Street, drunks crossing the roads, including hordes of distraught cats and dogs, there were always copious accounts of his outrageous highway meanderings – but never an indication of his origin or destination.

'Auchterlony, are ye sure you're searching out this scooter nutter with utmost vigour?' asked Sergeant Ratley just as Angus was going on to the back-shift.

'I'm doing the best I can, Sergeant,' replied Angus testily.

'Paying attention to details, with vigour?' queried Sergeant Ratley relentlessly.

Angus, resenting the implication, replied, 'As vigorously as possible, Sergeant.'

'Well, come with me, Constable. I'll show ye something,' said Ratley smugly.

Sergeant Ratley led Angus at a fast walk to the Suspension Bridge across the Clyde at Carlton Place and stopped momentarily at the large stone entrance arch. Leading Angus on, Sergeant Ratley continued till they reached the central point of the river. Ratley regarded Angus strangely for a second, then enquired, 'You realise this is the extent of your beat, Auchterlony?'

'Yes, Sergeant, I know it,' replied Angus grinning, as if he was a pupil being quizzed by an eccentric schoolmaster.

'Well, turn round, right now, Auchterlony, and tell me what you see?' growled Sergeant Ratley.

Swivelling around Angus looked and was frozen in horror. There, in huge white letters over the archway lintel, was the painted exhortation – 'QUIT INDIA'.

'Holy Moses!' was all Angus could gasp.

'You see, Auchterlony, you missed that important detail,' lectured Sergeant Ratley. He reminded Angus of the drill-sergeant during his army square-bashing. 'Your beat extends to the centre of the river. That means walking to the centre of same bridge, and back again. Not bloody well peeping across it. Vigorous attention to detail. Are you receiving me, Constable?'

'Yes, Sergeant, understood!' Angus replied stiffly, thinking it's those bleeding Gandhi supporters from the University again. With that dressing down of his duly chastened subordinate, a smug and refreshed Sergeant Rat Ratley set off on his rounds.

Fate smiled on Angus, however, in the form of Popeye, his nark, who had very valuable information for him concerning the mad scooterist. Funnily, what Popeye was saying agreed with what many, including Kathy, had said about the offender being a local. A nervous Popeye announced in a low voice, as he glanced from side to side about the busy street, 'Yes, he's a local madskull. Rides a folding up scooter – just like the Paras used in the War. Keep an eye on Duffy's Bar, in Oxford Street, Auchterlony. He's said to frequent the place,' announced the diminutive bright eyed man.

Angus replied quietly, 'There'll be a few quid in this for ye, wee man, when we nab this nutter.'

Ed Moran of the CID was shocked to hear that Slogger Struth had left Glasgow suddenly and unexpectedly without informing him. After all, Struth was a key witness in their case, along with Kitty, Lilly Grant's friend, concerning Angus's vicious attack. Now, with Struth's withdrawal, Ed Moran feared that the frightened and vulnerable Kitty was bound to take cold feet. When Angus found out, his feeling of deep disappointment was outweighed by intense anger, caused by the thought of Dougal and Bakley getting away with their assault on his person. Angus just had to find out why a tough man like Slogger Struth would change his mind at the last minute. There just had to be an explanation of some kind and Angus was determined to find out why.

Slogger Struth was known as a man who never backed away from anyone or anything. So what changed his mind? It must have been something big, thought Angus and his friend Ed Moran of CID firmly agreed. Jock and Lilly Grant had been informed by Detective Constable Moran and had agonised about Kitty. They had no option but to tell her.

'There's no way ah can testify now,' sobbed a fearful Kitty as she held onto Lilly's hands. 'Ah'll be all alone. That maddy Bakley'll do me in for sure, noo Slogger's disappeared. Why has he gone? Why?'

'There, there, lassie,' soothed Jock. 'Ye'll aye have me an' Lilly here.'

A near hysterical young woman cried. 'Naw, naw. Ah'll no testify if Slogger Struth's no along wi' me. Never!'

Angus meanwhile was waiting at a close mouth in Oxford Street, down from Duffy's Bar but on the opposite side. What a brass-neck, thought Angus of the culprit, to be operating so near the Police Training College. But where better to hide something than under the noses of the Police themselves. He remembered a film about a priceless stamp which everybody sought, and there it was hidden in an ordinary stamp album.

Around seven thirty-five, Angus's ears pricked up and he became galvanised by the sight and sound of a miniature scooter drawing up before Duffy's bar, pursued by a couple of barking dogs who stopped some ways behind. To his amazement, Angus observed a small, stocky man alight from the khaki two wheeled scooter as he whistled a tune which sounded like Wagner's 'Ride of the Valkyrie'. The dapper man wore a maroon beret and, without further ado, deftly folded the contraption into half its size, finally disappearing with it into the pub.

'Well, my Aunt Fanny,' cried Angus to himself. 'Can ye credit the gall o' it!'

Nevertheless, Angus would enter Duffy's bar with a certain trepidation. After all he was in pursuit of a culprit committing an offence, or offences. He waited for a short spell before entering, to let things settle before acting. Feeling justified and confident as he entered, Angus caught sight of the folded scooter, lying against a circular pillar. 'Ah, there's the "vehicle" – the evidence. Good,' he mused. 'All we need now is the accused.'

A sudden and immediate hush descended upon the bar, as happens when the villain enters a bar in a Western picture.

The dapper little man, in the faded maroon beret, had finished his Johnny Walker, and was drinking a beer chaser as he was engaged in conversation with the landlord, Daniel Duffy. Angus stood by the bar, saying nothing but observing. Although unknown to Angus, this was the very man whom Popeye had described to him as being the likely culprit with the scooter. Known as Madcap McNulty, the latter had been in the Paras, wounded in Normandy and had had a steel plate inserted into his skull after Arnhem. This was believed to have sent him off his rocker with consequent wild behaviour thereafter, according to his old mother, relatives and friends – and hence his nickname Madcap McNulty.

Angus addressed McNulty slowly. The latter kept staring ahead into the large silver mirror which hung on the wall opposite. The ex-Para said nothing, as he observed Angus, but continued drinking his pint.

'Are you, Sir, the owner of that scooter in the hall, back there?'

'Ye mean my Para folding bike, Constable?' replied the stocky man in clipped military style. 'Yes, that's mine. Anything wrong? By the way, just call me Corporal McNulty. The address of "Sir" is only for officers.'

'My apologies, Corporal. Can I have your name?'

'Michael McNulty,' came the clipped reply.

Angus wrote the details in his pocket-book. Without further ado he vanished into the hall. He returned to everyone's amazement carrying Madcap's scooter, laying it on the bar with a bump which made Daniel Duffy's eyebrows arch markedly.

'So you, Mr . . .er . . .Corporal McNulty are the owner-driver of this scooter, this vehicle. Am I right?' queried Angus in an official manner.

'Aye. I admit it. It's mine. Ah call it "Jimmy" an' it was wi' me at Arnhem,' replied McNulty, gazing at the bike and adding, 'Do ye remember the lines aboot us Red Devils at Arnhem. *Men defying cannon, facing Panzers of the line, for a bridge too far?'*

Angus felt deeply touched by what the man was saying and wished it was some other Cop who was in his situation. He couldn't help admiring the feisty wee warrior, but nevertheless he had to continue, watched by a hostile crowd of patrons.

'I have to warn you, Corporal,' said Angus in a softer tone. 'There have been many complaints about you causing a nuisance in the area with this thing.' Angus pointed to the scooter.

'Why? I don't see why. I haven't knocked anybody down. I know that,' replied McNulty, shrugging his shoulders and taking a swig at his beer.

Duffy the barman laughed. 'By Jeeze, it's the first time I've ever heard of a road offence where the vehicle in question is placed on a pub bar.' Universal laughter erupted, breaking the tension. Even Angus had to smile.

'He's a very law-abiding soul. Never a bother at all, Constable,' said Duffy's blousey barmaid earnestly. But a strong dissenting voice broke the air.

'Thank fuck,' cried a grey thin old man at the far end of the bar. 'Lots o' us locals wullnae be sorry Madcap's copped it. We're lucky to hiv survived till noo wi' his bluidy crazy driving.'

'Yer face in a dunny, ye auld keech [shit],' roared a red-haired man. 'The puir bastard nearly got kilt in the War twice, fightin fer crappers like you.'

'Shut it, pal,' cried the old thin grey man. 'I did my bit in the trenches of the Great War. So ah did.'

Angus called for silence while he conducted his investigation, amidst simmering resentment.

McNulty sat there at the bar, protesting his innocence and continued, 'I don't see what's wrong here. You're making a mountain out of a molehill, Constable.'

'Nothing wrong?' exploded Angus in disbelief. 'Perhaps endangering the lives of pedestrians and road-users can be a start,' cited the Policeman, pausing before continuing, 'Not to mention driving the said vehicle without a proper driver's licence, no road taxation nor insurance cover. That should be enough to be getting on with.'

'Och, I was going to wheel the bike home, no' ride it. Honest, Constable,' pleaded Madcap piteously.

'Shall I continue,' said Angus. 'No number plates, no lighting and now, you're likely to be in charge of a vehicle under the influence too.'

Several of the pub patrons started to crowd around Angus, shouting, 'Ach, let him alone, Constable. Can't ye see he's no' well.'

'That's all the more reason to protect him, and the public too,' said Angus sternly, warning them to back off as this was Police business.

'Right lads, leave off,' warned Duffy the landlord. 'It's Police business. I want no trouble here.'

'Well, Corporal McNulty. I'm acting under my authorised powers of arrest, in spite of what you and your pals here think.' Angus quoted reference to the Glasgow Police Act of 1866, and the Further Powers Act of 1892, and added, 'Just in case you think I'm being unfair. You, me and your bike are now going to the Station just along the road there. Okay?'

'Okay, okay, Constable. Right,' croaked 'Madcap' submissively. 'Just let me finish my drink.'

Back at the Grant's house in Bedford Street, Lilly was in conversation with her pal Kitty. Jock was playing cards with a couple of friends in the kitchen. Lilly's bedroom afforded the two friends the privacy needed at a time like this.

'Kitty, ah know you have troubles of yer own, hen,' said Lilly softly. 'But ah've got real problems now.'

'Just tell me, dear,' said her friend, looking directly into Lilly's pretty tearfilled blue eyes.

'Ah'm pregnant. And ma da will throw me oot into the street, if he doesnae kill me first.'

Kitty quickly quipped, 'Yer dad Jock's no the kind o' man that wid do that tae ye.'

'But he'd die o' shame, Kitty,' cried Lilly, with head bowed. 'He always said he hoped ah'd find a decent Proddy boy tae marry.'

Kitty laughed. 'Ma parents want me to find a good Catholic boy, tae.'

'Just like the song, Patsy Fagin – a decent Irish boy!' came Lilly's reply.

'Och, any suitable Scotch boy would do me fine,' replied Kitty.

'And ah'm sure there are lots of Scotch boys who wid love to do ye fine,' Lilly laughed. Seeing the point of the joke both girls broke forth in a riot of laughter, relieving their pressures.

Lilly explained how she had missed two periods, and sometimes felt sick. When Kitty enquired about the father, Lilly had replied simply, 'It's Con Dougal's.'

'Ah think ye should consult yer doctor, hen. They have their oaths to keep, and cannae say onything tae others,' confided Kitty.

Lilly, conscious of Kitty Cullen's problem, tactfully asked about Slogger Struth's whereabouts. Kitty just shrugged her shoulders and said it was rumoured that he had left Glasgow with his wife, possibly for London. Why? Kitty had no idea. 'Slogger was at school wi' my dad. He's no the kind o' guy tae be frightened off. God, he was into body building and boxing as a boy – he was a Scottish Amateur Champion.'

'Maybe he has family problems,' replied Lilly.

Although Lilly did not know it she had hit on the core of the problem. Angus and his colleague in the CID, Ed Moran, had heard rumours from their informers that Struth had been warned off from testifying about the attack on Constable Auchterlony. There had been a secret meeting with Con Dougal and his henchman, Bull Bakley. According to Angus's nark, Popeye, Struth had a son and a daughter living locally in Glasgow. His son was in the shipyards, married to an attractive lassie with a two year old son. Struth's daughter was at the Commercial College training to be a secretary. It was not difficult to see why the big bruiser had backed off giving evidence under such circumstances, where 'people could easily have an unfortunate accident' as Bakley had warned.

Slogger had looked both Dougal and Bakley straight in the eye at the time and replied, 'Believe me, they're not the only people who could have accidents.' The big fellow was not willing to put his vulnerable family at risk and so had fled to London to protect them. Kitty had said to Detective Moran. 'Ah'm no willing to gie evidence. Count me oot. If Slogger's no there – forget it!' Hence the solid Prosecution case now lay in tatters, and the Police's crusade to bring the perpetrators to justice no further forward, after so many months of hard work.

Con Dougal and Bull Bakley seemed to be holding all the high cards as their well paid, very sharp, lawyer struck a deal with the Procurator Fiscal. The Police forced entry without a warrant, including the charge of assault on his client's person would be dropped. Instead, Bull Bakley would be charged with assaulting a Police Officer with a fine of ten pounds or thirty days, at the local Police Court.

The time had come for the annual Police Ball which was held in the Glasgow City Chambers, attended by all the bigwigs, the Lord Provost, magistrates, councillors, lawyers and senior Police officers. Dress was *de rigueur* evening wear, and many ordinary Cops below the rank of Sergeant or Inspector felt out of place rubbing shoulders with the big wigs. For the social climbers, yes men and career merchants, the Annual Ball was a must, just as it was for Sergeant Rat Ratley and his crony, Snakey Flockhart and their better halves. Fortunately, most Police officers of all ranks including their wives gave solid support to the Annual Ball in one way or another, selling tickets and raising funds for Police charities. In this, Chief Constable McCulloch gave generous and unstinted support.

When Kathy asked Angus if he was going to the Police Ball, he replied with a sigh, 'Aye, I have no option. My gaffer, Inspector MacAlee, more or less ordered me to. And, by the way, I've to bring my partner too.'

'Well. I'd be delighted, Angus, old boy,' smiled Kathy, her blue eyes shining with pleasure.

'It's all formal dress, you know,' replied Angus, pausing in thought. 'Do you have enough coupons for a new dress?'

'Oh, I'll beg, borrow or buy some if I must. My mum will give me hers, no doubt,' quipped Kathy impishly.

Angus replied in mock surprise, 'Don't tell me you're admitting to a

Police Officer that you're into the Blackmarket!'

'Come off it, Angus,' laughed Kathy as she went on. 'The whole country's in on it, otherwise we would all be walking around wearing curtains, or nothing at all!'

'I'll kid on I didn't hear that, dearie,' retorted Angus with a sly smile.

Angus looked very handsome in his evening-suit some weeks later, with black dickie bow and pristine white shirt. When Nan opened the door she cried,

'Well, look who's here, Kathy. I'm sure it's Prince Charming himself.'

Kathy just looked and cried, 'Wow! You look great!'

Angus just stood there mesmerized at the sight before him, oblivious to the waiting taxi meter running up expense.

'Kathy, you . . .you look like a dream,' whispered a stunned Angus.

There stood Kathy in an off-the-shoulder narrow waisted emerald satin dress, complete with bow at her neck, her red hair set in high bouffant style highlighting her sparkling blue eyes and peach complexion. To a totally beguiled Angus, Kathy's diamante necklace and long matching earrings, with her orange-red lips, completed the dream. Helping Kathy and Nan with their coats, Angus gallantly escorted his Cinderellas to their coach.

The Police Ball was held in Glasgow's City Chambers and Kathy, Nan and Angus felt elated as they approached the magnificent front façade, with its porticos and Roman pediment. As they entered the sumptuous loggia or entrance hall, done in the Italian style with pleasing mosaic tiles, smart ushers clad in Corporation green and wearing spotless white gloves welcomed them, as they walked across a depiction of the city coat of arms done in yellow, brown and white ceramics, where their coats were taken.

An usher conducted them to the Banqueting Hall in the upper floor, by way of magnificent marble stairs made of Carrara marble with alabaster balustrades. Passing polished red granite pillars capped by green marble in the Ionic style, the trio felt a sudden swelling of the chest. A very impressed Nan exclaimed, 'Gosh, it makes ye feel like royalty?' A starry-eyed Kathy and Angus nodded in agreement.

It was as they entered the Banquet Hall that the trio reached their apotheosis of awe and sensual climax. Kathy exclaimed, 'My God, isn't it beautiful!'

'Magnificent!' was all Angus could exclaim, mesmerised by the huge sparkling chandeliers hanging from the massive arch of the ornate roof.

Nan regarded the huge murals depicting the city's history, and remarked, her eyes welling, 'It makes ye real proud of dear old Glasgow toon – so it does.'

The meal in the Banqueting Hall contained a good choice of menus, wines and refreshments, considering the post war restrictions, with a wide selection of meat, fish and poultry.

Angus was surprised to see certain civilian guests sitting among the throng, hob-nobbing and buying drinks. How did they get in, he wondered – they should have been in Barlinnie. But that's politics, and after all they were helping to contribute to a good cause. At least here you can keep an eye on them, he thought.

'Angus, you old reprobate,' came a voice from behind.

Angus turned round, laughing. 'It's Tam Cahill, himself. My old pal.'

'Holy Moses, who is this stunning lady you have here?'

Angus graciously introduced Kathy and Nan to Tam and his wife Madge, and presently took a table together with another two couples with whom they were friendly. Tam Cahill was in his element with his corny jokes, for which he was famed.

'Three men walked into a pub in the Sou'Side. One was an Englishman, one an Irishman and the other a Welshman. The publican refused to serve them, saying, "Is this some kind of joke?"'

'Very funny, Tam,' cried one of the women who had one pink gin too many.

Tam, now fortified with another double whisky, continued 'We arrested a man for robbing a bank and Toffylegs asked the criminal why he had sawn the legs off his bed. The crook replied, 'Ah had to lay low for a bit, with you on my trail!'

The joke brought several loud gaffaws from Angus's table. Kathy and Nan laughed as they thought it was funny. Angus rolled his eyes as if he had really heard them all before, but their clamour brought disapproving glances from Sergeant Ratley's table. Mrs Ratley, a large woman with huge bust, looked fit to burst as she remarked,

'Some folk don't know how to behave in civilised company.'

This remark only brought forth further giggles from Angus and Tam's table, subsiding as the band struck up with 'Forty-Second Street'.

'May I have the pleasure of this dance, miss?' The invitation came from none other than Inspector MacAlee himself. The dance was a quickstep and Kathy took an instant liking to MacAlee and his humorous banter. It seemed Kathy was the talk of the place, according to what the Inspector was saying. And it proved true, as she, Nan and Angus were invited over to meet Mrs MacAlee, a fine outgoing woman.

MacAlee remarked to his wife with a laugh, 'This is the chap who solved the case of the crowing cock, ye remember?' His wife nodded her head vigorously as MacAlee continued, 'and he located the Indian Pedlar Johnny, Mr Ali, who now comes to our house wi' all those shirts, pullovers and socks!' The table erupted into laughter.

It was as Tam passed the ornate 'Satinwood Salon', so named after its opulent Australian satinwood finish, that his eye caught the chatting figures of Angus and three former pals from the Training School. The trio – Billy Armstrong, Rab Dingley and Jim Gibb – planned to have some fun at Tam's expense, for there, smoking a fat cigar and toasting his rear in front of the large alabaster fireplace, was their target: none other than the Chief Constable himself, dreamily puffing his huge Havana cigar.

Billy remarked to the inebriated Cahill, 'Hey, Tam, do ye see him there?'

'Whit's it yer on aboot?' answered a tipsy Tam, looking round.

Rab interjected. 'The Chief Constable's actually smoking in there, and what does the sign say above the fireplace?'

Tam stared and repeated, 'It says . . . No Smoking. Aye . . . No Smoking.'

Jim quipped slyly, 'You know, Tam, a good Cop is never off duty. It's very bad when the Chief himself breaks the rules. Gives a bad impression tae the troops!'

'Aye . . . bad example to the Force . . . an' Ratley's aye on aboot that,' replied Tam slowly, his chin beginning to jut out . . . always a sign of trouble!

'Now if someone had the guts to tell him, he'd probably be given a commendation for a real sense of duty, and for no being feart,' quipped Billy with a wink.

'Aye . . . yer right. Ah'll just away over . . . and have a word in his ear.'

Angus attempted to grab his arm, shouting, 'No, Tam, stay. Don't be a fool!'

It was no use. Tam, the drink in him, strode boldly over to where the Chief was deep in the clouds of his smoky heaven.

'Excuse me, Sir. A word in your ear?' said Tam as if about to give a felon a friendly warning.

It took fully several seconds for the Chief to emerge from the clouds before he realised he was being addressed.

'Yes, can I be of assistance, son?' replied the Chief Constable, as he enquired. 'And who am I addressing?'

'Constable Thomas Cahill, Southern Division, Sir.' Pause, then: 'Are you aware that this is a non smoking area, Sir?' replied Cahill briskly, pointing slowly to the sign.

The look on the Chief's face was one of utter amazement. He quickly doused his cigar in embarrassment, propelling the offending butt into the open fire.

'Thank you . . . er . . . er. Good work. A Police Officer is never off duty.'

Tam his chest heaving markedly, announced, 'Glad you took it that way, Sir.'

'Well, Cahill . . .Yer name is Cahill is it not?' confirmed the Chief, pausing as he answered. 'I shall certainly remember you, Cahill of Southern Division. You can depend on that.'

'That's very kind of ye, Sir,' slurred Tam proudly.

The clique nearby, his so-called pals, could hardly contain themselves.

As Kathy returned with Angus to his flat in Partick for a glass of wine and cheese appetizers, he told her about Tam's extraordinary act of drunken folly.

Kathy said reproachingly. 'Ach, Angus. Ye might have tried to stop him making a fool of himself.'

'I tried, but Tam was in his cups and I failed,' replied Angus, feeling really guilty and bad about the incident. Angus finally added, as if a foregone conclusion, 'Tam'll be lucky if he ever makes Sergeant this side of eternity, after that!'

Angus decided to change the mood by putting on Frank Sinatra in romantic mood. Kathy was willing to play along in his romantic interlude for a spell, until she announced, looking at her wrist-watch, 'No squeezing. Watch the dress, Angus. This has cost me an arm and a leg. Mum wants to borrow it next week. We're the same size.' Kathy finally said, 'Great night, Angus. Thanks, it was really super. Are ye going to see me to the taxi? It's late.'

'Yes, even though I didn't even get dancing with you as I'd expected,' said Angus sadly. 'That outfit really turned all those guys alight.'

'Never mind, D 93. I'll make it up to ye some other time,' chuckled Kathy with a wink.

Angus suggested, donning his coat. 'Let's walk along to Peel Street. We'll get you a taxi there.'

CHAPTER 12

Jock Grant sat listening to the wireless as Lilly regarded her dad. How secure she felt with him. She loved him dearly for his gentleness. Jock was not only her fond father, he was her surrogate mother too, lavishing loving care on her since her mother died in the accident when she was a child.

Lilly was deeply upset but didn't show it to her old man. Here she was pregnant and about to bring hurt and shame on the very person whom she loved above any other person in the wide world: Jock, who had fought so bravely in the Great War, losing a leg in the process. Her father who had almost crawled up the stairs of Bull Bakley's close to rescue her in the shebeen, and suffered cruelly for it at the hands of the evil Bakley. Then there was the disappointing outcome when the Dougal's slick lawyer, Kane, managed to get Bakley off because of lack of evidence. There were four of Bakley's witnesses who swore Jock had come up to their house looking for drink, swearing abuse. They told him to go home, they had no drink, and no, his daughter was not there. Grant had obviously been tipsy, lost his balance, and fell down the stair. As the programme Jock was listening to drew to an end, Lilly said, 'Now, Da, would ye like a cheese roll and a nice cup o' tea?'

'Oh, aye, lassie. That would be smashin',' said Jock, rising from his chair. 'That was a real interesting programme aboot William Wallace.'

'Aye, we got him in oor history,' said Lilly putting the kettle on the gas.

Jock said solemnly, 'Wallace was a true Scottish patriot, lass. He fought, not for any crown, but for Freedom alone.'

Lilly carried on with the buttering of the rolls, saying nothing, but felt touched by the way her father had spoken.

At length Jock said, 'Lilly, is something bothering you, hen?'

'Naw, naw, Da. Whit makes you think that?'

Jock replied, 'Lassie, I've raised you since ye was a wee girl. I know you like a well kent book. And ye didn't go oot dancing this Saturday night wi' Kitty and yer pals.'

Lilly just laughed, crossing over from the kitchen table to give her dad a hug, saying, 'Dinnae worry, Dad. It's just ma monthly, and I prefer yer company sometime, ye ken!'

'Dinnae worry, Lilly hen,' chuckled Jock feeling reassured. 'You'll get yer breakfast in bed to-morrow. Your favourite, potato scones wi' toasted cheese and hot sweet tea.'

Lilly gave her dad a fond smile, not revealing her suffering but putting a face on it. How was she going to solve her problem, God only knew? Her doctor had confirmed she was three months gone. So that was that, and there was no doubt.

Meanwhile life went on as usual. One night in Alexander's Bar, it had been a year to the day that a number 27 blue tram (doing the loop from Commerce Street into Bridge Street and back into Nelson Street) had jumped the rails smashing through the Alexander's lounge bar window. The landlord John Clancy had found old regular Mick McGrath, snoring through the whole incident with the Noon *Record* on his lap and four pints of black velvet under his belt. When Clancy had shaken old Mick awake, he had brushed shards of glass off his bonnet, exclaiming excitedly, 'They're oot to get me!'

'Calm doon, Mick,' said Clancy trying to soothe him. 'Who do ye mean?'

'The tramcaur people, fur sure. They feckin' bastarts from the Corporation. Ah hiv been nicking off the blue trams wi'out payin'. They're oot to get me, fur sure!' wailed the demented Irishman, fleeing from the bar crying, 'Mother of Jesus, preserve us!'

And no wonder. Six months previously, the same Mick had been in his other favourite local along the road, the Bonnington Bar, when a number 22 blue tram had smashed through the bar window, jumping the rails as it rounded from Commerce Street heading for Paisley Road.

That time he was reading the *Daily Record* and had only consumed one black velvet, so he was still compos-mentis when it had happened.

Angus was on patrol at the time and had to deal with the details. Luckily nobody was injured, the damage mainly to property for which the Corporation Tramways would be held liable.

Another episode involving the Corporation happened as Angus was called to an old tenement which was being demolished locally. The foreman of Safe Demolitions had the demolition ball machine on site, ready to commence immediate operations under a Corporation dangerous building order.

'When I did a final check, before starting, Constable, I found this old guy,' said the big, rough bearded foreman. 'Thank Christ I did.'

Angus went up to the second floor, and there covered by bundles of newspapers lay a man in his late thirties, on his back and unshaven, wearing a woolly balaclava, hands in mittens and clad in an old sailor's coat tied round with rope. White foam issued from his mouth.

'Is he dead?' queried Angus, hand on chin.

'As dead as a doornail,' replied one of the two ambulance men. The foreman nodded in agreement, saying he'd seen enough dead men in the War.

Angus immediately set about searching the man's clothing. This was not easy as the victim wore two pairs of trousers, two pairs of old army socks, a jacket under the overcoat, and finally a heavy shirt with two vests under that.

'Be careful, Constable, you're liable to become infested. And I don't mean to be disrespectful, ye ken,' said the other ambulance man quietly.

Angus imagined an itchy feeling all over his body but continued with his search. He could find no proof of identity. All he found was the tattered picture of a young fair haired woman, holding a blonde baby on her knee, in his inside jacket pocket. On the back of the picture, was written in copper-plate script, 'To Danny with Love, Dina and Baby May, Clydebank 1939.'

Further searching brought forth a ball of twine, a beer bottle opener, various coins amounting to nothing much and a medicine bottle smelling like cough mixture.

All around lay empty wine bottles, like Lanlic, VP and Eldorado, with an empty container of 'Bel-Air' hair lacquer side by side with empty bottles reeking of methylated spirits.

The deceased's right hand clutched a battered mug which announced 'Happy Days at Dunoon'.

'Poor old bugger. He looks as if he was once a fine looking man,' said Angus solemnly.

'Aye, just look at his white hair. He's no really old either,' added one of the ambulance men.

Angus concluded. 'Maybe they were his family. Perhaps killed in the Clydebank Blitz?'

'Aye, and maybe that sent him over the edge. We'll never know,' said the foreman.

Turning to the ambulance men, Angus said, 'I think you can take him to the morgue now. There'll be the usual examination there. And we'll need to let the demolition work continue. I'll get my Inspector's clearance.'

A short broad man strode into Alexander's Bar and looked around. Tank Mulgrew was as tall as he was broad, with a fearsome reputation as a battler. Even on a good day, he displayed the temperament of a bulldog with a sore paw. Spotting Bobby Lettin sitting at a table with a couple of cronies, Mulgrew approached and announced in his rasping voice. 'Whit is this I hear from wee Mikey here aboot yer brither?'

'Yer wee pal? Where is he?' replied Bobby, cheekily looking around.

'Ma wee pal here. Mikey's his name,' rasped the Tank, pointing to a midget wearing a large tartan bunnet who stood at his side.

'Oh aye, him,' was all Bobby said as he continued with his beer.

Tank addressed wee Mikey, saying, 'Whit did he say about his brither, Shug, last night in this very bar?'

Bobby piped up. 'Aye, ah remember noo. Ah said ma brother, Shug, could beat the hell out o' ony man in the Sou'Side.'

'Whit . . . whit!' roared Tank, rubbing his fists together, and roaring, 'Your damn brither has'nae met Tank Mulgrew yet.'

'Yer right, Tank. Dead right. Naebody can live wi the Tank,' squeaked his diminutive companion adding, 'This Shug better make arrangements fer his funeral before he meets oor Tank.'

'Ye better believe it,' snarled his bulldog companion, looking directly at Bobby Lettin. 'I'll be in to-morrow. Tell yer brither to meet me outside here.'

Bobby replied in a very casual manner, 'OK, Mulgrew, if that's the way ye want it. But it's your funeral, pal.'

Tank Mulgrew departed with his little friend, swearing under his breath.

It was a week later that the Tank managed to catch up with Shug and brother Bobby as they emerged from the Alexander Bar at closing time. Tank shouted, 'Ah've found ye at last. Ye dodgy wee nyaff.'

Surrounded by pub patrons eager for the impending fight, his brother Bobby egged him on, crying, 'Right, Shuggie, noo show this windbag whit you can do!'

'Windbag is it,' roared Tank Mulgrew. 'Right . . . to the vacant ground . . . Right the noo!'

'Lead on, pal, efter you,' shouted Shug heroically.

John Clancy decided to run out and search for a Constable, for he feared for Shug's ability to remain in one piece after his meeting with Mulgrew.

As the small number of pub patrons swelled with the inclusion of passersby, the two men threw off their jackets and, with sleeves rolled up, prepared for battle on the vacant muddy bomb site. The shadows cast on the assembled gathering by the glare of nearby street lamps adding a macabre quality, as if some primeval ritual was under way.

As a grinning Tank waited with fists about waist level, a game Shuggie Lettin attacked with left jabs to his opponent's face. To Shug's surprise, Tank took all his punches with a laugh. Shug took a number of heavy punches which sent him down into the mud, but he was soon up, encouraged by his brother's cries of 'Up, Shuggie, up. Gie it tae him!'

Tank Mulgrew, tiring of fisticuffs, launched into his famous bear hug, and soon the two battlers were rolling about in the wet mud. Shug felt as if he was being squeezed by a boa constrictor. Mulgrew's dwarf, Mikey, was yelling, 'Squeeze the shit oota him, Tank!'

In spite of raining a series of punches on Mulgrew's pug-face, his tormentor just kept squeezing with gritted teeth.

The sounding of Police whistles caused the crowd to scatter as two Cops arrived on the scene with batons drawn. It was Constables Auchterlony and Dingley who arrived. The beams of their combined flashlights revealed two figures totally covered in mud, only the whites of their eyes showing, like minstrels from a Southern Showboat.

'Stop this bloody nonsense, now. Get up. What's it all about?' shouted Dingley. Rising slowly, like two naughty schoolboys before a teacher, the muddy figures stood awkwardly before their inquisitors.

It was Tank who spoke first. 'Sure, Constables, 't was just simple Irish fun. Ah wis jus' teachin this fellah here. Connemara Wrestling 'tis called.'

'Aye,' added a pained Shug, rubbing his chest.

'This is not Old Ireland, boys. Let's be having you down at the station and we'll sort all this out,' said a grinning Angus, interjecting, 'Come on. Ye both look like things from the horror films – creatures from the swamp.'

Later as Angus related the episode to Jock Grant, he cried out in laughter.

'Och, that's Shuggie Lettin getting into a fight again. Terrible wee bugger. He's a distant cousin o' mine, didn't ye know!'

When Shug recovered from his bruises a week later, with a court fine too, he immediately took his brother Bobby into the back close and gave him a good tanking. Finally he shouted a warning at his recumbent sibling. 'Don't ye bluddy-well get me intae any more scraps, with yer boasting aboot me in pubs. Do ye hear!'

Some time later, Jock Grant found himself in a bit of a quandary as he took his daughter's breakfast in at six-thirty a.m. He normally woke her up with breakfast to set her up for work at the nearby Twomax factory. This particular morning all he found was a folded note on her bedside chair. All it said was, 'Dear Dad, I'm going away. Do not try to find me. I love you. Lilly.'

Jock sat down in a faint, knocking over the teacup on the tray, crying in panic, 'Holy God. What does this all mean?'

As he came on back-shift, Angus was given a message that Jock Grant had phoned asking to see him as soon as possible about an urgent problem. Arriving hurriedly at Grant's ground floor flat, Angus found Jock shuddering, in a state of shock.

'Lilly's gone. Lilly's gone, Angus!' cried the distraught father, showing him the note.

Angus read the note carefully, then said softly, 'Had she any problems, you know, Jock?'

Jock replied Lilly was always a happy carefree lassie, and he couldn't fathom it out.

'I'll make some enquiries right away,' replied Angus. 'We usually like to leave a day or so to let things settle. Family tiffs and things like that, you know. But I'll see to it right away, Jock.'

It didn't take long to find out what happened. It seemed Lilly was observed jumping off a bridge into the Clyde at five thirty that morning. A passing shift worker, who happened to be a good swimmer, unhesitatingly dived in and pulled the struggling and weeping girl to safety.

As soon as he was alerted that she was in the Royal Infirmary, Angus went down to inform Jock without delay, taking a half bottle of brandy with him.

'Jock, sit down. I have bad news for you. But it's also good news in a way,' said Angus like a son.

'It's Lilly, isn't it?' cried Jock piteously, continuing, 'I knew it.'

Angus took a chair and related what he knew. 'Jock, Lilly tried to take her life. She jumped into the Clyde.' Before he could continue, Jock stood up and screamed loudly, 'Holy God in Heaven! My wee lassie's gone! First her mother, now my wee daughter too!'

Angus rose, seizing the crazed man by his shoulders, finally making him sit down again as he soothed, 'Jock, Jock. Listen to me. Lilly's alive. She's in the Royal.'

With tear filled eyes, Jock Grant ceased sobbing as he beheld Angus holding a half bottle of brandy before his lips.

'Take some sips of this, old fellah. Yes, yes. Your Lilly's alive. She's under care presently. You'll be seeing her soon, Jock.'

Jock took the brandy in small sips and said softly, 'Thank God Lilly's all right.'

What they both did not know was that whilst Lilly was recovering physically, she was mentally in great anguish, about her pregnancy and the shame she felt before her father. She had also lost her baby which had miscarried. When Angus had gone up to see her in the Royal, sounding her out about letting Jock come to visit her, she finally relented.

Lilly had been interviewed by the CID after her recovery, and Jock especially wanted to learn the name and address of the young electrician who had saved her. The hero's name was Harry and he lived in the South Side, was all Jock was told, but the old soldier made it clear he wanted to thank Harry personally for saving his daughter. With Angus in tow, Jock carried a huge card announcing 'With Love from Dad', along with grapes and flowers. Lilly's eyes sparkled, her face lighting up like a tree at Christmas at the familiar sight of her dad and friend Angus.

'Oh, Dad, it's great tae see ye. I've missed ye,' sighed Lilly, her father hugging and smothering her with kisses like he did when she was a wee girl.

'Remember, Lil. Yer old dad, Jock, will aye be there for ye, hen. No matter what,' said a tearful Jock. Angus, felt the tears welling, but managed to effect a smile as he pecked her on the cheek with. 'We're all missing ye, lassie. Especially yer dad.'

'The doctor says I'll be out soon, but ah'll need to attend the Outpatients for a while,' replied Lilly with a smile.

Angus was about to meet a criminal, yet amusing situation on his patrol that night. But he wasn't fated to know it.

Standing in a close mouth in Dunmore Street, just at the corner with Gorbals Street, Angus was observing the quiet surroundings for signs of suspicious movement. It was around midnight, during midweek, with little pedestrian activity about. Only the occasional dark form of a fleeting cat broke the stillness.

All of a sudden, the sound of shattering glass caused Angus to move instinctively to its source, towards Gorbals Street. As he rounded the corner, he glimpsed something to his right, his startled eyes refusing to believe what was happening sixty yards up the road. There on his side of the street a young man was lifting a fully clad tailor's dummy from the shattered window of a well known male fashion shop. As the window lights were still burning brightly, Angus was able to discern that the dummy was clad in a smart grey suit, and wearing a check black and white waistcoat, its feet clad in black shiny shoes. Angus quickened his pace, shouting. 'Halt, thief. Police!' How silly he thought, running towards the shop, as if the bugger was suddenly going to stop and obey. By the time, Angus had made it level with the shattered plate glass window, still with many displays intact, the culprit had disappeared round the corner into Bedford Lane near the public baths. 'Stop, thief,' cried Angus intermittently, blowing his police whistle.

As he turned into Bedford Lane, Angus imagined he saw movement in one of several closes on the side of the pavement where he stood. He hesitated, trying to choose the right close, as the crook had a warren of exits whereby to escape.

Presently, a cry was heard, 'Haw, help! Police! Anybiddy, help!'

Angus hurried up the lane some distance, past an old tramp dozing on the pavement, just as an elderly woman emerged wearing a headscarf and carpet slippers, with a dog on a leash.

'What's up, Missus,' cried Angus.

'Thank the Lord, the Polis,' shrieked the woman, pointing up the close. 'There's a naked man standin' in the back close!'

Angus hurried on, his flashlight at the ready, followed by the woman and her barking dog. The old wino, further down the lane, now struggled to his feet to join in the fun. Cannily entering the close in question, Angus shone the beam of his torch towards the rear, letting out a roar of laughter, which made the barking dog even madder.

'Love a duck!' guffawed the big Cop as he examined the figure leaning against the close wall. 'It's a . . . a dummy, Missus. A bloody dummy!'

'Whit a dummy?' shrieked Missus Headscarf and Slippers. 'Ah had'nae mah glesses on.'

A slurred voice behind them, which accompanied a strong whiff of hooch, cried, 'Ah thought . . . ah saw a man kerrying . . . a well dressed joker a minute ago.' The old wino went on in a hesitating tone, 'the guy was kin' o' stiff lookin'.'

Angus took details but couldn't help bursting into fits of uncontrolled giggling the rest of his shift.

All Sergeant Ratley said was, 'The thief probably needed a new suit fer a wedding.' Regarding Angus intently he added. 'We'll keep the dummy. It'll give us an idea of the thief's build. All we need now is to arrest some bugger wearing a slick grey suit with check waistcoat.'

Angus said nothing. He thought to himself – this case seems to involve two dummies, not just one!

The time for Lilly's release from the Royal arrived as Jock came in a taxi, laden with a huge box of chocolates for the doctors and nurses.

'I've come to take ye away hame, lassie,' said a happy Jock, greeting his daughter with a kiss on her cheek.

What Lilly didn't know was that Jock and his friends had set up a big surprise for her back at her house. On the front door was a sign announcing 'Welcome Home Lilly' which made her heart leap. As they entered the kitchen a roar of love and welcome erupted from her friends. There was Kitty, her pals from Twomax's, neighbours and Jock's band of cronies, as well as an off-duty Angus dressed in sports jacket and flannels.

Every one had a glass of spirits, wine or soft drinks and a huge iced cake announced Lilly's name. The simple kitchen table groaned under its generous bounty of sandwiches, made-up rolls, sausage rolls and pastries. Beside the cheery fire grate stood a figure which caused Lilly's already excited heart to go into fibrillation. There a tallish, fair haired young man smiled at Lilly, as he held a glass of beer. Jock led Lilly over and said simply, 'Lil, this is Harry. This is the chap who saved ye, hen.'

All Harry said was, 'Nice to see ye, Lilly. I hope you're feelin' much better.'

Lilly liked the quiet way Harry said that, with his gentle smile and hazel eyes.

'Have another beer, Harry?' enquired Jock like a mother hen.

The following Monday, Angus popped into the Fruit Box to see Kathy and Nan, to relate the good news about Lilly and Jock Grant.

As Angus entered, Kathy let out a screech. 'Whit in the name o' heaven have ye been up to, Angus?'

She was referring to Angus's prominent black eye, and bruised cheek.

'It was the rugby, ye ken. We were playing against the RAF at West Freugh, down in Wigtown,' replied Angus sheepishly.

Nan interjected, 'Ah thought rugby was a gentleman's game. No' like soccer?'

'Oh aye, the guys we played were RAF trainee pilots. Officers and Gentlemen,' grinned Angus adding with a sly wink, 'Except when the ref wasn't looking, and we had a difference o' opinion.'

Kathy said, 'Sean Robb also had a whopper, a few months ago. Black eye I mean, playing the Navy, the submarine boys I think he said.'

'Och no, the RAF boys and us got together at the wee local later. We had a great sing-song before coming home in our rickety old bus,' laughed Angus, making light of the matter.

'Surprised yees weren't stopped by the local Polis, with all yer carryings-on,' said Nan in mock solemnity.

CHAPTER 13

Angus called round to see a shopkeeper he knew well in Portugal Street. Josef Mikulski was a Pole who ran a cobbler's shop with his Scots wife, Sadie. Mikulski was affectionately known as 'Joe the Pole' locally and produced first class workmanship. Kathy and Nan used him regularly and had recommended Joe to Angus, bearing in mind all the pounding his police boots had to take.

Mikulski had been born in Lodz and had fought as a young conscript in the Polish army when they had been overpowered and encircled by the Nazi Blitzkrieg at Warsaw. Luckily he had managed to escape through Romania to France, then later to Britain when France was invaded. Joe joined the Polish Brigade in Scotland where he met his future wife, Sadie, who was then in the ATS.

Mikulski fought through the war in North Africa, and Italy, winning a medal at Monte Cassino. Sadly, his older brother, an officer, was murdered at Katyn.

A fine handsome man with a mane of white hair, he invariably greeted his customers with a welcoming smile.

As Angus entered the cobbler's shop he was greeted by Sadie.

'Hello, Constable Auchterlony. Glad you came. Josef's in the back shop.'

'Come, come, my friend Agnus,' came the highly accented voice from the rear. Suddenly Angus was welcomed by Mikulski, with his smiling brown eyes.

'Joe, good to see you. How are you and the missus this weather?' enquired Angus, shaking hands.

'We not so good now. I explain you problem,' replied Josef, his face momentarily grim. Joe shouted, 'Sadie, how bout you give Agnus [he could never say Angus] some *chleb z kielbasa z herbata?'*

'What's that?' asked Angus, intrigued.

'Sorry, Agnus, I meaning black bread and Polish sausage with tea,' replied Josef, laughing loudly.

After finishing his delicious sandwich (*kanapka* in Polish) Angus questioned Josef and Sadie about their problem. Sadie explained that two Heavies had come in two months earlier, enquiring whether they needed insurance cover. They had declined, saying they were covered already by the Co-operative. Angus asked what had they replied.

'They say you could having serious accident if not suitable covering,' said Josef in his broken English.

Sadie revealed that they had been broken into twice now, as he probably knew. The insurance company had forced them to put iron bars and grills on their shop windows to continue cover. Now she and Josef thought he should know that the Heavies had come in again before the bars were put up and threatened them. Other shopkeepers had been similarly approached.

'Yes, we've heard,' said Angus gravely. 'Sounds like a protection racket. But who's operating it?'

Josef said bravely, 'I tell to the men, you go to Hell. I fight Hitler, now I fight you two crookeds.'

'He means crooks,' said Sadie smiling. 'But Josef did tell them to get out and never come back!'

Angus asked, 'And what did they say?'

'We'll be paying you a visit,' replied Sadie.

Josef suddenly said to Angus. 'Agnus, you come to our house above for Polish dinner, some time. No?'

'Very nice, Joseph,' smiled Angus.

'Brink Kathy too. We cooking *zupa jarzynowa* [vegetable soup] first. Then havink *pieczen wolowa* [roast beef], then with *budyn* [milk pudding]. Afterwards we all drinkink *wodka.'*

'Very good, Josef, great,' replied Angus, adding with a serious look, 'Is it true you are a friend of Johnny Ramensky?'

'Yes, he is friend. We talk when you come,' finished Joseph, as two customers waited for their shoes.

144

At a short distance from Gorbals Cross one Saturday evening, a happy wedding celebration was in full flow in the local Co-operative hall. The bride, Emily McLuckie, was in her seventh heaven as she sipped her umpteenth gin and tonic, gazing with longing into the expectant eyes of the bridegroom on whose knees she was resting. Cecil Smith, her newly acquired husband, was a year older than his seventeen year old bride, a tall dark boy who supported Rangers, liked his bevvy, smoked his Woodbine, and was into his final year as plater's apprentice in John Brown's shipyard.

Emily's feet ached after dancing non stop with husband Cecil, family and friends, to the great quartet who reeled off all the popular tunes of the day. As Emily rested on Cecil's knee, her shoes discarded for comfort, she said, kissing her inebriate swain.

'Dinnae take too many, Cece. Ye'll no want tae fall asleep on yer honeymoon?'

Cecil smiled, saying, 'No way that'll happen. Ah've waited too long fer the night.' Emily was a short, thin blonde with blue eyes and a nice personality. Her name Emily meant 'worker' and she had worked long at winning her new man. Perhaps the word 'entrapping' her new man would be more apt. Cecil's name meant 'dim sighted' and this aptly fitted the way he'd been caught by his spouse's wiles.

In spite of the austerity, the meal had been fair with a choice of soup, steak pie, fish and chicken, followed by jelly and fruit. The bride's parents, Flora and Dave, typical working class folk, had put themselves in hock to pay for their daughter's sudden decision to get married. The young newly-weds had managed to rent a top storey single end in Hospital Street, out of her wages in the John Fraser's 'Hair Works' or 'Coffin Works' in Ballater Street, as it was known locally (owing to its shape) and from Cecil's meagre wage as an apprentice.

The bridegroom's parents Ina and Jim had been pleased with the way things had gone. The minister, Reverend Barr-Shaw, had made a pleasant speech toasting the newly-weds, as did his wife Janette, with glasses of Harvey's Bristol Cream sherry. Dave, Emily's dad, was in his cups, but had made a funny speech, in spite of mislaying his bit of paper. Nevertheless he had made a number of sly remarks such as 'Noo, Cecil. Ah want nae hankey-pankey the night wi' oor Emily. Mind, familiarity breeds weans!' Huge roars of laughter broke out from all present. Even the Reverend Mrs Janette Barr-Shaw tittered, gaining pleasure from this verbal impropriety. Even friends Tim Riley (Twinkletoes) and his wife Sandra were there, tipsy and happy, with Tim dancing with all the women, especially the young ones.

Emily, star-gazing into the eyes of her tipsy spouse, whispered softly as she stroked Cecil's dark locks.

'You know, Cece, you were worth waiting for.'

'Damn right. And ye'll fin' oot the night,' replied Cecil, straightening perceptibly in his chair and continuing, 'Lots o' burds were after me, a' the time.'

A silky tongued Emily whispered against his cheek, 'Aye, Cece. Lots o' competition. That's why ah told you ah wis expectin'.'

Emily became alarmed as she felt Cecil's frame stiffen and shudder, as if ten megawatts of high powered electricity had shot up his anus. Cecil leaped from his chair, Emily falling unceremoniously with her wedding dress awry, her legs up in the air.

'You bloody bitch! Are ye saying ye're no pregnant efter all!' roared Cecil.

Suddenly all sounds of music, laughter and conversation ceased, as if an invisible magician had waved his wand.

'Dinnae fret, Cece. We can always hiv kids later,' cried Emily rising to her feet.

The look on the faces of nearby Reverend and Mrs Barr-Shaw was beyond description.

'You lying wee bitch. Get up. Ah'm gonna do ye here and noo,' shouted Cecil, taking off his dress jacket.

At this challenge, Emily's parents, sisters, brothers and friends formed a protective cordon like a herd of threatened wildebeest, shouting, 'Whit's this aboot? How can ye be pregnant? God, ye cannae be. Yer only just bloody married!'

A similar wildebeest cordon was formed by Cecil's family and supporters in opposition. Some screamed, 'Cow! Whore! Ye bliddy slut! She worked a fast wan on ye' there, Cece!'

One shabby geezer, with a marked Irish accent, who had been chatting and partaking of the couple's largesse for most of the afternoon, now stood between two hostile blocks.

'Who the hell are you? Who invited you here?' cried Chick, the best man.

'Who am I?' cried the untidy middle-aged man, shouting, 'Ask the bluddy bride. Ah've bin wid her, more times than yees hiv had fish suppers.'

An incensed Emily was now on her feet, waving her fists and screaming, 'Ah don't know who this bastard is! Ah've never seen the scunner before in ma life!'

'Intae the bletherskeits!' screamed the interloper, and without further ado the opposing factions closed into a full scale donnybrook, mobs of men and women with fists flying as tables and chairs overturned and glass and crockery smashed all over the place. The sneaky geezer who started it all now did a bunk through a fire exit, taking a half bottle of JP whisky and a satisfied grin with him.

Meanwhile, Jim Smith, Cecil's dad, faced up to the taller Dave McLuckie, Emily's father, shouting, 'Your daughter's a bloody disgrace. She should be thrown in jail. Bloody un'erhand way to get a man!'

'Even we didnae know,' screamed the McLuckies. Apparently the Smiths weren't buying as fists and handbags flew in all directions whilst scuffles raged all over the hall.

Meanwhile a distraught reception manager had phoned the Gorbals Police Office. Soon a beat Sergeant and two Constables, including Angus, were hot-footing to the scene of the disturbance. Entering the hall with batons drawn, the Sergeant rapped his baton on a nearby table, blowing his whistle loudly, calling. 'Police, Stop!' then bang . . . bang . . . bang with the baton. 'Quiet, quiet. Cease immediately!' then the sound of a whistle again. 'Stop or ah'll have ye all arrested!'

The last exhortation for peace did the trick, as all parties broke off hostilities. The bride's dress was in tatters, her face scratched as if by a demented moggie. The bridegroom's shirt lay open and torn, a big red welt mellowing over his left eye, and his rubbery lips swollen and bleeding. The parents and friends of bride and groom were in equally dishevelled condition, with some members even *hors de combat* being revived by the Constables. Angus was beside the Reverend Mrs Barr-Shaw who was slowly coming out of her swoon. He lifted her half-full sherry glass to her lips and she smiled gratefully.

'My God,' announced the Sergeant, continuing, 'What a way to run a wedding!'

A thoroughly roughed-up Twinkletoes piped up as he regarded his missus. 'It reminds us of oor ain wedding, doesn't it, Missus Riley.' A wave of laughter broke forth, soon relieving the tension.

Meanwhile, to everyone's amazement the bruised bride and groom stood arms entwined, kissing passionately, oblivious to the scene around them. Even the Sergeant and Constables broke off, gazing like grannies at this unexpected interlude. Finally the Sergeant, clearing his throat, announced: 'Right, would the bride and groom, followed by their parents, come over here. We will be taking statements. No one has to leave till we take their details and statements. The Inspector is due any minute.'

It was some weeks later that the Police announced to the families concerned that the interloper who incited the stramash was a well-known party-jumper from the Calton. The eccentric Irishman was thought to have a drink problem, and was believed to work on building sites. The Police were keeping a sharp look-out for the culprit.

As Angus patrolled his beat in Gorbals Street one Saturday afternoon, Sergeant Ratley came hurrying up, and quickly said, 'Follow me, Auchterlony, we have an urgent call!'

The two Policemen were soon picking their way up a stair, which split left and right, through a warren of single-ends in a tenement which lay in a side street off Gorbals Cross.

Sergeant Ratley knocked on a door with a polished brass plate. 'A woman phoned to say she had a fight with her husband, and had hit him,' he said to Angus.

A woman in her late thirties answered the door, appearing as in a daze. 'Aye, officers, come away in. He's in the kitchen, ben the fire.'

As the two officers entered the tidy well kept kitchen, they caught sight of a man sitting in front of a roaring fire, as if he had dozed off. A newspaper lay in his lap. However, drawing nearer, the two Cops gasped at the sight on the wall to their right. Large scarlet spatters of fresh blood stained the faded wallpaper, running haphazardly to the floor. The fair hair on the back of the middle-aged man's head was soaked in blood which dribbled onto his newspaper.

Sergeant Ratley felt the victim's wrist pulse, then checked for a pulse at the throat. Taking a small mirror he found no sign of breathing and then said, 'Looks as if he's dead. Hurry down and phone for an ambulance right away, Auchterlony. Give the CID boys a ring. Hurry back.'

As Angus departed, he observed the woman sitting on a chair opposite, looking very calm, her gaze fixed on the Alexander stove. For there, gleaming and caked with blood, lay a brand new claw hammer.

Sergeant Ratley was sitting, drinking a cup of tea, as Angus entered. The quiet woman, who looked older than her thirty years, asked, 'Do ye want a cup o' tea, officer. The pot's still hot.'

'Aye,' said Angus, as if he was paying a social visit.

Sergeant Ratley drained the dregs from his cup, then took his notebook from his breast pocket. 'Can you tell us what this is all about, Missus?'

The woman looked at the figure of the deceased, his head resting on his chest, and said in a firm, unemotional tone, 'Fer two bloody months, ah was askin' him tae mend the wean's shoes. He's got a cobbler's last, and ah got him the sole leather and the new hammer ower there.'

'Did he fix the shoes?' enquired the Sergeant.

The woman answered vehemently. 'Did he hell. Ah asked him again this mornin' and he just sat there filling oot his bookie's lines, so ah hit the bastard over the heid with the bloody hammer!'

'Bloody hammer indeed,' thought Angus.

Soon afterwards the St John's ambulance men arrived to check out the victim. They confirmed the man was dead, just as a couple of CID detectives arrived on the scene.

'Are you right or left handed, Missus,' asked the detective in the wrinkled mackintosh.

'Right haunded, why?' replied the woman with a puzzled look on her face, adding, 'Ah'll need to take the wean's shoes tae Joe-the-Pole's noo. Mair bloody money.'

'Right, Missus, once your child comes home we'll send a Policewoman to take you down to the Police Office,' said Sergeant Ratley gently. The CID surmised she had hit the rear of her husband's head as he sat reading at the fireside. Being right-handed, the blows had landed on the back of the skull, hence the spatters on the wall to the right.

The outcome of this tragedy was that the poor woman was sent to a local asylum and her daughter placed into local authority care where she cried herself to sleep every night with, 'Mammy, Mammy. Haw Mammy, where hiv they took ye?'

The hunt for the riotous interloper at Emily McLuckie's wedding continued. One Sunday morning early, as Angus stood at Gorbals Cross, he spotted a figure he knew leading a whippet on a leash. It was none other than Tim Riley, Twinkletoes.

'You're out early, Tim. Hope ye've got a licence for that mutt,' teased Angus, smiling.

'Och aye,' replied Twinkletoes. 'Ah'm looking efter the dug fur a neighbour in hospital. I hid tae get up. The dug wanted its walkies. It wouldnae stop barking.'

Angus asked the wee man if he would spare a minute to help him out.

'Sure, pal. Ah'll aye help the Polis ony time,' replied Twinkletoes.

'Well, all the boys will be coming out of early mass from St John's soon. Can you help identify the geezer who ruined the wedding reception, if he's there?'

'Aye, if'n he's there,' said Twinkletoes, pulling to keep the whippet from wandering off.

Sunday morning was always busy and interesting at Gorbals Cross. From 7 a.m. onwards, fleets of construction lorries would assemble nearby, ready to collect the scores of fresh looking Irish workers coming from early mass, taking them to their various job-sites. As well as this crowd, there were the local Jewish population going about their business. Having closed on their Saturday Sabbath, Sunday was just another working day for them, and there would be freshly baked bread, bagels and mouth-watering cheese cakes from Morrisons and Fogells.

Presently the sound of hurrying feet revealed crowds of workers who dashed to their respective lorries. As Angus gazed up at the big clock which symbolized the Cross, he heard a yell from Twinkletoes who pointed to the gents' underground toilet.

'Hey, Angus. Sorry, Constable. Yon geezer just went doon there for a pee!'

Angus hurried across to the pedestrian island as he shouted. 'Follow me, wee man. Follow behind me. You can identify him!'

As they ran down the stairs there was no one at the urinals. As he peeked under the cubicle door, Angus spied a pair of working boots. In a poor imitation of a Donegal accent, Angus laughed, 'Sure, Mick, are ye gonna be in dere all dis fine day?'

'No, bejasus. But how did ye know me name?' came the reply.

Presently, the snib slid open and there stood the very man himself.

'That's him! That's the blighter!' screamed Twinkletoes excitedly.

'Are ye sure?' quizzed Angus intently.

Twinkletoes replied, 'As sure as sugarollie-watter!'

'Now whit is dis all about,' said the suspect truculently.

'Remember the weddin' and all your shenanigans? You're an evil nutter!' screeched Twinkletoes, his straining whippet barking excitedly at the suspect.

'Pure Blarney,' blurted the suspect, moving to leave and muttering, 'Ah've me work to go to.'

Angus blocked him and said in a firm voice. 'I'm taking you down to the Station for questioning. Are ye coming quietly, or is it the hard way?'

'Okay, okay. Ah'm comin'. But 'tis mistaken identity, fur sure. An ah'll claim you feckin' Polis fer loss o' wages!' came the rough reply.

It didn't take long to prove the suspect's identity. Twinkletoe's wife, the newly-weds, and their families pointed him out with ease in an identity parade. Angus was praised by Inspector MacAlee who said, 'This will certainly not look bad on your record, Auchterlony.' Sergeant

Rat Ratley made no comment whatsoever.

Kathy had informed Angus of surprising news. When she had called in to see Josef Mikulski, the cobbler, with an old pair of shoes needing repair, she had remarked that she was looking forward to their invitation. Kathy had inadvertantly mentioned that she had a friend who was Polish-American, a USAAF flyer. Kathy related how Josef's instant reply had been. 'Brink him alonk too.'

Joe Cherkowski had been informed of the invitation by Kathy and gladly agreed to come. Angus hid his surprise at this development. After all, this guy's a competitor, a potential threat, he mused. I do not know if I want to make this guy's acquaintance. Ach, it would really be a good idea to meet this Yank, to assess the opposition, to see what qualities Kathy actually saw in him. Presently Angus said, 'Great. Two Poles will make interesting company. We'll probably learn something.'

On the night of the invitation, Angus went to Kathy's home to await Joe's arrival, planning to escort the duo to Josef and Sadie's home in Portugal Street. Surprisingly, he found Joe Cherkowski there already, having a scotch on the rocks. Joe was dressed in light brown slacks, pale yellow shirt and flowery tie and wearing light tan shoes. His bomber jacket lay at the side of the settee.

Joe Cherkowski rose at once as Angus entered, extending his hand in welcome. 'So you're Angus. I've heard so much about you from Kathy.'

'All good, I hope,' replied Angus smiling, taking Joe's hand. Both men were of similar build, Joe a half inch taller but Angus leaner in build.

'So you're the guy who stopped the runaway horses,' praised Joe, continuing. 'Any guy who can pull such a feat is worthy of salutation.'

Calling for Kathy to bring glasses, Joe poured Angus and Kathy a drink from a bottle of Haig's Dimple which he had brought along. Nan was away seeing friends. After a couple of rounds, Angus felt himself warming to the big, cheerful Yank. Yes, he reckoned he liked Joe. He had liked Ike when he was in the war. Now he liked Joe too. So let the best man win, Angus was thinking. Kathy sensed the empathy growing between her two friends, and was very happy and relieved.

'Man, that sure is some suit you have there!' said Joe admiringly. He was referring to Angus's double-breasted navy pin-stripe suit which he was wearing with white shirt and plain red tie.

'Yes, I paid five pounds, eleven and six for it in the Glasgow-London Clothing Company up the town,' replied a flattered Angus.

Kathy, who was dressed casually in dark slacks, white blouse and light jacket, smiled as Joe enquired, 'What's that in real money? Dollars?'

Angus just smiled and shrugged his shoulders. 'No idea,' he replied.

When they arrived at the Mikulski room and kitchen in Portugal Street, the door was opened by an ebullient Josef who stood like a welcoming Santa Claus, with his familiar mane of white hair and sparkling brown eyes.

Kathy nudged forward, announcing, 'Mr Mikulski, meet Sergeant Joe Cherkowski. He's Polish too, you know. From America.'

'Kome, kome, Joe. Welcome. *Prosze.* Good evenink. We say *Dobry wieczor.*'

To Josef's surprise and delight, Joe answered, '*Dziekuje bardo* [thank you very much].'

The trio of guests were greeted by a happy Sadie who fussed like a mother hen over her guests. Could she offer them a drink? Kathy offered Sadie a large bunch of mixed sweet smelling roses. Angus hurriedly proffered his box of chocolates but it was Joe Cherkowski's gift that brought squeals of delight from Josef Mikulski. Joe handed his host a bottle of real Polish vodka and a carton of cigarettes.

'Ah, *Wyborowa wodka*!' cried Josef. This is real, very best Polish *wodka*!'

'Yessir, Josef,' replied Joe proudly. 'I got that from the Commissary. Special for my Polish friend.'

Josef could hardly contain himself as, in true Polish fashion, he walked over and hugged the big American tightly, tears welling in his eyes.

'So you Polak, hey. Where you from there?' quizzed Josef.

Joe replied smiling, 'Well, I'm American. Polish-American, really. My pop came originally from Kracow.'

'Kracow! Kracow!' cried Josef dramatically. 'Very beautiful place. Much history there.'

'Yeah, but we live in Boonton, New Jersey. Maybe you can visit some day and meet my Mom and Pop. You'd like them,' replied Joe.

'I comink from Lodz, in Mazovia area,' beamed Josef.

'Right, folks, dinner's ready,' announced the Mikulskis proudly. There, set out in a simple Scottish kitchen was a piece of Poland. There lay the starter, steaming plates of vegetable soup *(zupa jarzynowa)* with a huge plate of crusty bread *(chleb)*. The soup was a meal in itself as Kathy, Angus and Joe saw the soup plates vanish effortlessly, only to be replaced by the main meal, in true Polish style *(po staropolsku)*.

'*Pieczen wolowa z wieprzowa,*' announced Joseph as he and Sadie carried in large, steaming plates of roast beef and pork.

'Hey, what do you folks do for food coupons?' asked a smiling Kathy. Sadie replied with a wink, 'Our Polish friends all helped out when we told them our guests were coming.'

After the roast, which was accompanied by mixed vegetables and roasted and boiled potatoes, the guests lay groaning and inflated in their chairs.

'Next, we havink – how you call in English. Desertion?' announced Josef.

'No, no, Josef!' laughed Angus. 'Desertion is what I nearly did in the army because of the bleeding Sergeant-Major, ye know! It is called dessert. Two esses.'

'Very sorry, Agnus. My Eenglish is not good,' announced Josef, shrugging, with an embarrassing roll of his eyes.

'Oh, he gets by,' defended Sadie, in a fit of laughter. 'They love him round here.'

'Okay, we havink Polish dessert. *Budyn* [milk pudding] and *gelaretka* [jelly],' announced Josef proudly. Finally the happy band of friends sat at the table, hardly able to move. Two bottles of white French wines lay fully drained, Polish wine not being available locally. Producing his bottle of valuable *Wyborowa* vodka, which Joe Cherkowski had given him, Josef proudly proclaimed, 'My friends, we drink to all friends in my hoose. *Prosze* [welcome].'

'Cheers to the two Joes. And thanks to our hosts, Josef and Sadie,' cried Angus. The rest shouted, 'We'll all second that!'

'Thank you, my friends. *Dziekuje,*' cried Josef emotionally, tears flowing copiously.

CHAPTER 14

When Kathy told the bold Sean about the meal at the Mikulskis', as he appeared with the potato and veg delivery, he seemed uninterested until she mentioned that both Angus and Joe Cherkowski had also attended.

'What's that? Ma competitors ganging up on me!' said Sean, reddening perceptibly as he threw down a sack of spuds.

Kathy replied, 'Come on, Sean, it was just circumstances. Josef Mikulski is Angus's as well as my own cobbler too. He'd invited us both for dinner.'

'How very convenient. How come the Yank was there too?' asked Sean.

'When I mentioned my friend Joe was a Pole, Mr Mikulski suggested he come along too. Simple as that.'

Sean regarded Kathy unsmilingly, then finally remarked in an off-hand manner, 'How cosy. Maybe I should take ma boots to this Polish cobbler? I might get an invite and become one of the gang. Better gie me his address.'

Kathy sensed that Scan was boiling within, resenting that she had shared innocent enjoyment in the company of her two male friends. Sean considered Angus and Joe a double threat, Kathy knew that Sean did not like competition. Sean liked to keep his girls dangling on a line, disregarding them whenever he felt like it. Look how he treated Sybil, his old girl friend.

Kathy decided to humour Sean and reacted to his mood by saying, 'Come on, Sean. The kettle is boiled and Mum and I have some nice rolls ready.'

'Kathy, we can have a celebration of our own. I'm invitin' you to the Rogano on Saturday. You like the food there too. Okay?' said Sean, like an excited schoolboy. Kathy laughed and said that would be super, as Sean's mood lightened. Nan came in from the front shop smiling, preparing to make the tea.

A breathless Popeye met up with Angus as he pounded his beat in Abbotsford Place.

'Jesus, you're one hellova man tae find,' cried the wee fellow breathlessly.

Angus laughed, saying. 'What's bothering you now, wee man?'

'Slogger Struth,' came the staccato reply.

Angus's attention focused as he queried, 'What about Struth? I wish I could get hold of the bugger right now.'

Popeye took Angus aside into a nearby close entrance and advised him of what he'd seen. He'd seen Slogger having a furtive pint with a stranger in a local pub.

'Who was the stranger? Where's Struth staying right now?' quizzed Angus excitedly, gripping his informant by the shoulders.

'Take it easy, Constable,' replied Popeye shaking himself free. 'All ah can tell ye is Struth's mother was ill, and he come up from the Big Smoke tae see her,' he continued, informing Angus that Slogger had a pal in London, big in the Blackmarket business. The stranger seen with Struth could have been a London Heavy. Popeye wasn't sure, but would contact Angus when he found out.

Angus didn't waste time seeking out Detective Constable Ed Moran, in order to keep the CID in the picture as well, to ferret further information on the subject.

'Struth has a pal in London. An old South Side pal by the name of Scottie Dunn who's big in the rackets, we understand. They're very close. Both been raised in the South Side,' recited Moran like an encyclopaedia.

'Great, great,' cried Angus as he continued, 'I heard he had a tall Heavy with him, having a quiet drink and not wishing to be observed. Seemingly Slogger was up seeing his sick mother.'

Detective Moran replied that he hadn't known that, but would keep a watch on the mother's house for signs of the son. As for the Heavy, there were several Scottie Dunn used, and they were very dangerous individuals. Moran assured Angus he would contact his Police sources in London. He'd let him know as soon as he could. Moran finally said, 'You know, Angus, we are as desperate to nail those bastards who attacked you as you are. If we can get Slogger to talk then, probably, the lassie Kitty will talk too. Then we can tie up the case against those evil scum, Dougal and Bakley.'

Sean Robb picked Kathy up at her house in a taxi on the following Saturday night. He was dressed in a grey, pin-striped suit with wide lapels, his bright patterned tie set off by a navy shirt. On his head he wore a wide brimmed trilby, whilst on his feet he sported two-tone black and white shoes. Goodness, Kathy thought to herself, he looks like one of Al Capone's gangsters. Maybe we should be heading for Chicago?

Kathy wore a typical Norman Hartnell mass produced knee length utility look, light blue dress with Peter-Pan collar, black pill-box hat that matched her handbag and high court shoes. Kathy was glad of the coupons which Nan had no trouble obtaining from willing customers wishing to raise a bob or two.

'You look smashin', Kathy,' beamed Sean, touching his trilby, 'how about myself?'

'Extraordinary, Sean,' exclaimed Kathy, playing to his ego as he stood like a peacock. He's straight out of a Damon Runyon novel, she thought.

As they entered the Rogano Restaurant in Exchange Square, Kathy's taste buds awakened as she anticipated the delicious sea food they served there, amid the opulent Thirties decor. Some claimed the style was reminiscent of the furnishings in the *Queen Mary*, and this made Kathy feel great. The thought of Sean footing the bill added even more to her satisfaction. It was his idea – he had invited her, after all.

A young man at the cloakroom was standing in for the girl who usually took the coats. The sleek-haired fellow gave them a welcoming smile as he took their coats and hats. He quipped cheekily as he took Sean's hat, 'Take your trilby, Al?'

Sean didn't react. He didn't have a drink yet, but he riposted, 'Thanks, pal. Ah've left my violin case with the tommy-gun at home.' That wiped the smile from the joker's face.

A head-waiter simply said, as he led them to their table, 'Will you and your lady please come this way, sir?'

Happily, another waiter soon presented them with menus, enquiring of their choice of drinks.

'I'll have a Pimm's Number One,' said Kathy casually.

Sean simply said, 'Make mine a whisky and soda.' To the question of wine, he and Kathy chose a white French which the waiter strongly recommended.

'What do you recommend today, waiter?' enquired Sean eagerly.

'The Dover sole, really fresh. Or you can try the salmon or lobster, fresh in from the Highlands too,' replied the handsome waiter, rubbing his hands together expectantly.

Kathy said, 'I've been here before. I'm for the fried rice with the lobster, prawns and crab mixture. And a small side salad with bacon and parmesan croutons and garlic salad dressing too, please.'

'Oh you're an old hand,' quipped Sean adding, as he studied the menu, 'I'll stick with an nice Scottish salmon salad, with the usual cream salad dressing, thanks.'

The waiter queried, 'And for soup, Sir? We have some rich fish soup, very smooth.'

Sean looked at Kathy for a decision, then said, 'Okay, we'll both have the fish soup. Hope we've room left.'

After they had shamelessly gorged themselves on their piscine and crustacean repast, Sean said, 'Well, Kathy, was that to your liking, hen?'

'God, I can hardly walk or breathe at the moment,' came the reply from a ruddy-faced Kathy.

Sean said, his mood serious, 'Let's go into the lounge bar, Kathy. I'd like to talk to you. Do you think you can make it?'

'I think we could manage to wobble round there, if we tried,' laughed Kathy.

In the lounge, an air of pleasant ambience enfolded Kathy as she listened, starry-eyed, to a favourite song, 'I'm in the Mood for Love'.

'I love that tune,' said Kathy dreamily. 'It's – "I'm in the Mood for

Love".'

'Are you dropping me hints for later?' quipped Sean with a leer.

Kathy just laughed, closing her eyes till the tune faded.

'Kathy, Kathy are you still there?' came a voice. Kathy opened her eyes; it was a smiling Sean who spoke.

'Sorry, Sean. I must have drifted.'

'Kathy, I'm going to ask you something very important. Okay, are you listening?' said Sean gently. 'I'm not boring you?'

An alert Kathy now replied, 'No, no, Sean. Sorry. What is it you're saying?'

Sean said simply, 'Kathy, you know how I feel about you?' He took her hand, revealing a side she had never imagined. Looking into the depths of her eyes, Sean continued, 'I'd like you to be my wife, Kathy.'

Kathy couldn't believe what she was hearing. Her mind ran riot. What about Angus and Joe? What about her mother, Nan? Her blood was pounding. She was confused.

'We could get engaged first, then save for a house,' continued Sean. 'What do you think?'

Kathy remained silent. She just sat regarding Sean, her mind befuddled. All she wanted to do was run away and think.

'Sean, I'll need some time to think about this,' was all she said.

Sean smiled and said to the waiter, 'My girl has now woken up. Can I settle now. Could you call for a taxi?'

As he came off early shift, Angus entered Mikulski's cobbler-shop with a pair of well worn boots.

'Ah Agnus, nice to see you,' smiled the handsome Pole. 'How you are doink?'

Angus replied. 'Not too bad, Josef. I called in as these boots need repairing.'

Josef examined the boots and said, 'No problem. I fix these good, for sure.'

Sadie came in from the back shop and greeted Angus. 'Hello, Angus have you recovered since last week?'

'Oh, God, yes. Kathy and I thought it was super. So did Joe

Cherkowski too, I believe. I'd like to thank you both,' replied Angus.

'Don't mention it,' said Sadie continuing, 'Josef and I enjoyed doing it.'

'You'll have had no more problems with the protection racketeers, since they were sent down?'

Josef and Sadie replied with a positive nodding of heads. Thankfully that problem was behind them. Presently Josef said, 'Kome, kome Agnus for tea. Okay?' He lifted the counter flap to let him enter as Sadie said she would look after things out front.

As Josef heated the kettle on a small gas ring, Angus decided to ask him about a local Gorbals hero whom he had learned of since he'd joined the Police Training School.

'Josef, what about this fellow, Ramensky?' enquired Angus with an inquisitive grin. Josef filled the teapot with boiling water, stirring the contents thoughtfully, as if trying to gather his thoughts.

'Yes, I know Ramensky. Johnny we callink him. Very nice man,' started Josef as he continued, 'Johnny not Polish. He's people komink from Lithuania to Scotland.'

'He was from Lithuanian immigrants?' enquired Angus.

'Yes, yes. His father dyink when he baby. His mother, only one arm, raisink Johnny and two sisters. When Johnny yunk boy he go in coal minink, in Lancashire or something. Maybe Lanarkshire. Coal mine in Scotland. Is very hard vork,' related Josef sadly.

'Aye, you mean Lanarkshire. Lancashire is in England,' clarified Angus.

Josef continued, 'Yes, Lanarkshire. But Ramensky not likink miner's vork, he leave and go in crime. Too bad, too bad.'

'So what happened?' asked Angus.

'Judge puttink him into place for yunk people. Criminal activity, ye know,' said the Pole, struggling with the correct English terminology.

'It would be the Borstal, probably,' confirmed Angus.

Josef repeated parrot-fashion. '*Tak* [yes]. Borstal.'

Josef went on to say he had learned this information from Ramensky just after the War, when he had invited Johnny as a guest to the Polish Servicemen's Club for a drink.

'He move to Gorbals when younk man from coal minink place in Lanarkshire, because many Lithuanian people livink in Gorbals then,' continued Josef, rising to pour Angus another cup of tea.

'How did he drift into crime?' asked Angus.

Josef said, shrugging his shoulders, 'He try to get job when meetink good Scotch lady name McManus. He marryink her, but not gettink job – problem,' related Josef as he went on. 'Johnny go back to robbink bank and place like big store.'

Josef explained that Johnny Ramensky was jailed in Barlinnie and there he met an expert safe blower called Scotch Johnny who taught him all he knew. Consequently, Ramensky took to safe breaking with a will, armed with all this imparted knowledge of explosives.

'You wonder about mixing young criminals with the hardened ones. It's like sending them to an academy of crime,' concluded Angus.

'Johnny very physical man. Trainink body, very fit man. Always in gymnasium. When he go jail after first marriage, his poor wife havink shock. Heart attack, I think,' revealed Josef, shaking his head sadly.

'Poor woman,' was all Angus said.

'You know, Ramensky, tellink me how he escape from Peterhead Prison before war. He goink over high prison wall. What a kinda man!'

Angus, impressed, announced, 'Escaping from Peterhead is some bloody feat, I'll tell ye.'

'Yes, durink war, Government go see Johnny in Peterhead Prison for very special vork,' revealed Josef saying, 'Facts still very secretly.'

'He was parachuted behind enemy lines to blow enemy safes, we're told,' suggested Angus.

Josef thought for a moment, as if trying to remember, then said, 'Yes, Agnus. Army takink Ramensky for kommando trainink. He make parachute in France, blow safes for Nazi information.'

'What a guy! And what a story!' cried Angus exuberantly.

Josef revealed further. 'Yes, he blow all safes in embassies in Rome before German runnink away. Alzo, Allies make him doink special job on safe of Reichsmarschall Herman Goering in Karinhall. Many secrets inside!'

'What a bloody fine man to do all that!' exclaimed Angus. 'What a tragedy he couldn't find the straight and narrow.'

'Johnny not settlink down after war. He winning medal too. MM you calling name. Alzo, he making rank of sergeant in Kommandos.'

Angus enquired. 'What age was he when you met him, Josef?'

'*Ezterdziesci*,' came Josef s answer. 'Sorry, forty years about. I am always in Polish thinkink.' Josef went on, 'After end of War, Johnny go back to old trade.'

'Safe blowing?' enquired Angus.

'Yes, yes. But Johnny not wiolent man. He not hurt anybody. He never breakink in people houses. He only attack business, like bank and big shop store. He never hurting anybody, or fightink for police. Never!'

Angus replied, 'Aye. That's why they call him "Gentle Johnny Ramensky".'

'*Tak*. Johnny Ramensky now jail. But Johnny very brave, very good soldier. He fight Hitler, for him own country!' said Josef sadly, his eyes welling with emotion.

'Yes. Pity his talents couldn't have been given the right lead,' concluded Angus as he rose to leave. 'It's been a tiring shift. I'm away home now to bed, Josef. Thanks for the tea – and for the story.' He left bidding Sadie goodbye.

A few days later Angus found a note from Detective Ed Moran to contact him. Angus went to see him right away.

'Angus, I've had the lowdown on this London pal of Slogger Struth's. Scottie Dunn is a big time operator in the London East End Blackmarket: booze, cigarettes, food and clothing coupons. Also uses picked Heavies for doing contracts on people – a difficult customer to nail,' concluded Ed Moran in his usual erudite manner.

'Any idea who the Heavy could be?' asked Angus.

Moran replied, 'According to our nark's information about the big Heavy, it could be a character who knows Glasgow, one Silent Turley. A tough guy of few words, but deadly with the knife and axe, and fanatically loyal to his governor Scottie.'

The two cops were puzzled. Why would this Heavy be in the company of Struth? And why in Glasgow?

'Could be he's protection for Slogger Struth,' suggested Angus.

Ed Moran looked thoughtful for several moments, eyeing Angus. 'Aye, it's possible. Could be protection against Con Dougal and his gang – a sort of warning off signal?'

'Aye, it sounds plausible, Ed. But there's more in this than meets the eye,' commented Angus grimly.

When Sean came in on his delivery round he sat and had his roll and tea and said little.

Kathy said, 'That was a great night at the Rogano, Sean. I'm sorry I fell asleep. It must have been a combination of the food and drinks.'

Nan was busy in the front shop so Sean decided to press Kathy on his proposal of marriage, enquiring gently, 'Have ye thought about what I said?'

'Oh yes, I have,' replied Kathy slowly, and adding, 'But I still need time to think about it. You know what they say – decide in haste, repent at leisure.'

'Och, I wished you'd have said yes. We could have gone shopping for an engagement ring,' said Sean disappointedly. 'H. Samuel have a great selection, too.'

'I know that,' countered Kathy, saying, 'When the time's ripe, we'll see.'

Sean rose, getting ready to leave with some old potato sacks. 'Hope you're still no thinking about the opposition. Remember a bird in the hand's worth two in the bush,' said Sean, pursing his lips.

Sean seemed to have a knack of knowing her thoughts, as if he was telepathic, mused Kathy. It was uncanny and unnerving. After all it was an offer of marriage in good faith. Sean was a handsome guy with prospects but she had reservations. He could be so unpredictable in his mood swings, especially when in his cups. She wasn't sure. She wasn't going to be rushed by anyone, least of all Sean. She hadn't told Nan, but would do so when she had thought things through.

One afternoon about 2 p.m., two men made their way purposefully down

McNeil Street towards the St Andrew's suspension bridge. As they crossed the short span over the Clyde, two men focused intently on their progress. One of the men at the Glasgow Green end held an alert Alsatian on a chain; a cigarette dangled from the lips of his shabbier companion.

The man with the dog was Con Dougal, dressed in an ex-officer's fawn overcoat, his habitual fixed grin belying his thoughts. His lieutenant, Bull Bakley, stood, lower lip hanging as it habitually did on his pig-like face.

'It's Slogger right enough,' muttered Bakley, straining his neck. 'But who's the big geezer wi' him?'

Dougal commented briefly. 'Wan of Scottie's Heavies nae doubt.'

As Slogger drew near he smiled and quipped, 'Hello, Con. Greetings, Bull. Nice dog. Hope it doesn't bite?'

'Only when I tell it to,' replied Con with a fixed grin.

Slogger laughed. 'Well, it better no. Ah've a lot to offer.'

Both Dougal and Bakley regarded Slogger's large Heavy with unease.

'Ah see you've got Scottie's big guy there?' said Dougal, raising his eyebrows.

Slogger smirked and said, 'Just a bit of insurance, ye might say.'

During these conversations, Struth's companion stood at arm's length. Silent Turley, a broad shouldered ex-wrestler, full six foot three in height, remained silent. He was the big London boss's chief Heavy. Turley was of mixed race, African and Irish and Dunn's faithful lieutenant. Feared in London's East End, Silent Turley was the deadly disposer of Scottie Dunn's enemies, always with knife or axe. He seldom spoke, but was known to have uttered, 'Use a gun. Bloody waste of bullets! Nothing can beat the sound of a blade slicing through flesh and bone.' The Police were never ever able to pin one of a dozen murders on him.

What was on offer at this bizarre meeting was a large amount of Blackmarket and stolen goods which Con Dougal was always keen to exploit. The fact that Slogger Struth and his family had been threatened by Con Dougal to remain silent, regarding the revelation of damning evidence in the Auchterlony case, was not allowed to interfere with business. What mattered here was that Struth had been chosen by his old Gorbal's school pal, Scottie, to conduct the negotiations. The big Heavy was there to give Struth the necessary clout and protection.

Scottie Dunn controlled London's East End and the good quality whisky, cigarettes like Camel and Lucky Strike, nylons from America, clothing, GI shirts, coats, officer's overcoats, shirts and shoes, coffee and you name it. Scottie could get anything – at a price! He also ran well organised gangs who highjacked lorries with valuable goods which a deprived British public, now flush with money, desperately craved.

Scottie also ran the flourishing prostitution racket, with its pimps and illegal gambling.

'What's on offer?' snapped Con Dougal.

'Whatever you've got dough for, pal,' Struth shot back.

Con Dougal regarded his adversary for a while, then said, 'I'll take good quality whisky, cigarettes, and Yanky fags, clothing for both sexes too. And watches?'

'Nae bother at all,' quipped Struth. 'Anything else?'

'Aye, nylons?' questioned Con expectantly.

Struth replied. 'Certainly, what figure do ye reckon?'

'Aboot five grand for a first delivery. Then a repeat order, most likely,' affirmed a confident Con Dougal.

'Fine, done!' cried Struth as he shook his hated enemy's hand.

'The guy wi' the nylons nowadays gets all the burds. He's their bloody hero,' cried a laughing Con Dougal.

As Slogger Struth returned over the bridge with his bodyguard, he rubbed his right hand in his pocket, as if trying to remove the remnants of Dougal's handshake from his skin. He hadn't forgotten Con Dougal and Bull Bakley: those evil bastards who had beaten old Jock Grant and terrorised Kitty Cullen, the daughter of his deceased pal. There would be a reckoning. Scottie had been upset when he learned of the evil duo's violence against friends of his childhood. And Scottie Dunn's powerful arm had a very long reach. But for the present, it would simply be – 'bizness is bizness' – as an old Jewish stall-holder at the Barras, Mrs Berkowitz used to say.

CHAPTER 15

Kathy had given Sean's proposal of marriage a great deal of thought. She had mentally agonised so much over it that the lack of her normal bubbly manner in the shop became noticeable. Customers wondered if she was unwell. Her mother knew that something was bothering her girl. Obviously Kathy did not wish to discuss whatever it was. Kathy had always consulted her mum, ever since she was a young child, later growing through puberty to adulthood. A close bond existed between mother and daughter.

One afternoon during a lull in the shop, as Kathy stood looking fixedly out of the shop window, Nan enquired gently, 'Kathy, hen, is there something you want to tell your ma?'

Kathy regarded her mother for an instant, like a schoolgirl caught daydreaming in class

'Och, yes, there is something that's eating me, Mum,' replied a relieved Kathy. She went on at length to reveal how Sean Robb had proposed to her in the Rogano. How he kept coming back, eager to become engaged and buy the ring.

'He a strapping, hard working lad,' said Nan thoughtfully, 'And he's got a good business mind, tae.'

Kathy's reply was interrupted by a regular customer, the fat talkative Minnie Curley who wanted cauliflower, tatties and beetroot for the visit of her son, his wife and their tribe of weans. They didn't like carrots. 'Pity that,' Minnie exclaimed. 'They're good for the eyes.' The first time she tried to feed them carrots, her eldest grand-daughter vomited all over the floor, and her young grandson tried to strangle the cat! Minnie sang the praises of the humble carrot. 'Ah canna un'erstand it? Look at mysel'. Ah've the best eyesight in Glesga.'

169

Aye, thought Nan. You're bloody right, missus. Ye never miss a trick.

A quarter of an hour later, Kathy was able to resume, her mood changed by the mention of carrots. She never liked them either. 'I'm so confused, Mum. I am really attracted to Sean. But he's a bit of a loose cannon. Especially when he's had a drink,' commented Kathy.

Nan enquired. 'And how do you feel about Angus and Joe?'

Kathy's drooping mouth and lack-lustre eyes showed her confusion. 'I love them both, too. At first I tried to say they were just "friends". It's not so simple as that.'

'Aye, ah know what ye mean,' said her mother nostalgically. 'It was the same wi' yer dad and another guy.'

Kathy, distracted from her own cares momentarily, enquired eagerly. 'Did you pick the right one?'

'Whit a silly question, hen. Of course, ah did. Yer da was a great guy. An' just look at ma bonny wee lassie,' laughed Nan as she cuddled her daughter.

'Begging your pardon, ladies, ah'm sure,' said a tall puzzled figure, as he regarded the two embracing women. 'Is my tea on the boil yet?' It was none other than D93, Constable Angus Auchterlony himself.

Following the meeting with Scottie Dunn's representative, Slogger Struth, urgent arrangements had to be made by Con Dougal and Bull Bakley for the impending consignments of black market goods which had to be safely stored. A perfect opportunity became available in the form of an old converted shed, presently a store for cleaning materials. Con Dougal paid the happy owner just over fifteen hundred pounds for the business, goodwill and stock. Included was an old van advertising 'Wonder Cleaning Materials - What Every Housewife Needs'.

'The perfect scam, boss,' exclaimed Bull Bakley, adding. 'Pure brilliant.'

A smug Con Dougal replied. 'Aye, no bad. We can carry on supplying existing customers, and at the same time use their "Wonder Cleaning" boxes and van for transporting the quality goods aboot.'

'Ah must say, boss, ah take ma hat off tae ye. Damn clever idea,' came the reply.

Con Dougal was pleased. Not with the sycophantic praise of his underling but by the potential of storing large amounts of illicit goods in ample and secure space. But valuable goods like whisky, cigarettes, nylons and clothing would need protecting. He would need to arrange for a watchman, and Old Fergus, a retired thief, would be the very man. A small bothy would be provided for Fergus with an electric heater and radio. To be sure, the ever canny Dougal would also install a burglar alarm. It would help reduce the insurance premiums too. Anyway, all these costs would soon be retrieved by fat profits flooding in from the booming Blackmarket. Con would have to organise things quickly. He addressed Bakley intently.

'We'd better get a move on, Bull. The goods are due here in a week's time.'

'Ah know, boss. But ye ken, Ah hiv doubts aboot that bastart Slogger. Especially considerin' oor hold over him an' his family.'

Con Dougal laughed, reassuring his man. 'Don't fret, Bull. Struth's boss, Scottie, is a big time operator, no some halfpenny cowboy. His word's gospel. Calm doon and take it easy. It's just business – there's nae personalities come into it.'

Angus was delighted to see the Café del Sole return to its normal routine as the Lombardi family returned to business. Emilio, the café owner, had just come back from Italy with his wife Francesca, and son Alberto, where they had been to bury his son Franco, killed fighting the Nazis with the Italian Resistance. He had decided to take Francesca too.

'Emilio and Francesca, it's great to see you back. How did it go?' queried Angus, beaming broadly.

'Angus, *paisano*. It's so good to see you again,' cried Emilio with emotion as he hugged his friend, thanking him. 'My cousins were very thankful for you keeping an eye on things. *Grazie.*'

A smiling Francesca greeted Angus with a kiss on the cheek '*Come sta?* I go now an make you nice toasted sandwich.'

Presently, as Angus was getting stuck into his sandwich and hot tea, he listened intently to Emilio giving an account of how he found and buried his son Franco.

'The Graves people identified Franco's body with the help of the Italian Resistance,' related Emilio gravely. He continued, 'Franco had been wearing a crucifix with a special prayer, inscribed by me and Mama.'

Angus queried, 'Where was Franco buried then, Emilio?'

'Franco was buried in my father's village near Bologna, in our family ground, among his ancestors,' said Emilio emotionally. Then he added poignantly. 'They laid Franco alongside his cousin Augusto, in the quiet graveyard under the tall cypress trees.'

Angus said nothing. He was overcome emotionally, but did not show it.

'You remember the story, Angus, about the two cousins?' queried Emilio.

Angus remembered the tragic story of family and war. How could he forget? There were Franco and his cousin, Augusto, fated to face each other in battle at El Alemein. Both died in the War. Both now sleeping side by side in Italy!

'Gone are many old friends, so many old Italiani in Glasgow. Like Catani, Gizzi, Jaconelli, Porelli, Tognarelli, Tobias, Tomerelli, Verrichia, and so many other old *amici* whose dear names I cannot speak,' lamented Emilio tearfully.

Angus trying to cheer him, said. 'It's no that bad, Emilio. There are still many of their sons and daughters about. Like Verricos. One's a doctor and another in the wholesale business.'

'Yes, you are right, Angus. But the old ones, those who came same time as my mama and papa – they are no more. They are gone, but *non dimenticar* [not forgotten].

Sean Robb continued his routine of vegetable deliveries, having his early morning roll in the Fruit Box and going out with Kathy, dancing or to the pictures. He had asked her several times about marriage since their dinner in the Rogano. She hadn't answered. Obviously Sean assumed Kathy wasn't ready for marriage. Kathy just couldn't make up her mind. All she saw was a series of images of Nan, Angus, Joe and Sean whizzing by in her mind, as if each was competing for her love and attention. Try as hard as she could, she could not separate them into compartments in her mind, they always came together, not allowing their union to be broken. They were all friends, all loved; not one could be ignored. She loved Nan but in a different way from the others. She loved Sean in a different way from Angus. Same with Joe. If only she could have all the qualities in one, that would solve the problem. But that was 'pie in the sky' and not worth thinking about.

Sean had been acting strangely since the Rogano meal. His manner had become a few degrees cooler, in a way the most efficient thermometer on earth would be unable to measure. It was as if he was miffed. His habitual jokes, quips and comments were there but there was a slightly frosty air about him. Kathy could understand Sean's feelings, in the circumstances, and felt uneasy about the situation.

One day, about noon, Sean came in looking flustered.

'You're a bit late this morning, Sean. What happened?' said Nan, as Kathy looked on.

'The lorry had a problem,' said Sean. 'Blooming petrol blockage.'

As Nan went to serve a customer, Sean took Kathy aside and said, 'Kathy, I have something to tell you. I've a short break. Would you join me for a sandwich at Moscardini's along the road?'

Surprised and intrigued by Sean's behaviour, Kathy readily agreed.

When they had finished their sandwiches and tea, Sean regarded Kathy solemnly for a while, then said, 'Kathy I have something to tell ye. I know it's not going to be very pleasant for you.'

'For goodness sake, Sean. You make it sound like the end of the world.'

Sean coughed nervously, smiled and replied, 'It could be about someone you know, a friend of yours.'

Kathy said expectantly, with eyebrows raised. 'So who, or what, is it?'

'It's your friend Auchterlony, the Polisman,' replied Sean meekly.

'Well, what about him?'

Sean paused then blurted out, 'Well he's married. And has a wean too!'

'Ach, away with you. Nonsense!' came Kathy's response. 'Angus would have told me, long before now.'

'Would he now? Don't you think he was trying to hide it from ye?' smirked Sean.

'How did you find this out?' Kathy shouted peremptorily, tears welling in her eyes.

Sean looked sad as he said gently, 'Look Kathy, hen, ah'm only tellin' ye because I dinnae want to see you hurt. The information came from one of the Constables I meet on the regular beat.'

'Who was that then?' queried Kathy.

'Sorry, Kathy. But I promised not to reveal the source of the information, you understand? All the Cop said was Auchterlony was very touchy on the subject.'

Tears welled in Kathy's eyes, her emotions in turmoil, leaving her confused and vulnerable. How could Angus have done this to her? How could the gentle big Cop have been so underhand? Sean's words filtered through.

'Kathy, are ye all right? Forget the Cop, hen. He's no worth it. A bloody cheat, a bloody no-user!' cried Sean.

'Enough, enough. Please, Sean,' cried Kathy as she got up to leave. She was very distraught and not thinking straight. She would need to think this one out in her own time.

Kathy did not waste time before taking her mother into her confidence about what Sean had told her.

'Ah cannae believe it. Surely Angus wouldnae be so underhand, or two-time his wife,' exclaimed Nan.

'Seemingly he is very touchy on the subject,' said Kathy.

Nan said, with a puzzled look. 'Surely Angus doesn't expect to have his cake and eat it?'

'Could be,' mused Kathy. Then more determinedly she stated, 'Well, Ma, if he comes in here again, he'll get the cold shoulder. I'm not going to quiz him. That's no use in a relationship. Okay? Just so as you know.'

Shrugging her shoulders, Nan regarded Kathy blankly, saying simply, 'Okay.'

Knowing that Joe Cherkowsi was due to take Kathy dancing at the weekend, Nan smiled and said, 'Don't forget, hen, Joe's coming on Saturday.'

Kathy smiled weakly. 'Yes, I know. I need a bit of cheering up. And Joe's the guy who can sure do that.'

In a little known side street in Gorbals, Con Dougal inspected his new premises with Bull Bakley and the new watchman, the trusted Fergus.

'The place is great noo, Con, wi those fan heaters and the new burglar alarm,' remarked Fergus. He was allowed to address the boss on first name terms because of past association.

Con replied, 'Bags o' space and those company cartons, alang wi' the van, are perfect.'

'"Wonder Cleaning Materials". What a great cover, boss,' laughed Bull.

'The advert on the cartons and van says "What Every Housewife Needs". Little do they realise they'll be packed wi' nylons and ladies' drawers!' laughed Con heartily. They then discussed when Scottie Dunn's shipment was expected.

'The lorry's due next Wednesday. We three can handle the unloading. The less anyone knows the better. Right?' stated Con Dougal.

'Right, Con. Nae problem. Ah'll aye be here to keep an eye on things. There'll be no fiddling while ah'm on the job.'

Con replied, 'Aye. Just like yer old da, Fergus. Rest his bones.'

Saturday found Kathy and Joe in More's Hotel, India Street, enjoying dinner and drinks before making their way to the Green's Playhouse nearby. Kathy wore a light blue utility dress which highlighted her blue eyes, her red hair tied back with a white ribbon. Joe was dressed casually in grey slacks and azure shirt, standing out against the drab patrons. You could tell he was a Yank a mile away, Kathy thought as she fondly regarded Joe across the table. Finishing their meal of steak pie, with crab salad for Kathy, followed by apple pie and custard, the happy couple adjourned to the lounge for drinks.

'Kathy, honey, can I ask you a question?' Joe said gently. Kathy felt her heart flutter as she gazed into those smiling, hazel eyes which set off his sleek good looks.

Suddenly effecting a smile, Kathy replied, 'Yes, of course, Joe.'

Joe continued. 'You seem more withdrawn than usual. It's like you've got the blues.'

Kathy knew the reason. It was the thought of Angus being married and lying about it. She never believed that he could do that to her. Never. Then there was Sean's proposal hanging over her. She felt pressurised by these events as she sat there regarding Joe.

'If it's something I've said or done, honey, just let it out,' said her partner, smiling.

Kathy was touched and said, 'For goodness sake, Joe. Of course not. It's nothing. Maybe, it's been too much work and not enough play of late.'

'Well, I'm sure as hell gonna change that. To-night, you and I are gonna make whoopee at the Playhouse. Right, honey?'

'Sure, Joe. Anything you say,' laughed Kathy, returning to her usual ebullient self. 'We'll cut a rug, as you Yanks say.'

'Right. You got it, honey!' replied Joe, leaning back in his seat.

Joe ordered another round of drinks, a glass of white wine for Kathy and scotch on the rocks for himself, before leaving for the dancing. Joe had no idea what had been bothering Kathy, but having been on countless bombing missions during the war, he had seen the human psyche under pressure, and would always tread warily in such matters. In order to lighten things up, Joe said cheerily, 'Kathy, honey, have you ever been to the States?'

Kathy replied with surprise, 'To America? No, never, I'm sorry to say.'

'Never been to God's own country!' exclaimed Joe in mock surprise. 'Gal, you ain't never lived. We'll sure have to change that!'

Kathy queried, 'Can ye not sneak me aboard your aeroplane, what's it called?'

'Oh, you mean my B17 bomber? She's called "Jersey Lil", you know. Did I ever tell you?' remarked Joe casually, continuing, 'I've been through hell an' back, with Jersey Lil in all those raids during the war.'

'Is that not where you come from, Joe?' asked Kathy.

Joe replied. 'Yes Mam! I come from the little town of Boonton, in the great state of New Jersey!'

They both laughed at once, Kathy amused by his typical American bravado, and Joe because her laughing made him laugh. Presently Joe sipped his drink as he gazed thoughtfully at Kathy.

'What you thinking, Yank?' she asked.

Joe smirked at the mischievous way Kathy addressed him, replying, 'We always load supplies for our base in Germany, then fly Stateside with other gear. Maybe you would fit into one of the crates?'

'Oh, you're such a Charlie,' joked Kathy, her blue eyes sparkling.

Joe sheepishly shrugging his shoulders, replied, 'How can I be Charlie when my name is Joe?'

'You sure got a point there, partner,' quipped Kathy in a good American accent. At this, they both broke into another fit of giggling, like a couple of adolescents. Fleeting glances from patrons made it clear that over-indulgence in mirth by loud Americans was certainly not approved.

Taking Kathy's hands into his own, Joe gave her a look of deep intensity, with that far-away look in his attractive hazel eyes which turned her to jelly.

He whispered, 'Kathy. You know I'm very fond of you, honey. You're forever on my mind. Sometimes, I lie awake thinking about you. You know, hon, like the song says – "I Never Slept a Wink Last Night"?'

Kathy was strangely overcome and, surprisingly, embarrassed at the same time. 'Joe, I knew we were friends. I never thought you felt this way.'

'I guess, neither did I, hon,' sighed Joe. 'You know, Kathy, I'm sure gonna have you over to New Jersey, in the not too-distant future. My Mom and Pop would sure love to meet you.'

'Sounds really great, Joe,' smiled Kathy enthusiastically. 'I'd like that. But now it looks like time we were going?'

Joe replied eagerly. 'Sure, honey. This is Glenn Miller night. Whoopee!'

The Green's Playhouse had one of the biggest picture houses in the country and adjacent was its roomy dance hall which always attracted the most popular dance bands of the era. The Playhouse was one of Kathy's favourites, much preferring it to the Locarno or the excellent but staid Albert. That night as they entered, they were thrilled to hear the Squadronnaires giving a great rendition of Glenn Miller's 'Pennsylvania 6-5000'. The music drew them like bees to honey. Joe and Kathy were on the floor in a trice, thrilled by the nostalgic music.

'Gee, I used to dance to the real Glenn Miller band back home,' shouted Joe like a college fan.

'Sad he died in that plane crash. Great band leader,' said Kathy.

Joe sighed. 'Yeah.'

The couple enthusiastically danced their way through 'Moonlight Serenade', 'Say Si Si' and 'It Happened in Sun Valley'. It was during 'Perfidia' that Kathy felt a tap on the shoulder and the unmistakable voice exclaiming, 'In the name o' . . . Kathy . . . Is it yourself?'

As she turned on her heels, Kathy couldn't believe her eyes. There, dressed in a blue pin-striped suit, was none other than a grinning Sean Robb, one arm around the attractive figure of Sybil Barr. Sybil, who looked like a million dollars in a blue and white tailored silk dress, matching her white high heel shoes, smiled and said, 'Hello, Kathy, what a pleasant surprise.'

A flustered Kathy, trying to hide her embarrassment, spluttered, 'Sorry . . . er . . . this is Joe. Joe Cherkowski from America.'

The two couples pulled off the floor so as not to impede the flow.

'Nice meeting you, Joe,' replied Sybil with a friendly grin.

Joe beamed. 'Yes, mam, glad to meet you too.'

'So this is your American friend, Kathy,' said Sean, shooting out a hand which reminded her of a gunfighter drawing a Colt, as he continued, 'You know, Yank, she never stops speaking about you.'

Joe laughed in his usual easy way. 'Well, I'm sure honoured. It seems I've hit it big over here.'

'Yeah, just like the rest of your guys. With all yer nylons, cash and Yankee patter,' came Sean's biting response.

Joe didn't like the way Sean Robb had said that. Had he not been in the present company, he would have walked away to save any unpleasantness.

'Please forgive him, he's had one too many,' excused Sybil, reddening markedly.

Suddenly, it was a lady's choice. Sybil said, 'Joe would you like to try this one out?'

The band struck into the romantic 'A Nightingale Sang in Berkely Square'.

'A pleasure, honey,' replied Joe as he led Sybil on the floor.

Kathy took Sean aside, and said, 'Sean, what on earth are you doing here to-night?'

'I'm just giving Sybil a night out. She's a real smasher, isn't she?' slurred Sean.

Kathy's colour heightened perceptibly as she enquired, 'Yes, but you knew Joe and I were coming to-night, and you didn't say. We could have met beforehand.'

'Ach, it's a free country, lass. Surely a fellah doesn't need permission to take a friend out dancin'? Look at your Yank friend there, Joe Cher . . . Cher . . . whatever his name is. You didn't need my by-your-leave.'

Kathy said nothing but her mind was racing. This was one of Sean's twisted devices which she was unable to fathom out. Anyway leave it, for the present, she mused.

'Gee. You got one helluva dancer there, Sean man!' cried Joe admiringly.

Sean laughed loudly. 'Okay, Yank. She's yours for a bottle of Jack Daniels and two pairs of nylons, Joe. Joe Polaski . . . or . . . whatever yer name is?'

Joe controlled his urge to let fly, ignoring Sean's insult by saying, 'Sybil, hon, do you want to skip the light fantastic again?'

'Sure, Joe. I'd love to.' They danced off to the romantic strains of 'Stardust'.

Sean, his face as mean as a bad smell, produced a hip flask, guzzling the whisky noisily. He blurted out, 'See for yerself. Yer bloody Yank friend is now after my girl, tae!'

'Don't be so damn silly, Sean,' replied Kathy, shaking her head in disgust.

'Ye had better watch it, Kathy. He'll probably dump you and bugger off wi' Sybil,' said Sean as he rambled on. 'They really fancy one another. Ye can see it.'

Kathy, irritated by his comments, thought what nonsense. That could never be true, as she chided, 'For goodness sake, Sean, sober up. Joe is a friend and you're embarrassing both me and your friend, Sybil!'

'Oh, aye. You know about friends. You've tae be careful with friends. Look at that Auchterlony fellah. A bloody two-timer, if ever I saw one.'

'Stop that. Stop that now, Sean!' cried Kathy, her eyes filling. 'Joe and I are leaving when he comes off the floor with Sybil.'

Sean just mumbled and rolled his eyes.

'Another super dance, Kathy,' beamed Sybil. 'Joe here is a real Fred Astaire.'

Kathy laughed. 'Yeah. He sure is. We'll have to leave now. Nice to meet you.'

Joe could see Kathy had been crying but said nothing. Any dispute had been between friends; he did not wish to intrude. All he said was, 'Yeah, folks. I've to make it back to base to-night.'

'Oh yeah, it's been mighty fine, mighty fine meeting ye, Joe,' said Sean in a mock American accent.

As Kathy and Joe departed to the strains of 'String of Pearls', all they could hear was Sean mumbling something about bloody Yanks winning the war, and taking all the women with the dosh, nylons and fancy Yankee patter.

Kathy felt ashamed of Sean's conduct. He had insulted her friend Joe and spoiled her night out which up to then had been an enjoyable evening. What kind of friends did Joe think she had?

As Joe saw Kathy home by taxi, he made no comment save, 'Boy, Kathy, your friend Sean sure ain't partial to us Yanks.'

Kathy blushed, and could find no reply.

CHAPTER 16

'Hey, Angus did ye hear the news?' said Constable Rab Dingley as he met Angus coming on the two to ten shift.

'No, what news are ye talking about?'

Dingley's reply sent a surge through Angus's frame. 'Con Dougal's been found murdered. They fished his body out of the Clyde in the early hours. CID are handling it.'

Angus's feelings for the death of a fellow human being was not charitable nor Christian in this case. Dougal had been an evil crook, a defiler of young innocents, and the brain behind the vicious attack on his person in Carlton Court. Frankly, he was glad.

'That's one down. One to go,' he muttered to himself as he started his beat. 'Now for that bastard Bull Bakley.'

Angus made his way along to the CID in the Gorbals Police office, and Kate, one of the clerical staff, said, 'Ed Moran's out at the moment, Angus. They fished a body out of the Clyde this morning and he's investigating. Is there a message?'

'Can you say I want a word?' said Angus, then departed.

As he prepared to exit the building, Angus froze as he heard a dreaded, and familiar call. It was the cry of Sergeant Ratley. 'Auchterlony. Are ye no on yer beat yet, man?'

'I was checking on the news of Dougal's body, supposedly found in the Clyde this morning, Sergeant.'

Ratley replied, 'That's CID business. Leave it to them.'

'Yes. But it did affect me. You know the attack *was* on me,' retorted Angus determinedly.

Sergeant Ratley did not reply, but called the figure of a young Constable over who stood nearby.

'Auchterlony, this is a new chap, Constable Clark, he'll be assisting. He wasn't at muster as he was filling out some forms,' said Sergeant Ratley formally.

Angus gave the rookie a firm handshake, and smiled. 'Nice to meet you.'

Beckoning Angus aside, Sergeant Ratley said in hushed tones. 'Watch this fellah, Auchterlony. He's a Christian, one of they do gooders ye know. Keep an eye out!'

As he left to resume pounding his beat, Angus pondered on Ratley's remarks. He came from Campbeltown, a place with more churches per acre than Heaven itself. He knew Christians. Goodness, he was one himself. We probably do more good than harm. Think of the Salvation Army for one, he concluded. This new fellow, Constable Clark, was a dapper dark haired chap, with a shiny keen face bursting with enthusiasm. Angus resolved to help the young sprog as far as possible.

'Auchterlony, Auchterlony!' cried a familiar voice as Angus patrolled down South Portland Street. Angus was delighted to see Detective Constable Ed Moran hurriedly approaching.

'Ed, the very man,' laughed Angus.

'Yes, I got your message,' replied Moran, taking Angus aside. 'I suppose you've heard Con Dougal's body was fished out of the Clyde early this morning?'

Angus nodded in agreement and asked, 'How did it happen. What do you think happened?'

'It looks like foul play, for sure,' affirmed Moran. 'The back of his head was mashed to pulp. He was obviously hit from behind. The pathologist is working on him to-day.'

Angus rubbed his chin thoughtfully. 'Who would do this. What's the motive?'

'Christ! They were queuing up to do Dougal in!' blurted Moran.

'Aye, you might put me on yer list too,' said Angus, adding, 'But I'm innocent in this instance.' He added, 'Do you think he was attacked nearby, or by somebody he knew?'

Ed Moran paused before replying, 'I don't rightly know. He was well dressed at the time. His wallet was stuffed with notes. He had a half-bottle of whisky in his crombie overcoat pocket too. He was deep into the Blackmarket, as you know, and was starting to muscle into other gang bosses' territory, so I'm informed.'

'What about his side-kick, Bull Bakley?' queried Angus.

Moran answered. 'He's probably crapping himself, not knowing who has done this to his gaffer.'

'Could he not have done the deed?'

Moran replied, 'I don't think so. Bakley was too dependant on his gaffer. Con Dougal had all the brains, money and know-how.'

'Well, this could have a big influence on my finding the bastards who laid me out,' said Angus vehemently. 'Maybe our witnesses'll come forward with Dougal out of the way, and Bull Bakley lying low.'

'Oh aye, I think it will, Angus. Our boys in CID are searching high and low for Bakley right now,' replied a determined Moran.

Whilst Angus continued his beat, often in the company of a Sergeant or Senior Cop like Constable Sharkey, the Fox, now it was Angus who followed unseen behind the new young rookie, Constable Clark, on Sergeant Rat Ratley's orders. Again it was like the Keystone Cops and the farce of Mr Ali's cockerel. So here was the picture – the beat Sergeant was being followed on his rounds by eager young Constable Clark who in turn was finally followed by blood-hound Constable Angus Auchterlony himself!

Angus knew that Sergeant Ratley always popped into one of three pubs on his rounds for a fortifier, particularly on a cold, dreich night. He was sure to receive his glass of favourite double malt whisky, welcome sustenance from an oasis in the great Gorbals Desert. The first oasis was Joe Dodd's in the Robin Bar, Norfolk Street; next came Jon Clancy's Alexander Bar, Bridge Street; and finally there was always succour at McCann's Mally Arms in Eglinton Street. After all Sergeant Ratley, or whoever it happened to be, was only checking on a problem, calling in to enquire if there were any particular complaints, or again supervising a licencee's tardy closing times.

As Angus shadowed young Constable Clark, he noticed him standing outside the Robin Bar in Norfolk Street, notebook in hand, copiously taking notes. Coming on the young Cop suddenly, Angus said, 'Clark, old boy. What are ye doing. Writing yer memoirs?'

'Oh, no. I'm noting that Sergeant Ratley entered the Robin Bar at the said time,' replied the young cop.

'Why?' queried Angus.

Constable Clark looked puzzled, then replied, 'Good Police procedure. If he runs into trouble in there, I'll be on hand – and I'll have it on record!'

Taking Clark aside, Angus whispered, 'If you're wise, you'll continue on your beat.'

'But what about the Sergeant?' pleaded Constable Clark.

Angus quipped. 'He's really in there for a "refresher", you silly bugger. But you don't record things like that. Officially Sergeant Ratley is in there investigating a complaint. And, believe me, he'll soon be out and hot on your trail, kicking yer rear-end.'

Without further ado, young Constable Clark was on his way, tail between his legs and much wiser in the ways of Cops on a city beat.

Angus was at his wits' end. For several days, he had been experiencing 'the cold shoulder' from a source he'd least expected, namely Kathy. Kathy had been acting out of character, and Angus found it totally unfathomable.

Entering the Fruit Box one morning, Angus greeted Kathy and Nan with, 'Good morning, ladies, can you spare a cadger a cup o' tea?'

'Mornin', Angus. Aye, come in, come in,' smiled Nan. Kathy said nothing, barely nodding as Angus went into the back-shop.

This had happened for about a week. Angus hadn't reacted to her mood, save asking Nan variously, 'Is she not feeling well?' or 'Have I blotted my copy-book?' or 'Will she not tell me what's wrong. What have I done?' Angus got no response from Kathy when he greeted her, just a nod and no conversation.

'Nan, there's no change,' remarked Angus disconsolately, not receiving Kathy's usual welcome. 'She wouldn't give you light in a dark corner to-day, Nan,' he added.

Nan just shrugged and smiled. 'Ach, she's not feeling herself this weather. Give her time, Angus. She'll come round.' After all it was not for her to give advice. It was Kathy's business, and her problem to sort out. As much as she felt for both parties, Nan wasn't going to make the error of intruding in this matter. She was too experienced.

During that week of gloom, two occurrences on his beat gave Angus relief. As he was passing by a close in Buchan Street, Angus clearly heard the cry of 'Edge up, Polis!' He slowly made his way to a back court. As he did, he observed men scattering through various rear exits. Only two boys, around twelve or thirteen, were visible. One boy was busily gathering piles of betting money, abandoned by the fleeing pitch-and-toss punters, as his confederate sat on a midden roof. Spying Angus emerging from the close, the look-out cried, 'Haw, Jamie. Polis edge-up!'

An unconcerned Jamie shouted back. 'Ach, Wully, there's nae need to act the mug noo. They're all awa' and we hae the money!'

It was only when Angus's heavy hands gripped his shoulders that Jamie squealed like a rabbit seized by a fox. 'Haw, ma – Polis!'

His pal Wully exited at high speed, shouting. 'Ah warned ye, stumer!'

Angus said gently. 'Now son, what's yer name? Is it Jamie?'

Initially dumb, the young boy said, 'Aye. Ah'm Jamie. Are ye taking me to the Polis station? Ye gonna lock me up?'

Angus said, 'Well, I may be forced to. But if you tell me what you and your pal were up to, I may be able to help you.'

Jamie started to cry. 'My ma will leather me!'

'What about yer dad, son?' asked Angus gently.

Little Jamie cried. 'Ma da ran away when me and ma sisters were wee babies.'

After a pause he explained to Angus that he and Wully had a great money-making game. When the adults played 'pitch-and-toss' in the backs, they volunteered as look-outs. Wully would shout 'edge up' and when they all scattered, Jamie quickly scooped up the betting money. Later he and Wully would split the money.

Angus queried, 'And what did you do with the money, Jamie?'

Jamie answered with a grin. 'We bought fush an' chips, and ginger fer oorselfs.' Pausing he added, 'Aye an' fer mah ma and sisters tae!'

Taking the boy's name and address, with a view to warning his mother, Angus said. 'Run along now, Jamie. Be a good boy and ye'll not get the jail.' He warned, 'And tell your pal, Wully, I'll be watchin' him too from now on.'

The second piece of good news was when he met Mrs McKistry whom he had previously dealt with over problems with her two boys fighting.

'Hello, Mrs McKistry. How's those boys of yours? Behaving themselves, I hope?'

Mrs McKistry answered. 'Oh, yes, their da leathered them. That sorted them oot.' She then informed Angus that her daughter and Danny Desai were now married. The couple had a comfy room and kitchen nearby and Annie was pregnant. Danny was still driving a Corporation bus, providing a steady income and secure future for her daughter.

Knowing of her husband's fanatical leanings, Angus enquired, 'How's Mr McKistry taken it all?'

'Och, he'll never change. He never went tae the weddin' like myself,' sighed Senga, continuing, 'But he still gave her fifty pound fer a weddin' present, even though, as he said, "I'm gonna have a darkie grand-wean".'

Angus bade her good day and continued on his rounds. He gave the Fruit Box a miss, feeling cold as he passed by. Not seeing Kathy and Nan was like having a death in the family. How could Angus even try to fathom the problem? How could he know that Sean Robb's viperous tongue had caused all the problems, Sean Robb who had told Kathy that Angus was married and had a child back in Kintyre. Had he known this, he would have run all the way to Kathy's door to expunge the evil calumny, and bring the light back into their lives.

The CID had concluded from the Coroner's findings that Con Dougal had been murdered. The back of the victim's head had been stove in by a heavy instrument with a sharp edge, like an axe, and he showed no injuries to the front of the face or head. There were no defence cuts on the hands. Blood samples showed the victim had consumed considerable amounts of alcohol. As Detective Moran commented, 'His wallet was still intact with over a hundred pound in notes. It's clear robbery wasn't a motive. Looks as if he was murdered, attacked from behind, by somebody with an axe.'

'Aye. Someone with a grudge?' wondered Angus.

Ed Moran suddenly said, 'Angus, this is still under wraps. But the "low down" from CID sources is that Dougal had been muscling in on someone's Blackmarket patch in Glasgow with stuff he was bringing from down South.'

'Obviously they took objection?'

Moran replied. 'Oh no doubt. But there's more in it than that. Seemingly he owed the other geezer, who we're not sure of yet, dough for a deal they'd already done.'

'Obviously, it's going to be hard to finger who did Dougal in?' remarked Angus.

Detective Moran answered laconically, 'Proving it. Impossible!'

Screaming headlines in the local newspapers soon found their targets, as Kitty Cullen poured over the details of Con Dougal's murder. Not far away, Jock and Lilly Grant had seen the headlines, unable to contain their surprise and relief.

'We'd better go round an' see Kitty right away, Da,' blurted Lilly excitedly.

That night Jock and Lilly Grant discussed with Kitty how Dougal's murder would now affect their plans of giving evidence.

Kitty said nervously, 'That's no' the end of oor worries. Bull Bakley is still around!'

'Aye, an' could gie us loads o' trouble, tae,' replied Jock cautiously.

'If only ah could contact Slogger Struth,' sighed Kitty. 'He would help me, fer sure.'

Forces were presently at work, forces which the three worried friends could not envisage. Fate would take a hand and show them a way out.

Some weeks after Con Dougal's grisly death, the CID watch on Bull Bakley's haunts paid off. Bakley was trailed by a ragged drunk (a detective in disguise) to the store nearby which his late boss, Con Dougal, had set up.

Fergus the storeman greeted Bull warmly. 'Good tae see ye, Bull. The place is packed full noo with the last load from London.'

'Aye, ah'll be in regular frae noo on. We've to sell the stuff, quick as possible tae raise cash,' said a concerned Bull Bakley.

'Most o' the cash was in the Boss's hands. A real problem,' replied Fergus.

'Aye, an' the bank accounts was in Con's name. And he had loads of hidey-holes for the cash tae,' sighed Bull heavily. 'Tae beat the taxman.'

Bull Bakley was now really out of his depth, and old Fergus knew it. Bull was all right for taking orders, arranging for the Heavies to sort out recalcitrant customers, or carrying out orders from his past departed boss. He was in a state of inner panic, wondering what to do. All eyes were on him, looking for leadership. Whether he was competent to seize control of operations was dubious. Fergus had his doubts as he suggested, 'Con said before he departed that we should remove the identification numbers on some of the packages, Bull.'

'Good idea. But noo there's only two of us wi' Con away,' said Bakley sadly.

Fergus asked. 'Ye werenae at Con's funeral, Bull?'

'No, ah was real sorry. But ah'd tae lay low. The fuzz were efter me.'

With the need to sell the stored goods on the Blackmarket to raise capital, Bull Bakley was observed arriving daily around 9.30 a.m. in the morning, disappearing through a wicket gate in the metal sliding door.

Angus and his colleagues were briefed by Inspector MacAlee and a CID Inspector about a coming operation. Details would only be released on the morrow, for security reasons.

Life at the Fruit Box went on, but it can't be said as usual. There were only two men in Kathy's life now, Sean and Joe. Angus no longer called in for his tea. He had decided not to. He just couldn't take not seeing Kathy's blue eyes beaming up at him as he entered. All he got was a deadpan nod, as if he was *persona non grata*, and Nan trying to put on a face. The result amounted to a feeling of unease and tension which Angus found distressing. It was as if he had died and was now walking about in an unrecognisable body. He missed Kathy so much, unable to fathom the reason for her strange behaviour. He had not raised the subject because Kathy herself saw fit not to raise it with him.

Kathy was no happier. She sadly missed Angus, but her feeling of anger at his supposed marriage would not allow her to have further contact or dialogue. Nan had broached the subject several times, as she enquired, 'Kathy, hen. Why don't ye ask Angus outright about his marriage?'

Just the mention of the word 'marriage' used in association with Angus's name was enough to send a tearful Kathy fleeing to either front or back-shop with an uncharacteristic cry of 'Mum, please. Do you mind? This is my problem!'

It's also mine, thought Nan, but she did not attempt to reply nor follow after her daughter.

Angus had gone to Jock Grant's, after coming off backshift, to discuss the implications of Con Dougal's murder, and to find solace and advice with a friend about his problem with Kathy, whom Jock knew well as one of her customers.

Jock poured Angus a whisky and water, saying, 'Now Dougal's gone all we need is that scunner, Bull Bakley.'

'Agreed,' retorted Angus, relishing his whisky. 'But if we could find Struth, and he'd testify, we would have it made.'

'Kitty Cullen would come forward, as sure as little fishes,' said Jock raising his glass. 'Here's good health tae ye, Angus.'

Back at the Fruit Box, the routine continued without Angus's presence. After his shameful behaviour at the Green's Playhouse, Sean managed to inveigle himself back into Kath's favour with flowers and apologies, pleading about 'wit being out when drink's in'. As usual, Kathy forgave him (as he knew she would) with a shrug and a smile, thinking Sean was basically a nice fellow, when the drink was not in him. After all, was it not Sean who had alerted her to Angus's despised two-timing? Sean who, in spite of his faults, always looked to her best interests. Angus, of course, was totally unaware of Sean Robb's revelations to Kathy about his being married with a child, nor the circumstances which had brought about the change in Kathy's behaviour toward him. So poor Angus went about his duties, suffering and oblivious to the spell which Sean had cast over him.

Since 7.45 a.m. a dozen cops, detectives and excisemen had been hiding in plain vans and up closes, their attention focused on the recently deceased Con Dougal's store. They had been tipped off by a telephone call to the local CID about a Blackmarket store being operated by the late Con Dougal's gang, at a certain address in the Gorbals.

The Cops strained for signs of Bull Bakley, having earlier observed Fergus the watchman entering at his usual time of 8 a.m. along with his Alsatian guard-dog. Present were Inspector MacAlee, Sergeant Ratley, Detective Moran, Angus and the other members of the disparate team whose aching and weary limbs yearned for action.

Just after 9 a.m., Inspector MacAlee straightened suddenly and said, 'There he goes now!'

It was Bull Bakley. Giving three bangs on the access door of the main door, he glanced round furtively as Fergus opened the door.

'Morning, Bull,' said Fergus, ingratiating himself with his new boss.

'Aye,' replied Bull laconically. 'Let's get the van loaded now. The customer's waiting for delivery around ten thirty.'

It was just before 10 a.m. that the big metal gate slid open, revealing the 'Wonder Cleaning Materials' van, driven by Bull Bakley who paused as Fergus strained to slide the big gate shut. At that precise instant, Bull Bakley, his man Fergus, the big ginger tom licking its paws across the road, together with the whole neighbourhood, shook as an ear shattering cacophony of Police whistles split the airwaves. Suddenly myriads of heavily booted figures sprang from stationary vans and from the mouths of apparently deserted closes, quickly surrounding Bull and Fergus beside their puttering van.

'Right, Bakley. Out, out. Quickly. Lay yer hands on the bonnet,' screamed Inspector MacAlee. 'And stop that bloody dog barking!'

'You too!' shouted Ed Moran to an obviously shaken Fergus, the big gate ajar and the keys still in his hands.

The head detective ordered the van doors opened, and Fergus reluctantly obeyed.

'Ah hope you bastards have got a warrant for this,' shouted Bull Bakley as he continued, 'Can't you fuckers see this is just a cleaning materials store?'

A thorough search of the contents of the van revealed a surprise, as did the store. There, stashed in cartons similarly marked 'Wonder Cleaning Materials' were American whiskeys, good quality Scotch whiskies, cigarettes, nylons, cardigans, pullovers, ladies' and gents' suits, and including Maxwell House coffee, all desperately awaited by an expectant and hungry clientele.

A dejected and shaken Bakley and Fergus stood like schoolboys caught in the act, as they were read their rights, with the crowd of locals and passers-by growing by the minute and muttering in wonderment at what was happening.

'Ah want ma lawyer, right this minute. For me and ma man, here!' hissed Bakley between clenched teeth.

'Okay, Bakley. You can phone him from the Station,' replied Inspector MacAlee formally, adding with a smirk, 'You are both going to need one, judging by the Aladdin's Cave you have here.'

Detective Moran joked to Angus, 'Strange how that tip-off came like that. Out of the blue and anonymous.'

'Someone's obviously had it in for Con Dougal and his successor, Bakley,' stated Angus as he went about examining the store and its contents.

A Police guard was immediately placed on the store, where considerable time would be expended by CID and Excise Officers preparing itemised lists of the illicit and stolen goods, in preparation for criminal charges and for the impending Prosecution Case.

Over a week later, a group of people surprisingly appeared at the Gorbals Police office.

Slogger Struth had returned from London and was accompanied by Kitty Cullen, Joe and Lilly Grant. Struth informed an amazed CID Inspector, 'We're noo ready to gie evidence in the case of Constable Auchterlony's attack.'

'Curiouser and curiouser,' said the smiling CID Inspector, beckoning the group forward. 'Come in, folks. We're very pleased to see you.'

CHAPTER 17

Angus had been warned by a sour faced Sergeant Ratley at muster that crack-down time had come for the local, illegal bookies operating 'pitches' on his pad in contravention of the Betting and Gaming Acts.

With such outmoded regulations, the Police would use their own discretion, letting it be known that a raid was planned. Such knowledge would allow the bookie to substitute his regular 'runner', he who collects the bets and lines, with a 'dummy' – often some unemployed fellow with no previous convictions. The 'dummy' would be placed near the close at the 'pitch' with planted lines and money. The real bookie would later slip him a few quid, also paying his fine which was normally very light as it was a first offence.

In consequence Auchterlony had been watching the comings and goings at Rab Galloway's close in Warwick Street, from a close entrance further down on the opposite side of the street.

'Rab's in full swing there, but it's catching the buggers,' mused Angus to himself. He knew wee Rab Galloway worked as 'runner' for Big Bob Droy, the illegal bookie who centred his activities on a pub in Norfolk Street. Droy had been 'mysteriously' tipped off about the raid and had doubled his 'watchers'.

Angus pondered on how he could make his way up to Rab Galloway's pitch without being observed by the enemy. A heaven sent opportunity presently came trotting by in the form of Quin's coal horse and cart. Quin's big black Clydesdale, Meg, was always well groomed with shining harness and a docile and obedient nature. She always knew when to stop at the right close, when her master shouted 'whoa!' Meg knew Angus well as the big cop always fed her sugar lumps which he carried in a bag especially for her.

As the small wiry Quin heaved a bag full of nuts up to the top of a four-storey single-end, Auchterlony, knowing horses from his labours in Kintyre, took the bridle and gave the horse a friendly 'clicking' sound with his lips. Meg moved forward, effortlessly stopping in front of the close entrance before Rab Galloway's, as Angus whispered softly, 'Whoa, good girl, Meg.'

Screened by the remaining coal bags Angus entered quietly up the close before the bookie's close, bent on stealthy ambush, but unseen eyes had spotted the intruder. Immediately a sudden cry of 'Edge-up, Polis!' rent the air. As he passed through the dingy, smelly close with the flaking whitewashed walls, he could hear the rush of pattering feet disappearing into the rear entrance of the adjacent close. Instantaneously, he just caught sight of the 'edge-up' man's clean pair of heels disappearing off the wash-house roof, like snow off a dyke with a faint laugh of 'Teuchter tumshie' fading into the distance. Up a first landing opposite, another 'watcher', a wraith-like figure with chalky face, dissolved mysteriously into thin air.

Meanwhile Rab Galloway was seated in Big Bridey Mulheron's first floor single end of the bookie's close in question. All his lines and money were secure within the belted confines of her limitless khaki ex-ATS bloomers, as she poured him a MacEwan's ale, and herself the precious red Eldorado. The other punters had meantime fled into Willy Smylie's ground floor single-end below where he packed them in like sardines. Known as Holy Willie, Smylie had once played the organ as a young man in the local kirk but had taken to drink. He had long since repented, and was now preaching an improvised sermon, in the event of a sudden visit from the Police.

All Angus Auchterlony encountered as he did a 'heavy dreep' off the wall were three solitary figures whose attention seemed riveted on a pencilled up edition of the *Noon Record* tacked to the wash-house door. The principal figure, a young man, smiled and said cheerily, 'Is there a soapy bubble [trouble] here, constibul?' Auchterlony looked them over closely before questioning them.

'What goes on here? Where did the rest of them go. Where are they all?'

The old codger with battered bunnet, clay pipe clamped in smoked teeth, just shrugged his narrow shoulders saying, 'We wis jus havin' a squint at the paper. Some joker left it up. Is that no richt, Davie lad?'

The large sandy haired youth, with a fixed smile, uttered, 'Aye, Danny, that's whit happn'd. They all gone tae heaven! They wi' Jesus noo!'

Angus stated he had reason to believe that illegal gaming had been taking place, and said sharply, 'OK lads, out with the pockets, empty the pockets!'

As Auchterlony had expected, from the 'old stained-teeth' came a small tobacco knife, a couple of old pipe cleaners, a ball of string and grimy half-crown coin. Davy laughed with glee as he produced a half eaten piece of bread and a white mouse by the tail.

'This is Mickey,' Davy laughed.

'I doubt whether Micky's a fan of the dogs and horses?' replied the astonished Auchterlony while Davie just stared blankly, not fully comprehending his comment.

'Oh aye, Mickey loves horses, and dugs tae,' smiled Davie, with, 'Look, he likes Polis tae.'

A quick search of the young man's pockets produced the desired result. He seemed to Auchterlony to be overly cooperative. Soon coin, silver and notes came flooding out along with the wad of paper slips. As Angus expected, they were bookies' lines with nom-de-plumes such as 'Dicky Bird', 'Canny Sanny', 'Liza M' and 'Vulgar Vic'.

'You're nicked, my man!' said Auchterlony to the 'runner', and warning 'smoke-teeth' to accompany him to the local Gorbals Office for the purposes of evidence.

It was a bad week for Angus which had only been made bearable by his success with the arrest of the 'runner'. He hadn't seen Kathy for weeks, she was away visiting her cousins in Inverkeithing, and to make matters worse, he had got human excrement all over his hands twice the previous week, courtesy of the local yobs, whilst rattling shop locks on night-shift. So Angus's expectations of praise were swiftly disabused by Sergeant Rat Ratley who sneered disparagingly.

'Auchterlony, that guy you arrested, did you not suss he was the "dummy" runner?'

'Well, he was carrying all the damned evidence!' replied Auchterlony defensively.

'Well, he's no' the only dummy in the case!' replied Ratley caustically. 'You're like a fart in a trance, D93!' The Sergeant laughed loudly, 'The bugger'll get off wi' a five pound fine at Craigie Street, and oot the same day, and there'll be a tenner frae big Droy the bookie for his pains too!'

Auchterlony looked blank, not finding a suitable response which would suit the spot he found himself in, especially with a superior whom he despised, and who was mutually disliked by him in return – one who could make it very awkward for him, and did so daily. Why, Auchterlony wondered constantly, was Ratley so hostile to him? Eventually he concluded it was simply down to human chemistry.

Angus was going about his duties feeling downcast. He pondered whether he had made a blunder in joining the Police. Perhaps he would be better to return to the fishing in Kintyre where he could buy a share in a trawler. His small savings would give him a start, and he had friends in Campbeltown and Carradale who would take him on. He also had a heavy heart, not being able to see Kathy. She didn't want to see him any longer, and what made it worse – he was given no reason why. She simply was not open to dialogue! Then there was Sergeant Rat Ratley with his 'goings-on' about the Tallymen (not Italian males!) and the spate of shop break-ins and hold-ups plaguing the area.

News came in which galvanised Angus out of his lethargy. Jock Grant's brother, Mickey, had been found badly beaten in a back court, next to a Cumberland Street boozer. Before sinking into oblivion as he was rushed to the Victoria Infirmary in a badly beaten condition, with slashed cheek, black eye and body severely bruised all over, Mickey had gasped, 'Ah know weel they bliddy bastarts that did this tae me!'

Later, after Mickey's regaining consciousness in the Vickey, Jock told detectives and Auchterlony that Mickey had related he had money problems, losing heavily on dogs and horses recently. Also Macfie, Mickey's factor, had been chasing him for rent. Mickey had asked around his pub pals for a 'bung tae see me ower' but they couldn't help him. He had appealed to Jock but even his usually obliging brother was short of funds, owing to Lilly's birthday, and couldn't come to his aid.

Mickey had been seen in heated discussion with Sluch Docherty in the pub adjacent to where he had been discovered after his attack. Sluch Docherty, known for the way he slurped his beer, was a well known Tallyman who worked with Con Dougal and his gang. Repeated extensive enquiries in local pubs, and on the street by the CID, failed miserably. As Detective Moran related to Auchterlony, 'They're all shit scared to speak. They know who did it tae Mickey. We know who did it – but they won't come forward. We're up against a frightened wall of silence!'

'Can ye blame them, Ed?' was all Angus replied.

The Tallymen were money-lenders with a vengeance. They would oblige the desperate punter by lending him money at the rate of interest of five bob in the pound per week. This would double for each week the punter failed to pay back on time. After a warning, and the unfortunate punter still hadn't 'coughed up', the Tallymen would waylay their victim and give him a 'good doing', leaving the poor soul dead or crippled and defaced for life: a signal warning to all other potential recalcitrants.

Sluch Docherty was the head of such a Tallyman punishment squad and often boasted of his pearl handled pal 'malky' (razor) who had 'ripped many a bastard's cheek'! On other occasions his weapon would be called 'Ma hoosie frazer (razor) which I got frae the Hoose o' Fraser.' He always said it as a big joke and all his drunken cronies and sychophants would laugh themselves silly over it – otherwise they might end up in stitches!

As if to compound the horror, Sluch Docherty worked for Con Dougal through his henchman Bull Bakely, the very same evil duo who had been Lilly's abusers and from whom Auchterlony had rescued Lilly from their shebeen in Nicholson Street, thereby earning their undying enmity.

Lucky we mortals that are not destined to forsee the future. Had Auchterlony glimpsed what was to occur that day he would have doubtless remained in bed.

Into the second round of his two to ten beat, Angus stopped off at

Grace's Fish Restaurant in Norfolk Street as he habitually did. Seated in the backshop, a smiling Angus chatted with Dan who had prepared him his favourite haddie fish supper, to fuel him on his way on a cold damp night.

Dan smoked his favourite Gold Flake in between gulps of tea as he watched with satisfaction Angus wolfing away his fish supper, washed down by copious gulps of his beloved Barr's Irn Bru. Angus finished his meal with a sigh of satisfaction, 'Och I'll tell ye. Ye canna beat a good Scottish haddie supper wi' the old Irn Bru. Ye can keep all your fancy foreign foods and wines tae!'

Dan's wife, Grace, an attractive fair-haired, middle aged woman, came in from the front shop every so often for a brief word, as intermittant customers came and went. Grace replied, 'Well, Constable Auchterlony, thanks for the compliment, we can see you enjoyed it as usual, and there isn't a drop left in the bottle either.'

Dan, a smart handsome man in white coat, white shirt and dark tie, broke into a guffaw as Angus inadvertently pulled two large French onions from his pocket and said, 'I got these from the Onion Johnnie who comes round the closes on the big black bicycle. I think his name's Marcel?' remarking finally that, 'I'm taking them back to my place in Partick to make some nice mince and onions!'

Dan laughed as Angus replaced his two onions in his big coat pockets, like a broody hen with her eggs, and chirped, 'Don't forget to take them out or they'll root in yer pockets!'

In all the time that Grace and Dan had been in business in the Gorbals, they had experienced no serious trouble, just the usual drunkenness or rowdy who refused to pay for his fish suppers or lemonade. This was due to the strong support of their regular customers, like the local residents, the late dancers, the picture-going fans, the pub clientele, the passing trade and the like of the Cops from the Police Training School around in Oxford Street. The Police and even local gang members would tell Grace and Dan, 'Let us know if anybody gives you any bother. We'll soon sort them out!'

That night as Dan and Angus sat having a chat, they suddenly became aware of the front door banging shut and the sound of a male voice raised in anger. Dan immediately got up and ran into the front shop, looked and screamed, 'God Almighty, it's a hold-up!'

'Shut yer trap, or ah'll chib ye!' snarled the figure in the hooded black balaclava who was holding a knife to Grace's neck as he shouted, 'Open the fucking till, dae ye hear, and put the dosh in this bag. Hurry an' ye'll no get hurted!'

His companion, a slim, small man, similarly dressed, stood cursing as he held the front door, shouting to Dan, 'Hurry for fuck's sake!'

'Don't hurt her,' shouted Dan. 'Take the money and go!'

'Make sure the door's ready,' screamed the big robber to his small accomplice. Pointing the knife closer to Grace's neck, he roared, 'Hurry, ye bitch, yer too slow!'

Meanwhile, unknown to the crooks, Angus had released the Yale lock of the rear shop door, sliding quickly through the close out into the street, and drew his trusty baton, whom he had named 'Hamish'.

Suddenly like a raging tornado Angus was using full bodily force to blast aside the front door with a resounding crash.

'Fuck me, the Polis!' shouted the big robber with the bag of money. Meantime Auchterlony had given the small crook holding the door several thwacks across the back of his neck and shoulders, which immediately laid him out.

'Keep back, ye bluddy Polis,' yelled the big hooded robber, 'or she gets it!'

It was then that a miraculous unrehearsed attack took place, as if co-ordinated by one master-mind. Angus, who was a cricketer of some skill back in Kintyre, withdrew one of his large French onions and launched it at the head of the robber threatening Grace. An audible loud thud immediately knocked the culprit off balance as Dan, seizing a bottle of Kola from under the shop counter, hit the villain in the crutch and the latter folded with a gasp. Grace fled past him into the back-shop, just as the US Marines, in the form of Auchterlony, leaped over the counter and attacked the kneeling bandit across the shoulders with his baton. The latter raised his arms and cried: 'Enough, for God's sakes. Stop, ye bluddy heidcase!'

Almost like a Hollywood Western, the seventh cavalry arrived in the form of a Sergeant and two Policemen who rushed from the Black Maria which had drawn up outside Grace's front door.

'Auchterlony, are you all okay?' said the Sergeant as the other three Cops raised and hand-cuffed the two broken robbers, escorting them to the awaiting Black Maria.

A large crowd had gathered outside Grace's Fish Restaurant, some of whom had witnessed the action through the large shop window from the street pavement, as had Miss Ida Campbell, the old biddy who lived above the shop.

'I heard the racket below, an' came doon tae see if it was yon bloody drunks peeing up oor close again!' said Miss Campbell.

'She was the one that ran round to Oxford Street and alerted us to the trouble,' announced the Sergeant, proudly pointing to the old spinster.

'You've got plenty of witnesses too, Auchterlony,' said the Sergeant, 'so it will be an award fer ye. We are taking statements now. Come round to the Station and we'll make a report for the Inspector, then ye'll be off duty.'

'Constable Auchterlony certainly knows his onions, Sergeant,' replied Grace with a beaming grin!

A physically drained Auchterlony returned home to his room in Merkland Street with one good onion; the other lay mashed on the floor of Grace's Fishey, crushed by the head of the unfortunate baddy. There would be no mince and onions that night! Nevertheless Angus felt like a hero, but he was sad, regretting he could not relate his adventure to Kathy in person. She would not be sharing in his triumph.

The spunky Miss Ida Campbell returned to the normality of her pipe-clayed close and she, thanks to her prompt and alert action, would never ever again be charged for a fish supper by the grateful owners of Grace's Fish Restaurant.

News of Auchterlony's valiant deed at Grace's Restaurant was in all the local papers next morning, and an elated Angus poured over the reports in his copy of the *Glasgow Herald*, a paper his family had read for generations. Some distance away in Norfolk Street, an equally excited Nan and Kathy wrestled with each other for the *Daily Record* during breaks serving customers.

PC Auchterlony was the undoubted local hero of the hour, 'the cat's pyjamas'. He was greeted, smiled at, and slapped on the shoulders by colleagues, local men and woman, shopkeepers, men pushing barrows, coalmen heaving bags up high tenements, young women with weans in shawls, old women with cotton bags – even dogs seemed to bark greetings at him, Angus imagined in his state of euphoria.

Only Sergeant Ratley's stony countenance belied abnormality, as if Angus's universally accepted feat had never really happened. From both Ratley and his stooge, PC Flockhart, there was never a flicker of recognition nor a word of praise, but Angus ignored the situation, riding the waves with satisfaction.

As Angus patrolled his beat he resolved to 'have it out' with Kathy – her attitude of ignoring him suddenly just didn't make sense. He had done nothing wrong and there had to be an explanation. And Angus was determined to find out why!

Angus entered the Fruit Box with a little trepidation, for the first time in a month.

'Hello Angus, long time me no see,' quipped a smiling Nan. Angus was relieved it was Nan, and not Kathy, whom he met as he entered.

'I see you're the flavour of the month this morn,' continued Nan as she shouted, 'Kathy, look who's here. Ah'll away an make the tea!'

Kathy, who seemed engrossed in sorting out fruit, turned and smiled, saying nothing. Presently Angus, whose eyes were drawn once again to the welcome sight of that lovely face, spoke earnestly in a gentle voice.

'Kathy, I have got to have a word. It's very important and . . .'

Before he had finished, Kathy said tersely, without looking up, 'I have nothing to say to you, Angus Auchterlony. It's no use.'

Angus was taken aback, but not showing it, simply said, 'Kathy, for old time's sake. Please give me a chance to talk to you!' There was a period of silence before Kathy looked up. They stood regarding each other for a long moment.

'Look, I'll be off at two o'clock, Kathy. We can go along to Knott's for a meal,' said Angus smiling. 'Okay? And it's on me!'

After a pause, Kathy replied, nodding her head in agreement, 'Fine,

Angus, I owe you that, at least.'

Angus pulled on his faded fawn gaberdine with shoulder straps and, clad in white shirt and black tie, complete with black serge trousers and thick soled boots, hurried to meet Kathy. Thus accoutred, Auchterlony was the archetypal cop coming off duty, in the disguise of the Cop in mufti, and as conspicuous as a ham sandwich on the shelf of a Kosher delicatessen.

In no time Kathy and Angus were on their way, after bidding Nan farewell, as they walked briskly along Norfolk Street towards Gorbal's Cross. Quickly crossing the busy Main Street the pair strode down Ballater Street, past the Green's picture house on the opposite side of the road, Knott's drawing them on like a magnet.

They soon crossed over Crown Street, quickly turning into Florence Street where the lure and promise of Knott's lay. Knott's: so plain from the outside but so good on the inside. It was not long before Kathy and Angus were tucking into the kind of hearty meal that made Knott's name legendary throughout the Gorbals. As the meal was on Auchterlony, he insisted on having the whole hog.

First they had the steaming hot Scotch broth, in large deep bowls with spoons like paddy's shovels with thick slabs of bread – a veritable meal in its own right, bedad! This was followed by hefty plates of steaming pink ham bones, cabbage and big Kerr's Pinks with their jackets on, served by a cheery waitress upon scrubbed wooden tables.

The sighs emanating from both diners showed they were full 'to the gunnels' and wondering how on earth they were to manage the mighty finale – the famous Knott's dumpling!

After a pause, in which Angus fumbled under the table, furtively opening a notch of his belt, both he and Kathy tucked into heaped plates of brown steaming dumpling, made to Bobby Knott's own recipe of best flour, suet, eggs, raisins, sugar, treacle with cinnamon and nutmeg, all bound with breadcrumbs. The dumpling came with hot, sweet steaming mugs of tea.

The meal finally completed, their faces flushed with satisfaction, each sighing with pregnant bulges, Angus immediately sensed a relaxation in Kathy's demeanour. Her facial muscles eased as she smiled across at him.

'Kathy, what's been up with you, the past while? Why have you given me the cold shoulder? I can't see what I could have done wrong?'

'Can you no guess? Surely ye're not having me on here. Me of all people!' Kathy encountered sharply.

'What is it with you, woman? What are you saying? Just spit it out,' replied Angus testily.

'Simply this. You didn't tell me you were bloody married,' cried Kathy excitedly, throwing in, 'I cannot abide a man whose life is a living lie either!'

'What!' roared Angus, his face turning scarlet with rage.

'Aye, a married man with a child too. Trying to get off with "a piece of crackling on the side",' replied Kathy mockingly.

At this diatribe, Auchterlony stood bolt upright, fists clenched and screamed. 'Who the Hell says so? Who has told you this?'

'It was big Sean. Sean Robb who told me at our Rogano dinner!' snapped the red-faced Kathy.

'The lying bastard!' echoed the enraged Auchterlony.

Silence descended upon Knott's Restaurant, and surprise too, as diners turned to see what on earth was going on at the adjacent table where, only some minutes earlier, mirth and quiet conversation had been happily in progress.

'For God's sake, Angus, sit down and calm yourself. Remember you are an officer of the law, so act like one!' chided Kathy through clenched teeth, gaining her customary composure.

The cheery waitress came across to enquire if everything was to their satisfaction and Kathy reassured her with a ready story of a slight difference of opinion, now all sorted out.

A pacified Auchterlony regarded Kathy for several moments and said simply he had a story to tell. Angus related at length how he had become engaged to a local girl back home in Campbeltown in 1939, just when the War started. His fiancée had already given birth to a baby, a year earlier before he had met her, the father being a fisherman from Carradale. It had made no difference to him, Angus explained, as he truly loved Rona. When he was away in the War, Rona had died of a ruptured appendix, before they could marry. The baby was adopted by the natural father's family.

'Oh, Angus,' sighed Kathy, taking his hands in her own, 'how was I to know?'

'Well, you could have asked me,' replied Angus fixedly.

'Aye. You're right. And I am going to have words with Mr Sean Robb directly!' said Kathy ominously, her jaw tightening markedly.

'You're not the only one, either,' said Angus to himself.

CHAPTER 18

Angus was his old self again, now that he and Kathy were reconciled. He was extremely pleased with himself, with the fact that he had tackled the problem head-on. He was never the type of man who could sit on the fence, or act in a wishy-washy kind of way. That is why he played rugby, rather than the more sedate game of soccer. He preferred the hard physical contact of the game. Luckily Angus and Kathy had worked out their problem. The sun had returned to both their lives. It showed in the gleam of Kathy's blue eyes and the spring in her gait. Even the customers noted it, commenting, 'My, Nan, your Kathy's lookin' chirpy the day,' or 'Kathy, hen, glad yer feelin' better.'

Of course, Angus was doubly satisfied as Kathy fussed over him, her guilty conscience not letting her forget that she had thought the worst of Angus in believing Sean.

Sean Robb was not the flavour of the month either. Kathy was now daily contemplating how to deal with him. Did the gullible Sean believe the source of the story, whoever he was? Sean said he couldn't reveal the source, as he had sworn not to. Did Sean tell her out of genuine concern, to protect her and save her from pain? Or again did Sean tell her because he knew it would spell curtains for her association with his rival, secretly enjoying every minute of it? She had to find out. Sean was generally a decent and generous fellow, she had found. They had shared fun, laughter and some intimate moments together as they got to know each other. She would give Sean the benefit of the doubt for the time being, but she would have to confront him when the time was ripe to learn the truth.

Angus had never liked Sean from the first. Robb's attitude had been cold, on the several occasions they met, as if he was saying, 'This is my patch. This is my girl. You're not welcome, trespasser out!' It was like a feline leaving his scent to deter rivals.

Come what may, Angus would have to sort it out with Sean Robb. He had to arrive at the truth so his relationship with Kathy could continue, without any niggling question marks hanging over them. He would confront Sean at a convenient moment. After all, he didn't wish to upset Kathy.

'Angus, it's about time you arrived,' cried Kathy, chiding the big cop like a schoolboy. 'Nan's had the tea ready for ages.'

Angus replied, 'I had a wee problem with a wino in Portugal Street. He was singing in the middle of the road. Well, that's Police work for ye.'

Nan came in and greeted Angus warmly as usual. 'Nice to see ye, Angus. You're late this mornin'?' Angus recounted his tale about the wino, managing to get off the hook.

'Next week's the big dance, you'll remember, Angus,' said Kathy smiling. 'Are you looking forward to it?'

'Aye and no. Especially as I'll not have you as my partner,' replied Angus flatly.

Kathy replied wistfully, 'Sorry, Angus, you and I can't be together. But you'll be Nan's partner. Mum's really chuffed you invited her. But Sean did ask me first.'

'Well, Nan's great company. And a real good dancer too,' answered Angus.

Kathy went on. 'Still that was very kind of you. But we've been havin' an awful time trying to find something to wear.'

Angus said mischievously, 'Still looking for clothing coupons, no doubt?'

'Ach no, Nan can buy as many as she needs from customers,' answered Kathy, adding, 'But Mum and I found a good tailor locally and she's doing something nice for us.'

'Women! Women!' cried Angus, putting on his helmet to resume his beat.

Kathy said nervously, 'Angus, I hope there won't be any problems at the dance?'

There was no reply for several moments, as Kathy observed Angus blush.

'There'll be no problems, Kathy,' Angus replied. 'Nan and I will only be there for a good time.'

Kathy replied, 'When I told Sean you were going, that you were taking Mum to the Highlanders' Institute, he just looked kind of strange. All he said was "Jolly good".'

Angus did not reply. He sensed Kathy was concerned. Why she even bothered with Sean was a mystery to him. Sean always spelt trouble with a capital 'T'.

'Don't worry, Kathy. Everything will be hunky-dory on the night,' smiled Angus, giving her a reassuring peck on the cheek as he departed.

With the incarceration of Bull Bakley on an array of charges, the principal ones being Blackmarket racketeering, and resetting stolen goods, the CID's suspicion also alighted on him as a possible suspect in the case of Con Dougal's murder. In their eagerness to nail Bakley, the Police even threw in the charge of keeping a dog without a licence! And that was only round one Bakley had to face.

Round two would consist of the bigger and more serious charges of his involvement in the vicious attack on Constable Auchterlony and the assaults on Jock Grant and Kitty Cullen, including charges of running illegal shebeens, prostitution and illegal money lending rackets with their strong armed Tallymen.

Prospects did not look good for Bull Bakley, as the witnesses queued to testify. First and most damning was Slogger Struth, followed by Kitty Cullen who had overheard Bakley's self incrimination. Then there were the assault charges against Jock Grant and Kitty Cullen herself. The attack on Jock Grant's brother Mickey was under investigation, and the Police were actively seeking witnesses. It was clear a real storm was brewing for Bull Bakley, and it was clear he would be put away for a very long time, even if he was tried by the most moderate judge and jury in the land. Heaven help him if that judge turned out to be Lord Carmont!

Meanwhile Kathy had also been seeing Joe Cherkowski regularly as a member of her trio of boyfriends, which she had named her Three Musketeers, but minus the cry of 'All for one, and one for all'. Sean was not for Angus or Joe; Angus was not for Sean or Joe; Joe was neither for or against Sean or Angus, being normally at a distance. Kathy, however, was for all three. And all three were for Kathy. That was all she cared about.

Joe, or to give him his full title, Flight Navigator Sergeant Joe Cherkowski of the USAAF, was stationed at Prestwick engaged in ferrying aircraft, personnel, materials and supplies regularly from the USA to bases in Germany.

Of all three, Kathy was fair taken with Joe's charm and dark good looks, with his outgoing personality and infectious laugh. Joe was always bringing Kathy and Nan presents of nylons, perfumes and American whiskey as well as Camel cigarettes (Nan's favourites) so that they nicknamed him 'Uncle Sam'.

Joe simply enjoyed dispensing pleasure, and not for any ulterior motives. After all, these folk had endured long, grim war years of shortages and rationing. And so 'Uncle Sam' Cherkowski was bringing some light and happiness into their lives. Joe always treated Kathy with respect, with that extra attention which made local girls fall for Yanks in a big way. During his short visits from the USA and Europe, he always spent generously on Kathy, taking her out for meals, dancing, or to any show of her choice. Then again it might just be to see a Hollywood film which they both fancied.

Though Kathy and Joe often kissed and cuddled in intimate embrace, Joe had never come across strong, like Sean for example. Although Joe could be passionate, he was a man of maturity and experience who understood womankind. They had never made love in the full sense of the word, and to Kathy's Presbyterian upbringing, that could only happen after marriage. Then a man and woman would raise a family and live happily ever after. Kathy was no prude, but that is how she felt and Joe accepted it. And Kathy and Joe respected each other because of it.

Two weeks earlier, at a dance at his Prestwick base, Joe and she had gone out to take the air during a break. Joe had said, 'Kathy, I've grown so fond of you during my time in Skatland, that I want you to come over to the States soon. How do you feel about that, honey?'

'Sounds great, Joe. I've never been to America.'

'Well, my Mom and Pop would sure be glad to meet you. I've told them so much about you,' laughed Joe, continuing after a pause, 'Do you know what Mom said?'

Kathy queried, 'What did she say? And by the way, what are your parents' names?'

'Well, Mom is called Marylin. An' she's a real cutey,' answered Joe fondly, continuing, 'My Pop is called Stan, short for Stanislaus in Polish. He's a real great guy and runs the family furniture store in Boonton, New Jersey.'

Kathy reminded Joe, 'So what did your ma, Marylin, say about me?'

'Mom said, "Eh, Joe, when are you and this Skatch gal getting hitched?"' replied Joe sheepishly.

Kathy blushed as she replied, 'Well, well. That's going to need a lot of thought.'

Joe had suddenly taken Kathy in his arms, fixing her with an intense gaze. He slowly said, 'Please do, Kathy. I'll be released from the Airforce soon and will be able to settle down. Remember, you only have to say the word, and we'll book your passage.'

When Kathy had told Angus about what Joe had proposed, the big Cop had blushed and simply said, 'Lucky girl.' Actually Angus had felt bad at Kathy's revelation, and she instinctively sensed how he felt. Not saying any more she had gone onto the subject of the Highlanders' Ball instead. She would never have dreamed of telling Sean the same story for fear of his exploding. But Joe's surprising proposal was her special problem, which only she could sort out.

Finally the Friday night for the Annual Ball, to be held in the Highlanders' Institute in Elmbank Street, arrived. Kathy and Nan, to avoid any conflict between their partners, had arranged that Kathy leave first. Sean had arranged to pick Kathy up at 6.30 p.m. for a pre-dance meal and drink at the Rogano, that fitted in well with Angus collecting Nan a half hour later.

Kathy had plans to have a tactful word in Sean's ear in the Rogano.

Kathy and Nan wanted no trouble on their night out. She didn't want an audience, nor loud music playing when she gave Sean the message.

In spite of the rationing, both Kathy and her mum had managed to arrange for Jenny Minkin to tailor identical long blue silk skirts which, with their long sleeved white satin blouses and MacDonald tartan sashes, fitted the occasion to a tee. Sean looked resplendent in his Highland outfit with Robertson tartan kilt and light skin sporran, dark short tail cloth jacket with silver buttons, black vest, light hose with the customary sgian-dubh in the right hand stocking, sporting black lightweight shoes with silver buckles.

'My, Sean, you're looking really braw the night,' said Kathy admiringly.

Nan pitched in with, 'Aye big fellah, you've got the height and the legs fer it.'

'Thanks. You two girls are looking quite a treat, tae. Where did yees nick all the coupons for that lot?' chuckled Sean mischievously.

Kathy detected a whiff of whisky when she greeted Sean; at least he was in good humour which was something. Kathy thought, I'll need to keep an eye on him, to make sure he doesn't imbibe too much.

The Rogano was Kathy's favourite restaurant, and Sean knew it. That's why he had chosen it to ingratiate himself into her favour after his previous bad behaviour. Finishing their meal of lobster and crab salad, followed by the white wine of the house for Kathy and several stiff whiskies for Sean, they sat half listening to the background music.

Kathy spoke first. 'The meal was just great, Sean. Thanks. I'm looking forward to a nice time at the ball.'

'Me too. I love the Scottish country dancing,' said Sean keenly.

'Sean, can I ask you a favour? You won't be angry?' asked Kathy in subdued tones.

Sean regarded Kathy with raised eyebrows. 'This sounds serious, hen. What's bothering you?'

'You'll go easy on the hard stuff? You know how it affects you, and I want no problems here to-night.'

Sean reddened perceptibly. 'My, my. Are you saying I canna hold ma drink?' he retorted, a smile crossing his face. 'Don't worry, hen. I'll be a good boy. Scout's honour.'

Kathy's ire rose as she found words suddenly bursting from her lips. 'You know, Sean, that was a real low trick to play on Angus.' With her dander up, she continued, 'Lying about him being married – with a wean and all!'

'Whoa,' cried Sean sharply. 'I was telt he was married by one of his own pals!'

Kathy probed further. 'Who was it? Come on. Who was it then?'

Hesitantly, Sean replied, 'Yon fellow, Flockhart, was the one. He heard it from one of Auchterlony's room mates at the Training School.'

'Flockhart!' hissed Kathy indignantly. 'Lies, all lies! He's no friend of Angus's. Just Ratley's damned stool pigeon!'

'Okay, okay,' cried Sean, raising his hands in mock surrender. 'I only told you what I thought was gospel.'

Kathy said no more as her anger subsided. Whether Sean was telling the whole truth, she would never fathom. However, in the circumstances she had lost her customary cool. She calmed down, concluding it wiser to raise the matter at another opportune moment, when both parties were cold sober.

Angus wore a plain dark suit with white shirt, sporting a MacInnes tartan (his mother's) tie as he collected Nan at her flat.

'My, Nan, you're looking stunning. I thought at first you were Kathy's elder sister, instead of her ma,' kidded Angus.

Nan laughed loudly. 'Ach away wi' ye, Angus Auchterlony.'

'The taxi's waiting, Nan. We'll pop into More's Hotel for a quick refreshment, just to put you in the mood,' quipped Angus happily.

The ball was in full swing as Nan and Angus walked up to the ballroom, entering a packed hall as the lively quintet was bashing out a Dashing White Sergeant. Their entrance was soon caught by a smiling Kathy who gave a welcoming wave. A straight-faced Sean hadn't noticed their entrance, for he was deep into the dance rhythm

Kathy and Nan had deemed it better to keep their two partners separated, like Siamese fighting-fish. After the following waltz had finished, an ebullient and smiling Kathy came over to say hello.

'Hello, young lovers,' teased Kathy, adding, 'Enjoying yourselves?'

Nan said, 'My, it's busy the night, Where's the bold Sean?'

'He's away to the Gent's room. That's the second time he's been since he arrived.'

'He's too young to have a prostate problem,' said Angus coldly.

Nan silently whispered to herself, 'I hope Sean's not at what I think he's at.'

Her mother's telepathic thoughts seemed to trigger off a suspicion in Kathy's mind. Why had Sean excused himself similarly at the Rogano? Maybe he had a weak bladder? No way! Sean was in perfect health. Maybe there was another obvious, and more worrying, reason.

There was. Sean was swigging secretly from a half bottle of Haig's whisky in the Gents' toilet which he had earlier concealed in his jacket pocket. With the intake of alcohol, Sean's character transformation was taking place. Sean was no longer the pleasant and good Mr Jekyll. He had been transformed into that saturnine Sean, who Kathy and Nan feared. And yet Sean had promised Kathy he'd behave! That was before the drink transformed him into the evil Mr Hyde!

It was not long before Angus began to experience hassle. It started with Strip the Willow, and continued through a Scottish Waltz and an Eightsome Reel as someone kept bumping him. Whenever he turned round, there seemed to be a smirking Sean Robb in the vicinity. Both Kathy and Nan couldn't help noticing Sean's behaviour. Angus's patience was close to breaking. He ushered Kathy from the floor, saying, 'Let's have a soft drink. I'm thirsty and your feet must be killing you.'

Kathy quipped. 'I'm away to powder my nose. I'll no' be a minute, Angus. Meet you in the hall, okay?'

As Angus entered the Gents', he caught his breath for there was the *bête noir* in person, Auld Nick, in the shape of a drunken Sean Robb, guzzling from a partially drained half bottle of whisky.

'Feck me, if it's no Auchterlony himself. Christ they're lettin' onybody in nowadays, even the feckin Polis!' slurred Sean, his eyes rolling madly.

'Aye, they're even letting folk like you in too, Sean,' quipped Angus in jocular vein, trying to humour Robb, not wishing to have a confrontation with a drunk man. Angus hurriedly washed his hands and departed to the sound of 'Bastard Polis' ringing in his ears.

The second half of the ball would prove unpleasantly memorable. Angus, Kathy and Nan were convinced Sean was deliberately bumping Angus, trying to provoke a reaction.

It was during a slow waltz that a passing Sean stuck out a leg, catching Angus off-balance. As Angus toppled to the ground a drunken voice could be heard roaring, 'Thar she blows!'

Kathy immediately broke free from Sean's embrace, crying, 'Let me free, Sean. I saw what you did there. You're nothing but a common hooligan. I'll be seeing myself home. Goodnight!'

Sean was grinning with glee over his rival's predicament, pleased at the sight of Kathy and Nan struggling to raise Angus back to the vertical.

'I'm okay, girls. I think it's time to leave,' said Angus rubbing his left leg, struggling to restrain his strong right hand from landing a punch on Robb's drunken visage.

Two burly ushers had been observing Sean, and came over to enquire if Angus was all right, then went directly for Sean.

Without a moment's delay, a loudly protesting Sean was being frog-marched from the floor, down into the reception hall and then ejected unceremoniously down the stairs into Elmbank Street. Lying on the bottom step, his kilt above his knees, Sean continued to shout drunken abuse at the closed door behind.

'Good God. What's the Highlanders' coming to, with riff-raff like that. He canna be a Gael. He's a disgrace to the national garb!' commented one usher to the other.

Outside, raising himself to his knees with great difficulty, the inebriated kilty lurched off unsteadily in the direction of Bath Street.

Meanwhile Kathy and Nan were in turmoil, as they quickly collected their coats, including Sean's.

Kathy pleaded, 'Oh, Angus, please run and see after that damn fool. He'll do himself an injury, or end up in the Clyde!'

'Okay, Kathy. You and Nan take a taxi home. Here's ten quid. I'll see ye all to-morrow,' cried Angus leaving hurriedly.

It did not take Angus long to locate the figure of the drunken, cursing Sean, his kilt and jacket stained with mud.

As Angus drew alongside Sean, he said gently, 'Come on, Sean. It's a hotel for you in Bath Street. Time for bed!'

'Adulterer,' blasphemed Sean. 'Away ye adulterous, two-timing bastart!'

Angus ignored Sean's ramblings, taking his arm in a lock, supporting his drunken weight, as he attempted to cut through the dark lane between the High School and Bath Street. There Angus planned to hail a taxi to a small hotel nearby.

'Polis, Polis. Help, Polis!' cried Sean. 'Leave me alone, ye bastart.'

'Come on, Sean,' replied Angus. 'I am the Polis. And you're for your bed.'

It was at this juncture that a passing Constable happened on the scene; as he shone his torch down the lane it caught two struggling men, like rabbits caught in a beam.

'Hey! What's going on here?' challenged the young Cop in a harsh official voice.

'This bastart's trying to rip me off, Constable!' shrieked Sean loudly.

Angus peered and suddenly shouted, 'Ken Hardie! It's me, Angus, Ken!'

'Holy Moses. Angus, is it really you? Surely you're no a Robin Hood on yer own account?' quizzed Constable Hardie excitedly.

Angus blurted, 'In the name o' Mercy, Ken. I'm just an off-duty Cop trying to help a drunken neighbour to a hotel in Bath Street. Please give me a hand.'

'Get him away quickly, Angus. I don't want to have to report this. I'll hail you a taxi. Wait in the main street,' cried Constable Hardie as he left.

It was minutes later that the taxi arrived, and a comotose Sean Robb was whisked away to a small local hotel. There Angus booked Sean in, then helped him to his room and into bed, before making his own way home to Partick.

It was a couple of days before Angus managed to see Kathy and Nan, after the Highlanders' fiasco, to inform them of his escapade with the drunken Sean. When they questioned why he was late coming, Angus said nothing but produced a small case.

'What's all this?' they asked inquisitively.

'It's the Corporation Medal for Bravery,' replied Angus in an off-hand manner, adding, 'I was presented with it yesterday by the Lord Provost himself. I didn't want to say.'

'Oh, yes. For stopping the runaway horses in West Street,' said Kathy, admiring the silver medal with green ribbon and red edges.

'See, his name is on it. Constable Angus Auchterlony – For Bravery,' cried Nan proudly.

Before he could utter another syllable, Angus was being smothered in kisses and hugged tightly by the two women.

'Ladies, ladies, I cannae breathe for all your perfumes!' pleaded Angus.

Nan said suddenly, 'I'm away to make ye the best cuppa tea, wi' the biggest roll and sausage ye've ever had, Angus ma hero. You deserve it!'

Kathy laughed at her mother's fussing over Angus like a mother hen.

Angus decided not to say a thing about the imminent Police Commendation which was in the pipeline for his gallant action in foiling the hold-up at Grace's Fish Restaurant. That would have been too much. Over the score in the circumstances. Besides, he would never have got out of the shop in one piece, with all the fuss!

Presently Kathy drew near and said in subdued tones, 'Angus, I've finished with Sean Robb for good. I told him on Monday not to come back. He was really upset but Nan and I have had quite enough.'

Angus replied, 'Too bad, Kathy. But I canna say I'm sorry. Robb was asking for it.' There was a pause, then he continued, 'You know, Kathy, when you stopped talking to me, the bottom fell out of my life. I planned to chuck the Police and join the Palestine Police, just to get away from here.'

'Goodness,' cried Kathy. 'I'm glad you didn't. You could have been blown up by those terrorists.'

Angus suddenly changed the subject as he queried, 'What about your deliveries?'

Kathy replied, 'Och, we've looked into that. We've chosen a supplier from the Fruit Market, by the name of Duncan Matheson and highly recommended.'

'Aye, he's redheaded. And a spunky wee bugger too,' laughed Nan as she entered with the tea and rolls.

Some time later, Angus had been through two busy weeks at the High Court giving evidence against Bull Bakley and his gang. As prosecution witnesses, Slogger Struth, Kitty Cullen and Jock Grant gave their damning evidence before a severe looking Lord Sorn, as the habitual smirk slowly but surely evaporated from Bakley's ugly, and increasingly distraught countenance.

The most damning evidence had come from the Prosecution's main witness, Struth, who had been propositioned by Bull Bakley to lead the attack on Constable Auchterlony in the first instance.

The jury found Bakley guilty of masterminding a premeditated and vicious attack on Constable Auchterlony, endangering life and limb and amounting to attempted murder. The accused was also found guilty of assault and intimidation in the case of Kitty Cullen and of assault in the case of Jock Grant who had gone to his daughter's rescue. Taking in the seriousness of the charges, together with Bakley's previous record, the jury accepted the judge's advice. Lord Sorn had no hesitation in sending Bakley away for twelve years' hard labour.

Bakley was led away, a broken individual. The witnesses would never forget the menacing stare which emanated from Bakley's eyes as he was led away to where expectant Prison Officers waited.

'Good riddance!' was all Angus said.

Kitty Cullen snarled, 'They should throw away the key with scum like him!'

'Aye, or hang the bastard,' said Jock Grant, finally adding, 'Thank God it's all over now.'

Lilly Grant said, 'Aye, Da. I'll sure second that.'

The case of Con Dougal's murder had not been solved. As Detective Moran said to Angus in confidence, 'We'll never really know for sure whether Slogger Struth or his big boss Scottie Dunn set Dougal up. Many of us think that they did, but we cannot prove it.'

Angus kept silent but thought to himself, scum like that are better out of the way. Presently he said, 'Aye, Ed, justice has not only been done, it has been seen to be done!'

'Yes, Angus. That's very important. Even in the case of Mickey Grant's attackers.'

Angus quipped, 'Aye, and that brave old witness, Liza Calder. She's the salt o' the earth. What would we do without such good people? Her evidence sure did for Sluch Docherty and his two pals!'

'They're all safely locked in the Bar-Ell [Barlinnie Prison] now,' smiled Ed Moran with satisfaction.

CHAPTER 19

Angus was down in the dumps since Kathy had surprisingly informed him of her impending visit to America.

Kathy had been seeing Joe Cherkowski regularly as a matter of course, along with Angus and Sean Robb too, treating them simply as 'men friends' with whom to enjoy a night out at the dancing or pictures.

To Kathy, Sergeant Joe Cherkowski was the one who knew how to appeal to a woman's needs in that special way which the other two local men could not. It was those minute courtesies and respects, his soft American accent and his lavishing attention on her all the time he was in her company. Then there were the gifts. It was unfair to expect the other two to compete with the Yank who had the resources of his Prestwick base commissary.

'Look, honey, I got you some nylons and the Chanel perfume you like from the States!' Joe would announce on his return, after ferrying aircraft and personnel from America and Germany, stopping off regularly at Prestwick. There were always Camel cigarettes and a bottle of Jack Daniels and Southern Comfort for Nan too.

Both Kathy and her mum Nan adored the tall, dark, handsome Yank with the infectious smile and outgoing personality. Joe brought a touch of glamour to the grey, still rationed Gorbals. When asked what he thought of the place, Joe would sigh.

'Jesus, Gorbals makes the Bronx look like Manhatten!'

Joe would frequently drop in unannounced, in his USAAF jeep with the big white star on it, shouting in a loud American accent, to the dismay and alarm of customers present, 'Yippee, folks. Look who's here. It's none other than your ole buddy Joe Cherkowski!'

'Joe!' was all an ecstatic Kathy and Nan could reply before being seized by the huge, leather jacketed Yank in a bear hug.

It was not as if the presents Joe brought were meant for buying privileges or favours. No, Kathy had fallen for the man himself. Sure, the gifts did make a difference to a young woman brought up in the grim war years of shortages and rationing. Joe brought a touch of romance into her life, like the Hollywood pictures. Perhaps she was infatuated with someone from a different world, but she liked the way Joe treated her and understood why all the girls fell head over heels for the Yanks.

But as Sean Robb would reflect, in the manner of envious British males mostly away during the War years, 'The trouble wi' them bliddy Yanks is they're over paid, over sexed and over here!' It never occurred to Sean that whilst the Yanks naturally availed themselves of what was willingly on offer by a male-starved female population, America also helped win the War.

Angus and Sean, Kathy mused, had always treated her just as a Glasgow lass would have expected a local swain to. A night out for a drink followed by the pictures, or perhaps a show or the dancing, would see either Angus or Sean escorting her home. Arriving at Kathy's close there would be the chat telling her of their adventures at work, or describing their cuts and bruises in the rugby. There was the ritual 'wee kiss and cuddle' under the gas mantle and, regardless of the intensity of their ardour, Kathy would permit nothing more, Angus or Sean eventually departing feeling on top of the world!

Joe treated Kathy like a million dollars, taking her to the pictures, or dancing to big bands like Joe Loss, Ambrose and Geraldo, or by taxi to the Empire theatre, followed by drinks and a slap up meal in the Rogano or Central Hotel, no expense spared. Though Kathy and Joe had often kissed and cuddled in intimate embrace, of all three, Joe was the only one capable of kindling the flame of her unfulfilled desires.

As Kathy stood enfolded in Joe's strong arms, pinioned against his broad chest, his gentle voice whispering loving things into her ears, she would become mesmerized and yearning for love.

Even though Joe would become passionate, he never came across too forcibly. Kathy would never have allowed that, even though at times she was on the edge. Joe was a man of maturity and experience who understood Womankind. He and Kathy had never made love and, according to Kathy's Presbyterian upbringing, this could only happen after marriage, when man and wife would raise a happy family. Kathy was no prude, but that was how she felt, and Joe accepted it. Kathy liked Joe because of it – and she knew Joe was the one for her.

Kathy had revealed the news to Angus, as gently and tactfully as possible.

'Angus, you know I have a great regard for you. You know, last week Joe Cherkowski asked me to become engaged after a dinner-dance in Prestwick.'

Angus just looked at her, flushing slightly and saying nothing.

'Joe has invited me over to Boonton, New Jersey to meet his folks,' continued Kathy hesitantly.

'Ah suppose that's where the engagement is to be held,' replied Angus in a casual manner, as if it didn't matter to him one way or the other.

'Yes, his folks, Stanislaus his Pop, and Marylin his Mom, are dying to meet the cute little Skatch lass!' replied Kathy limply, with a half smile. 'Will you come and see me off with Nan, Angus?'

'You can count on me. Ah'll be there by hook or by crook!' said Angus softly. But Auchterlony's heart had slid right down into his size 10 boots.

All Nan had said when informed by her daughter was, 'If that's whit ye want, hen, that's all right wi' me. Joe's a braw big fellah. He's a fine catch for any lassie. And he'll be returnin' to civvy life over in America tae.'

Deep in her heart though, Nan was as sad as Angus. How would she cope without her friend and companion, her Kathy, her own wee lassie!

Some claim trials and tribulations come in threes. Angus's third trial came when Constable Duncan Two-in-the-Hoose Gunn, another senior Cop, intercepted Angus on his early shift. The name Two-in-the-Hoose came from Gunn's instant reply, 'I hiv two in the hoose' whenever anyone claimed to own a certain thing. Angus had often joked he would say he had a wife at home in order to hear Gunn's reply.

On this occasion, there came an event which showed one of the sadder aspects of a Cop's duty, proving the old song that 'A Policeman's Lot is Not a Happy One'.

'Auchterlony, this is Mr McGuigan from the Blytheswood Shipbuilding Company in Scotstoun. I'm afraid we have some terrible news to carry to Mrs Lyall this day,' announced Constable Gunn grimly.

'Her husband was killed in the Yard this morning,' said McGuigan solemnly.

Thus a cruel Fate was leaving Molly Lyall, aged twenty-two years old, with five fatherless kids and the irreparable loss of the family's bread-winner. Only the previous night, Andy Lyall, a small cheery young man with a shock of fair hair, a shipyard riveter, had come home loaded with sweets for his bairns after a win on the dogs, and after a few pints at Hugh Boyle's pub in Gorbals Street. Andy was not a heavy drinker, and his only pleasures revolved around his wife and kids, having a few pints during the week with a few bob on the dogs and horses in which he just managed to keep ahead of Tich the bookie.

The Lyall children consisted of twins Willie and John aged four, Mary aged three, Tam aged two and baby Annie aged nine months.

The party of three made their way to upper Nicholson Street, formerly Apsley Place, to a run down close and knocked on the Lyalls' single-end door, two up with the name marked in pencil on the faded plaster wall. As soon as they entered the dark close with the water stained walls and grimy and peeling plaster, the smell of overflowed toilets assailed their nostrils. The owners of this slum property, living in the South of England, cared little for the plight of their poor tenants; neither did the local factor so long as the rents were paid on time. Molly Lyall sensed it was bad news immediately she opened the door, seeing three men standing there like birds of ill-omen.

'Oh God, it's no mah Andy?' she shrieked.

Mr McGuigan, the shipyard Welfare man, took Molly by the shoulder and said gently that he had some bad news for her.

'Mrs Lyall, I am sad to tell you that your husband Andrew Lyall was killed early this morning in the Yard.'

Molly Lyall, a small figure of five feet two, stood in frozen silence, supporting baby Annie rapped in a tartan shawl. On hearing the news she cried, 'Oh, Jesus in Heaven, no mah Andy!' then passed out.

Luckily the two constables reacted quickly, catching her and the baby before she fell backwards towards the grate.

'Is there any brandy in the hoose, I wonder?' said Constable Gunn urgently.

'I don't think so, not here,' replied Angus. 'I'll away to the nearest pub. I'll not be a jiffy!'

'Gie her some water, maybe that'll help,' said Mr McGuigan with concern as he held baby Annie, the latter regarding her siblings who milled around as if it was all a kiddies' game.

'Mammy gone bye-byes?' smiled John aged four.

Around ten minutes later, a breathless Angus returned with the brandy, and after a few sips Molly awoke to grim reality, unsure at first as to the identity of the men standing before her.

'How did puir Andy die?' pleaded Molly.

Mr McGuigan explained in a soft voice that her man had slipped on a frosty plate with his tackety boots, and fallen into the depth of the tanker's hold he was working on.

His last words were, according to the foreman-shipwright who held him in his arms, 'Jimmy, tell mah Molly and the bairns – ah'll always luv them.' Then Andy died.

This piece of news only brought on more chagrin, as Molly's pitiful laments increased.

'Oh God, ma puir Andy. Whit am ah gonna dae wi'oot ye? Deid, ah cannae believe it. Whit are me an' the weans gonna dae wi'oot ye?' she sobbed. 'Never gonna see oor Andy ever again!'

Baby Annie, in her mother's arms, just looked up into Molly's tearful face, and smiled sweetly as she pointed to the wee black and white kitten playing with a ball of wool. The three grown men, with heaving chests and bursting lungs, came near to tears as they comforted the distraught young widow.

A knock at the door introduced a homely woman who said her name was Senga, the next door neighbour, and could she be of help? Senga, after being appraised of the situation, immediately offered to fetch

Molly's doctor. Dr Gellen was not far away and could provide a sedative, Senga would look after the kids who knew her as 'Aunty Senga' until the Corporation Welfare could arrange for their temporary care, until Molly recovered.

Mr McGuigan explained. 'After your doctor's been, Mrs Lyall, the Welfare will arrange to come over with the Union man to put you in the picture. Just try to rest, hen, we'll take care of things.'

Constable Gunn explained subsequently to Angus about shipyard workers. 'They poor buggers don't get a pension, ye know, like us in the Police. Molly Lyall will get his wages due, his lying time. Likely his workmates will have a "whip round" for the widow.'

'I suppose the Union may help too?' suggested Angus.

Gunn replied. 'Maybe the Union, the Boilermakers' or whatever, will be seeking grounds for compensation – depends on safety at the Yard.'

On returning to his little room and kitchen in Merkland Street, Partick, Angus could neither sleep nor eat. The big fellah was weighed down with compassion for Molly Lyall and her bairns. He recalled the day he first laid eyes on the young freckled-faced mother, her long coppery hair flowing in the breeze as she played on the swings with her kids, that fine summer's day, a lifetime away, in the kiddies' play-park near the railway bridge in Cumberland Street.

'Look mammy, Polis, Polis,' shouted the twins as they pointed through the railings at Angus's tall helmet which fascinated them.

Angus was feeling in good spirits after coming off back shift. He had popped into see Jock Grant and things seemed to be coming right in his world. Lilly was fully fit and back to work at Twomax's and the great news was his brother, Micky, had been discharged from the Victoria Infirmary, though Micky unfortunately would carry the razor scar on his cheek, courtesy of Sluch Docherty, for the rest of his life.

What had really made both Jock and Auchterlony brim with satisfaction was Ed Moran informing them that a witness had bravely come forward regarding Micky's attack. An elderly woman named Liza Calder had seen and recognised three men emerging from the very same close in Cumberland Street where Micky had been found badly beaten shortly afterwards. Liza had informed the Police.

'It was yon Docherty, the wan they cry Sluch,' Liza had testified 'alang wi' Jim Pender and his pal, Chas McBroom. The three o' them, awright. I knew their mithers – a' deid noo. The puir souls would turn in their graves if they kent!'

Angus endured a ranting Sergeant Rat Ratley at backshift muster, going on about nuisances like stray animals, vandals and a street musician in particular, who were plaguing the area. It was obvious to most of the Cops who was the musician Ratley had in mind. It was none other than the one and only Twanky Macalister, most likely the worse fiddle player in the whole of the Gorbals and the Sou' Side – if not the World!

'Get the bloody high diddler, Auchterlony,' hissed Rat Ratley. 'Get the high diddler. He's on your beat now!'

'High diddler, Sergeant?' asked Auchterlony sheepishly.

'The bloody high diddler, man!' roared the Sergeant with screwed-up face. 'The fiddler, ye great loupin' stumer, Auchterlony!'

A sudden wave of tittering broke from the ranks of the dozen or so assembled cops who sneaked amused glances at the red-faced Auchterlony.

With Kathy's impending engagement in America, her need for a new wardrobe was paramount. So Nan asked a friend to look after things at the Fruit Box as she and Kathy set out early for the shops in town. They spent a tiring morning searching around Sauchiehall Street, visiting Daly's, Henderson's, Watt Brothers', Pettigrew's, Copland and Lyle's and Treron's, trying to find suitable travel wear and dress for Kathy's imminent engagement party. They were disappointed, however, with the limited choice of utility fashions on offer. After a quick bite to eat in Miss Cranston's Tearoom and a chance to rest their tired feet, Nan said, 'Kathy, why don't you take Joe's advice?'

'How do you mean, Mum?' came the reply.

Nan smiled. 'Buy your engagement dress in America, woman, it'll be a lot easier.'

'You're dead right, Mum,' replied Kathy who went on, 'And I'll have a wider choice over there, with no damn coupons to worry about. Brilliant idea, Mum.' So that's what Kathy decided to do.

It was not long before the day for Kathy's departure for America arrived. A subdued Angus arrived at the door, ready to carry Kathy's big travel case down to the waiting taxi, her large trunk having been uplifted by the shipping agents the day before.

'I see you're fighting fit, Kathy,' said Angus, trying to put on a brave face which belied his true feelings.

A quiet Nan greeted him with a kiss. 'Angus, nice to see you, son.'

Kathy looked smart in her brown tweed suit and tan felt hat as the trio alighted at the Central Station for their journey to Greenock. Nan was there to see her lassie off to America, after which she would return to business, a happier yet sadder mother.

On the way, Kathy explained all the trouble Joe's father Stan had gone to in arranging her passage. Stan had arranged, through a family friend in New York, a direct passage for Kathy from Greenock to New York on a fast cargo-passenger. The Anchor Line *Egidia* carried thirty-six passengers, rather than the twelve passengers accommodated aboard her sister ships *Elysia* and *Eucadia*. Joe had insisted on funding her travel fare and expenses but Kathy would have none of it, saying, 'Once we're hitched you can pay, not before, Joe.'

Joe had just shrugged and laughed. 'Okay, honey. You win.'

Arriving at Greenock Pier, Angus and his charges made their way to a big new ship tied to the dock.

'There she is. See the *Egidia*,' cried Kathy, pointing excitedly like a child.

Angus observed, 'She looks low in the water. She must have her cargo aboard.'

'Aye, I was told they load her up first before letting the passengers aboard,' replied Kathy.

'Well, lassie,' said Nan sadly, struggling to control her tears. 'Looks as if yon time's arrived?'

An equally tearful daughter replied, hugging her mum tightly. 'Aye, Mum. I'll miss you . . . and Angus here too.'

A smartly dressed purser beckoned them aboard. The trio made their way up the gang plank, Angus carrying her big leather suitcase till they met the purser on the deck.

'This way folks. I'll take that case, sir,' announced the purser, as he paused to ask, 'Is it Miss Kathleen MacDonald who's travelling?'

'Yes, that's me,' replied Kathy smartly.

The white clad purser showed them to Kathy's cabin, saying, 'I'll check your travel documents and passport, Miss MacDonald. Feel free to inspect the cabin.'

Nan and Angus were impressed by the passenger accomodation, with their private cabins and toilets. Other smiling passengers were already aboard, and they seemed pleasant people. The purser presently announced the vessel would be sailing soon, on the turn of the tide, and would visitors please vacate the ship. Exchanging light-hearted banter as Kathy leaned over the ship's rail, Nan and Angus finally left, waving cheerily.

'See ye in three weeks' time, hen,' cried a tearful Nan.

'Safe journey, Kathy and good luck,' was all Angus could call, his heart thumping against his rib-cage. He had never felt such an overwhelming sense of loss as pervaded his being at that moment.

As Angus departed, the figure of Kathy at the ship's rail etched itself into his mind, with her radiant smile and coppery locks flowing in the breeze. It was as if a beloved and precious dove was being released, never to return.

'This nearly was mine,' yearned Angus regretfully.

CHAPTER 20

Angus was soon back on the beat, and Nan to her cheery, chattering customers as life went on as usual. Angus was pining for Kathy, and his reaction was to redouble his efforts in the pursuance of his duties. First target in Angus's sights was Twanky MacAlister, the street musician who was a constant source of irritation and annoyance to local pub landlords and their patrons. Twanky had not been seen on Angus's patch for some time. The reason was simply that Twanky was plaguing victims in other areas, like Calton and Hutchesontown, until having had a surfeit of Twanky's music and singing he was unceremoniously ejected by popular demand, So what did Twanky do? He returned to his old stamping grounds in the Gorbals, and onto Constable Auchterlony's patch.

A few words of introduction to Twanky Macalister and his mangey, mongrel bitch would be in order.

Twanky was a street musician, using the word in its loosest sense, who played for the cinema queues at the Coliseum and Bedford in Eglinton Street and outside the Green's Picture House in Ballater Street. He afterwards installed himself, with his bitch Bess, outside the local pubs in the area, 'playing' his fiddle and holding pub audiences to ransom. The horrified punters, either too drunk or terrified of Bess's growls, would have to pay up to escape his screechings and vocal assassination of Old Scottish Songs.

Macalister, a diminutive balding figure, with the remains of a former mop of ginger hair, always sat on a three-legged stool at the entrance of his favourite pubs, with Bess tied to the legs by a long clothes line with an old bunnet for donations. Twanky and Bess had been chased or banned from more pubs than Father Mulrooney in nearby St John's had taken

229

Confession. The most virulent complaint emanated from Vogt's pub in Norfolk Street where Macalister had been swearing at punters leaving the pub.

After what Twankey had considered his delectable singing of 'Loch Lomond', with violin accompaniment, all of which had failed to bring forth any bounty from Vogt's unappreciative patrons, Macalister tried again. Presently the 'sound' of 'Bonnie Mary of Argyle' was followed by 'Will Ye No Come Back Again'.

At that moment, a bachle emerging from Vogt's bar exclaimed in agony, 'In the name o' the wee hairy man. Whit was that racket ye wis makin'? If that wis "Will Ye No Come Back Again", ah hope tae Christ ye and yer bliddy dug wilnae, by Jeese!'

Holding out his bunnet, Twanky pleaded for a few coppers.

'That's fur the dug,' mumbled the bachle sarcastically, throwing a penny into the hat. 'It sings far better'n ye dae!'

At that final taunt, Twanky lifted the coin from the hat, hurling it at the drunken bachle, screaming, 'Awa wi' ye, ye bliddy scunner. Ye dinnae know guid music when ye hear it! Ye wouldna gie a biddy a fright on a dark night!'

At this Twanky released Bess with wild exhortations to 'bite the bastart's leg!'

At this juncture Angus arrived on the scene. Quickly seizing the dog's rope leash and pulling on it, he yelled, 'Call off the dog now! Right this minute. Do you hear me!'

'Bess, get aff. Aff, aff dae ye hear. Ye heidcase basket, aff!'

The dog finally released its hold on the traumatised bachle who shot off without further ado, crying, 'Ah'm oota-the-way o' ye feckin' nutters!'

'People likes o' yon heid-banger disnae appreciate guid music,' said Twanky disgustedly.

Angus beheld the figure before him, and felt a kind of pity for the pathetic duo, replying, 'Well, that's a matter of opinion. Now what's your name and address?'

'Twanky – they a' ken me here aboots,' replied the wee man.

Angus challenged. 'It's your real name I want!'

By this time a crowd of pub clients and passers-by had gathered on the pavement.

'Constable Auchterlony,' screamed the pub owner, 'this bloody nutter should be locked up and the key thrown away!'

'That's enough, Bob,' countered Angus in a firm voice. 'Come on, folks, break it up. This is a Police matter!'

'The bum hasnae even got a licence!' accused a fat man with a beer belly.

Angus resumed his questioning and soon learned that Twanky's real name was surprisingly Jeremiah Macalister, and that he stayed in a single end in Hospital Street. As Angus entered his details in his notebook, he mused, 'Why couldn't the bugger plague the Central Division? He stays in their area.'

'Ah bet ye spelt mah name wrang!' said Twanky mischievously.

As Angus regarded the unshaven old fellah, he warmed to Macalister as he remembered people like him amongst the travelling folk in Kintyre. As a young boy, Angus would sit sharing their cans of hot tea with slabs of bread and corned beef as they sang round the bonfires on the beach overlooking Davaar Island of a summer's evening.

Angus showed the old rascal his notebook.

'Ah knew it. Yer wrang. Yer wrang. It's spelt Macalister no MacAllister!' laughed Twanky triumphantly.

'It's near enough,' replied an embarrassed Auchterlony.

'Well, no really. The Beak'll say you've got the wrang punter in the Court. An' besides there's an ell o' a difference. An' whit are the charges?' quipped Twanky impishly.

In a formal tone, Angus read out the following, viz: disturbing the peace; lacking control of a dog without a licence; dog attacking a member of the public; foul language; playing in a public thoroughfare without a licence; causing a public nuisance and obstructing the public footpath.

'I think that should be enough to be going on with, Macalister? I am taking you in on these charges. You will accompany me to the station, now,' concluded Constable Auchterlony.

'And whaur's yer instrument? An' aye, whit tune will ye be playing?' questioned Twanky laughing.

'What the Hell are you talking about man?' said the puzzled officer.

'Ye hivnae ony musical instrument or tune for me tae accompany ye!'

Suddenly the humour of Twankie's remarks made Angus smile. Unclipping his hand-cuffs, the big Cop held them high above the diminutive joker and said markedly, 'Maybe this particular instrument will play the right tune, if I slip them on ye?'

The little figure suddenly deflated as he said, 'Okay, Constable, you win. Ah'll come quietly. Lead on, MacDuff!'

As Angus came off duty, he paused wearily at the corner of South Portland Street as he spotted three wee girls playing. There was something very familiar about the wee, dark girl skipping the rope birled by her two pals. As a Cop's mind is never off duty, he knew there was something significant about this particular lassie. She wore a short cotton frock, a yellow ribbon in her long hair and dark 'sannys' with white ankle socks on her feet.

Angus smiled as he caught sight of her navy knickers every time she skipped the ropes. The dark haired girl didn't know, nor cared, that schoolboys across the street were having a good giggle too. The girl regarded Angus as she skipped, with a provocative smile, as if she knew something that he didn't, chanting rhythmically,

'I'm a little brownie, dressed in brown,

See ma knickers hangin' doon.

One, two, three, four

Shut the door.

Five, six, seven, eight

Here's she's coming thro' the gate!'

Then it hit him and he knew her. The wee skipper was the girl who had hired a bike from the well known cycle hirer, Darkie Marshall, and failed to return it on time. Her name began with an 'S' Auchterlony recalled. Something like Sally or Sadie, he wasn't sure which. But she took the bike back two days late, as she wanted to keep it, not having enough pocket money to pay for a longer hire. Her dad gave her a leathering for her pains, as Angus recalled.

Anyway, Angus was more intent making it back home to Partick for a roll, fried egg and tea, followed by a good sleep, as he strode purposely to the Bridge Street Underground.

The sight of the wee girls skipping made Angus think of Kathy, now far across the ocean in America. How great it would have been for him and Kathy to have been married, raising a family in blissful harmony. But that was impossible, mused Angus, remembering the Gilbert and Sullivan song about Constabulary Duties to be done. Kathy's lot would not be a happy one either, being a Cop's wife always worrying about her man's safety. Then there were the shifts, the unsociable hours and never a Saturday off like ordinary people. You became a social leper! Ach yes, Kathy was better off with Joe. He'll have a steady nine-to-five job too.

The next day a message awaited Angus from his pal, Constable Macrea who hailed from Beauly, to contact Nan at the Fruit Box as soon as possible. Passing on his beat, Angus slipped into the fruit shop in Norfolk Street to be met by an excited Nan who blurted out, 'Oh Angus, I phoned Kathy yesterday. She's arriving home next Friday. Can ye get time off to come wi' me and meet her?'

'You bet, I'll be there,' announced Angus excitedly, 'even if I've to resign the Force!'

Luckily Fate had seen to it that Angus would be able to arrange his shifts to suit that day. Nan phoned again later to learn that Kathy would meet them at the Central Station at the appointed hour, as she would make her own way by train from Greenock to Glasgow with light luggage.

Angus was on edge waiting for Friday to arrive when he and a highly excited Nan stood waiting expectantly on the Central platform for the arrival of the Greenock train. Presently with straining necks they watched with pounding hearts the engine steaming alongside the platform, hissing like a living thing. Soon all the carriage doors flew open like cages, releasing hordes of eager passengers. There, emerging from a rear carriage, was a sight which made them gasp. Kathy stood like a dream in a smart American outfit – light blue suit, white hat and matching white high heeled shoes.

A tearful Nan surged into Kathy's arms, as mother and daughter kissed

233

and hugged each other tightly, Angus hanging back.

Kathy stood regarding Angus from a short distance away. In that instant all her doubts and fears vanished forever. It was the sight of the big, self-effacing Cop with the round face, sandy hair and blue eyes that she had been missing all those weeks away!

'Och, Angus man. How I have missed you,' cried Kathy softly as she threw her arms around his neck, kissing him passionately on the lips.

Angus, holding her tightly in a bear-hug, and oblivious to the world about him, answered, 'Kathy, Kathy, I have missed you so!'

'Angus and I are treating you to a slap up meal in the Central Hotel over yonder, and we've reserved a table for three,' announced a radiant Nan.

Over a fine dinner, Kathy told them how she had enjoyed the trip both ways with the Anchor Line, and how good the service and accommodation were.

She explained that the Cherkowskis had arranged her return passage on the *Elysia*, another fast cargo-passenger ship with a smaller twelve passengers complement than the outward *Egidia*, but with equally good service.

It was then that Kathy released her *bombshell*. She said simply: 'It's all off between Joe and me! I realised it was a massive crush that I had for him. A kind of infatuation for the glamour of another world and way of life. The Cherkowskis gave me a great time showing me around New York, Manhatten, the Empire State Building, Ellis Island and the Statue of Liberty. The lot!'

Kathy explained how upset Joe and his family had been. They were very nice people, who lived in a grand house with two big cars as long as buses. She had bought terrific clothes in Macey's store, and presents for Nan and Angus too, but she wasn't telling. She had insisted on paying her own boat fares under the circumstances, but announced that she and Joe, and Joe's family, would remain firm friends. The news was like simultaneous thunderbolts striking from Heaven. In unison, Nan and Angus let out cries of sheer delight.

'Kathy. You're home again. That's all that matters,' cried a delirious Angus.

Nan, who'd taken earlier nips from Angus's flask, blurted out tearfully, 'Ach hell, Kathy. We're both chuffed to see ye back hame, hen. Back hame in Scotia, where ye belong.'

The trio were soon fortified with a several large whiskies as Nan said sadly, 'And all they claes tae ye bought for the ceremony!'

'Ach wheesht, Ma,' replied Kathy, winking at a blushing Angus. 'Dinnae worry, I may still find a use for them.'

Nan, soon getting the drift of the conversation, answered in kind, 'You're so right, lassie. There's other fish in the sea tae fry.'

As they rode home in the taxi feeling jolly after a fine meal, Angus recalled looking up into the roof girders of the station as they waited for Kathy's train. He remembered seeing a large cock pigeon courting his hen with loud cooing sounds.

Angus Auchterlony suddenly felt light hearted and silly. He felt happy and developed an overwhelming desire to coo like a cock pigeon! Maybe it was the whisky? Maybe it was because Kathy had returned home?

His Kathy had now returned home, home to the comfort of his bosom. Angus felt like throwing out his broad chest and cooing. Yes, cooing loudly like a cock pigeon on a roof, as he struts back and forth, head bobbing up and down before his chosen and favourite hen. To Angus that hen was Kathy, of course!

As a loudly cooing Angus serenaded Kathy home to the South Side, it wasn't long before the cries of Kathy and Nan's hysterical laughter filled the back seat of the taxi. A thoroughly alarmed taxi-driver was now convinced he'd picked up a trio of raving loonies. Nan observed that he was looking agitatedly into his mirror. She quickly reassured the poor fellow. 'It's okay, driver. We're no aff-oor-heids. Just celebrating the return hame o' ma wee daughter. An big Angus here is cooing because his wee hen has just flown hame frae America.'

'Och, ah see. Nae bother at a',' said the taxi driver, arching his eyebrows quizzically. 'She's just flown a' the way across the Atlantic. Bloody magnificent!' He suddenly burst out laughing at the idea. Ach well, it takes all kinds to make a world. At least they're all happy!